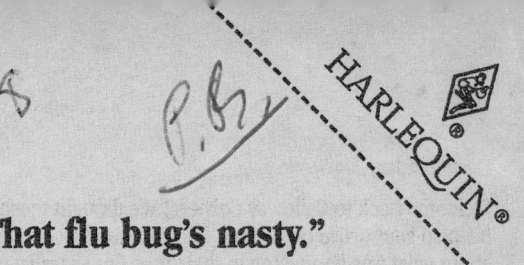

E-8  P.By

# "That flu bug's nasty."

Gabe skimmed the damp cloth over her pale face. "Mom and Jody both had it."

Tears spilled from Gretchen's eyes and ran down her cheeks.

He tried to concentrate on his task, but the look in her eyes was ripping his heart to shreds. "It doesn't last but a day or so," he said, putting down the towel and filling a paper cup with water. "'Course, you won't feel too great for Christmas morning."

He offered her the water, but she refused it with a shake of her head. Misery ousted the apprehension in her eyes.

"Still queasy, huh? I'll see if I can rustle up a cup of hot tea and some crackers. My mom swears by hot tea and soda crackers for an upset stomach."

He started to turn away, but she grabbed his arm.

"I don't have the flu," she said, her voice trembling and uncertain, the look in her eyes defiant. "I'm pregnant."

Dear Reader,

Welcome back to Calloway Corners! We thought those of you who'd been so supportive of *Mariah, Jo, Tess* and *Eden* might be curious about what was happening in their lives five years later.

Well, what we decided is that the Calloway sisters needed three drop-dead gorgeous male cousins who were the town's bad boys. RETURN TO CALLOWAY CORNERS is about Jericho, Daniel and Gabe, the town's "wild hearts." These are three of the sexiest, best-looking, wildest guys to come out of the little Louisiana town since—well, since their daddy! As they were fond of saying, they were "the bad time your mama always warned you about." But as all you romance readers know, even the wildest heart can be tamed by the right woman.

My "wild heart" was Gabe, the illegitimate son of Jesse Calloway and a young waitress. I wanted him to be in the rodeo—I love cowboys—but I wanted something different. I wanted him to be a rodeo clown. (What? A rodeo clown as a hero? Darn right!) I saw Gabe as a man who hides his aching heart behind a disguise of greasepaint and baggy clothes—laughing on the outside, crying on the inside. I fell in love with him and hope you do, too.

I loved writing about Gabe and the complex situations he had no part of and no control over, situations that made him the man he became, the man capable of bringing joy and peace to a woman like Gretchen, who is hurting as much as he is.

Also, there's a little lagniappe for the many readers who wrote to me after reading *Eden* and wanted to know what happened to Nick's sister Nicole and Lucas, the man she loved. Well, Patient Reader, your long wait is over.

I hope you enjoy these stories as well as reacquainting yourself with your old friends from Calloway Corners.

Have a great visit!

*Penny Richards*

# Penny Richards

# GABE

# *Harlequin Books*

TORONTO • NEW YORK • LONDON
AMSTERDAM • PARIS • SYDNEY • HAMBURG
STOCKHOLM • ATHENS • TOKYO • MILAN
MADRID • WARSAW • BUDAPEST • AUCKLAND

ISBN 0-373-70710-X

GABE

Copyright © 1996 by Penny Richards.

This edition published by arrangement with Harlequin Books S.A.

® and TM are trademarks of the publisher. Trademarks indicated with ® are registered in the United States Patent and Trademark Office, the Canadian Trade Marks Office and in other countries.

**Printed in U.S.A.**

This book is dedicated to Sandra and Terri—fellow laborers and good friends—and to Kathey. Sorry you couldn't make the trip. Maybe next time. You were with me during the writing more times than I can say.

Special thanks to Buck Thomas et al of Just Clowning Around Inc.—rodeo clowns, bullfighters, nice guys—for patiently answering my questions about your exciting occupation. You do a great and important job. Keep up the good work!

# CHAPTER ONE

THE FAMILIAR TENSION that knotted Gabe Butler's stomach eased somewhat as he turned off the highway and pulled into an empty parking spot next to Hank Hesterson's vintage Dodge. Flashing neon beer signs shot a gaudy rainbow of color over the row of rain-slick hoods, promising all who entered a good time.

For Gabe, the promise was a lie; the good time lasted about as long as the head on a freshly drawn beer. Even so, he switched off the engine.

The muted sounds emanating from the bar's ancient Wurlitzer pulsed through the graying cypress walls into the premature darkness of a winter evening, a deliberately twangy voice begging Daddy to please not get drunk this Christmas. The old tune and matching Christmas wreaths hanging on either side of the door were the only concessions to the holiday that was less than a week away. By all other standards, it was a typical Tuesday night at the Midnight Hour.

A sparse row of pickup trucks bellied up to the weathered facade of the bar, which was on Highway 80 between the Filmore and Doyline exits. Duke Boyd's Jeep resided in the place Jared Clements had parked back when he owned the honky-tonk. Hank Hesterson's Dodge occupied the same spot it had almost every night for the past thirty-odd years, and

Gabe knew that when he entered the dimly lit, smoke-filled room he'd find Hank—a walking testimonial of a misspent life—sitting at his usual table.

A landmark of sorts, the bar and grill had been in existence long before Gabe or his brothers were born. It was the place an ousted husband could cool off and grab a greasy burger and a few beers before he went back home to make peace with his honey. The place where Dallas/Saints football was debated and wagered upon autumn after autumn while others pitted themselves against the video poker and pinball machines. The place for the residents of nearby Haughton, Doyline and Calloway Corners to unwind after a grueling day at work. The place Gabe's dad had killed the Baptist preacher.

The Midnight Hour was also the first place Gabe headed when he blew into town to see his mother and sister, the first place he and his half brothers had visited when they'd learned their dad was coming home from Angola this past September. As they made the ritual detour into the bar, none of them knew if he was putting off the inevitable, looking for Dutch courage or just plain old hiding out.

Whatever their reasoning, it didn't work. Not for Jericho and Daniel, not for himself. No matter how stiff a drink Duke mixed or how many drafts he drew from the keg behind the counter, Jesse Calloway's boys eventually had to muster the guts to face the past.

Jericho and Daniel were well on their way to putting it all behind them, but Gabe was still struggling to come to terms with his dad. No matter how successful he knew he'd become since leaving Calloway Corners, the minute he crossed the state line, the old insecurities and paranoia began whispering through his mind.

"You'll never amount to anything."

"You'll always be Jesse Calloway's bastard."

"Loser...loser...loser."

He told himself he wasn't a loser, that as one of the most sought-after rodeo clowns on the pro circuit, he'd carved out a niche for himself. But he had to be reminded of that every time he came back to visit his family, which was every few months—unlike his two half brothers.

Jericho and Daniel had both left town the minute they got their high-school diplomas, and Jericho had been back as seldom as possible since then. As for Daniel, he hadn't stepped foot on Webster Parish County soil until this past September, when Jesse was released from prison after serving eighteen years of the twenty-five-year sentence he'd been handed.

Upon learning of his release and hoping they could make their peace, Sarah Calloway had called her two boys and asked them to come back and welcome their prodigal father home. Knowing Jesse would want the son he'd fathered with Hannah Butler there, too, both Jericho and Daniel had told Gabe about Jesse's return and urged him to join them. Like his brothers, Gabe had answered the summons, though he couldn't have said why.

Since that visit, his brothers were spending more time in the small community, and because it gave him a chance to be with them, Gabe was, too. Unlike his brothers, he had yet to establish an easy footing with either his father or the town.

Now he got out of the truck and stuffed the keys into the snug pocket of his jeans, wondering if he would ever be recognized as anything but Jesse Calloway's wild seed. The less than reassuring answer to that question was the reason Gabe made the ceremonial stop at the Midnight Hour whenever he came to town.

He pushed through the doorway and paused, letting his blue-eyed gaze pan the room. Through the smoke-dense air, he saw Jake Prescott, one of Jesse's former drinking buddies, huddled protectively over a shot glass brimming with amber liquid, and, as he'd known he would, he spotted Hank Hesterson homesteaded at his usual table. A woman with brassy red hair and old eyes looked up from her beer and gave Gabe an appreciative once-over. In a gesture that was as natural as drawing his next breath, Gabe tipped his hat and winked at her. Not expecting such blatant flirting, she looked away.

A framed poster of rock star E. Z. Ellis hung in a place of honor, with a portrait lamp aimed at his smiling face. E.Z. was Jo Calloway's husband. Jo and her sisters, Mariah, Tess and Eden, were Gabe's cousins, though the blood connection was rarely mentioned.

Via the jukebox, Kathy Mattea vowed she wouldn't be a clown in some guy's rodeo, while, on the tiny dance floor, a young woman in tight jeans and a "Wrangler butts drive me nuts" T-shirt executed a series of intricate spins and twirls beneath the expert guidance of her partner, a Tim McGraw look-alike.

"Well, I'll be the son of a biscuit eater!" boomed a friendly, familiar voice. "If it ain't the town clown himself!"

"Hey, Duke!" Gabe crossed the room and extended his hand over the bar, where it was taken in a crushing grip.

"I guess you're home for the holidays, huh?"

Gabe nodded. "Just got in from Vegas yesterday."

"Oh, yeah," Duke said with a nod. "The National Finals."

An easy grin lifted the corners of Gabe's mouth. "Right. So, how's it goin'?"

"Same ol', same ol'. How about you?"

"Nothing much changes."

Duke snorted and set a foaming mug of beer in front of Gabe. "I don't know how you can say that, considerin' all that's been goin' on with your brothers. Who'd've thought Jericho woulda gone and got married and Daniel would be thinkin' about tyin' the knot?"

Gabe lifted the mug and regarded it thoughtfully. "You've got a point."

As Duke had suggested, it was hard to imagine either of his brothers settling down—much less both of them—but that was exactly what had happened. Since their visit in September, both Jericho, an outdoor photographer, and Daniel, the head of an elite team of forest-fire fighters, had not only made their peace with the local residents, they'd fallen in love with local women—Jericho with Susan Quinlin, the parish sheriff, and Daniel with Becca Harris, none other than the supposedly compromised daughter of the preacher Jesse had shot in what the courts called a heat-of-passion killing.

At first, Daniel's decision to date Becca had gone over with Jesse like the proverbial ton of bricks, but lately it looked as if the time Jess had spent in prison had mellowed him somewhat. Both he and Becca were doing their best to exorcise the ghosts of the past. Maybe time really did heal all wounds.

Meanwhile, Daniel and Jericho forged full speed ahead with their plans to put down roots in the area. Jericho and Susan had eloped earlier in the month, and Daniel, who was trading fighting forest fires for a position with the local fire department, was planning a spring wedding, which thrilled their female cousins.

Eden was already knee-deep in tulle and lace and various wedding-cake recipes, while her husband, Nick, corralled their four kids. Jo was writing special vows for the couple to exchange, while E.Z. composed the music for the occasion. Tess was helping them design their new home, which her husband, Seth, would build. And Mariah stopped by almost daily, voicing her opinions on the pitfalls and the pleasures of every honeymoon spot from Bimini to the Swiss Alps. Her husband, Ford, a local preacher, had little to do until the wedding day, when he'd have the honor of performing the ceremony.

It was hard to imagine that Jericho and Daniel— who were now considered two of the town's most upstanding citizens—were the same two guys who, along with Gabe, had once been considered the town's premier juvenile delinquents and despoilers of innocent girls' virtue. Or, as the ever flirtatious Jericho had once put it to one of his female victims, the three of them were the "good time your Mama warned you about."

That memory brought another smile to Gabe's lips.

His brothers were the best. Considering that his very existence had brought their mother no small amount of shame and grief, Jericho and Daniel might have hated him. Instead, because of the way Jesse had incorporated them into one another's lives, the bonds of brotherhood had become too strong to be broken by the time they learned the truth about Gabe's parentage.

"I don't suppose you're thinkin' about gettin' hitched to some buckle bunny, are you?" Duke asked, dragging Gabe's thoughts back to the present.

Gabe's smile, this one more wry than genuine, made another brief appearance. "Not this cowboy."

But even as he said the words, Gabe's mind was filled with a memory he'd been trying to forget since early September. The memory of a soft, sweet-smelling body beneath his, of a warm, hungry mouth that clung and devoured, of a naughty smile and a throaty voice that whispered teasingly, *"I don't suppose you'd wanna marry me, would you, cowboy?"*

The recollection brought its usual response: rapid heartbeat, dry mouth, weak knees and a soul-deep longing for an ephemeral something he couldn't put his finger on and certainly didn't understand—like maybe for someone like Gretchen to say the words and *mean* them.

Gretchen West was no buckle bunny. She was a classy, savvy, highly educated businesswoman who headed her own country-music-video production company out of Fort Worth. He still didn't know how he'd managed to get her into his bed, or how, out of all the women who'd tried, she'd managed to worm her way into his heart. She was way out of his league, and she should have thanked him for realizing it, instead of storming out of his life the way she had the morning he'd heard about Jesse's release.

Gabe sighed.

"Woman problems?" Duke asked with the customary perceptiveness that seemed a requisite trait for bartenders and psychologists.

"Nothing a little time won't cure," Gabe said, raising his mug in a toasting gesture before taking a healthy swig.

Duke grinned. "That's what they all say." He wiped the immaculate counter with a rag, and Gabe focused on the hockey game playing on the muted television anchored high on the wall.

"Gabe, uh . . . Butler, isn't it?"

Gabe turned toward the person voicing the hesitant question. The rugged face looked familiar, but he couldn't place the tall, broad-shouldered man.

The stranger held out his hand. "Lucas Tanner," he said. "We met at the Calloway mill around Thanksgiving time."

As soon as Gabe heard Calloway mill, recognition dawned. "Yeah," he said, smiling. "You're Nick Logan's friend from Arkansas."

The man's answering smile was brief. "From Arkansas, via Tennessee and Mississippi. Nick's my boss now."

"You work at the mill?"

"I'm the new manager," Tanner told him. "I was here in November to interview for the position. I just moved in a couple of days ago."

"Welcome to the neighborhood," Gabe said. "For a small community it's not so bad. And it's close enough to Bossier City and Shreveport that you have the best of both worlds. Plenty of malls for your wife's shopping convenience."

"I'm divorced," Tanner said. "Six months ago."

Gabe saw the lingering pain in the man's dark eyes. "I'm sorry."

Lucas Tanner picked up his beer. "Yeah, so am I. But it was a mistake from the first. She deserved better than being second choice, but it took us four miserable years to realize that was the problem." He took a long pull from his bottle of Coors and rested his elbows on the bar with weary resignation. "I don't know. Maybe I always knew deep in my heart, and I just didn't want to admit it."

Gabe didn't think the comment required an answer and contented himself with taking another swallow of his own beer.

"What about you?" Luke Tanner asked. "Do you have a wife and a passel of kids waiting for you at home?"

"Hell, no!" The denial, made in a well-deep voice Gabe had been told was reminiscent of actor Sam Elliot's, was accompanied with a shake of his head. "I don't even live here anymore. I just come back to see my mom and my sister every few months."

"Where's home?"

"A twenty-acre spread west of Fort Worth, out near Aledo—not that I get to be there much, travelin' the rodeo circuit."

"Rodeo circuit?" Genuine interest filled Tanner's eyes. "What do you ride? Broncs or bulls?"

"I started out on both, but I gave up riding and became a bullfighter about five years ago." Seeing that Tanner didn't get it, Gabe added, "I'm a rodeo clown."

Instead of the chuckle of disbelief and the expected "Clown! You've got to be kidding!" Gabe had come to expect, Lucas Tanner said, "That's pretty dangerous, isn't it?"

The image of a man being tossed into the air like a sack of flour flickered through Gabe's mind. The picture triggered an ache that was as familiar as it was still painful, even after five years. "It can be."

Not anxious to pursue the subject, Gabe glanced at the Budweiser clock hanging over the bar. "Damnation! Look at the time. I'd better get out of here. Mom said she was frying chicken especially for me, so she's probably holding dinner." Rising, he reached into his pocket for a couple of wrinkled bills, which he slapped on the bar.

"Leavin', Gabe?" Duke boomed.

"If I don't get my butt home, Mama will be callin' Sheriff Quinlin to come haul it home," Gabe said, eliciting laughter from the other customers. The mental picture of the pint-size sheriff routing any man Gabe's size from the bar was hilarious, though there wasn't a man there who didn't doubt she could do it—especially since she'd laid flat a drunk and obnoxious Jericho in September, two months before she'd married him.

"In case you don't know, our sheriff is a woman who's no bigger than a minute," Gabe said by way of explanation to the town's newcomer.

He held out his hand for a farewell shake. "Nice to see you again, Lucas. Good luck with the new job."

"Thanks. Maybe I'll see you around."

Gabe recognized the loneliness in Lucas Tanner because he'd had years of close association with the emotion. Loner that he was, his true friends were scarcer than hen's teeth. Getting more was not a priority in his life, but the new mill manager seemed like a nice guy. Maybe this would be one acquaintance worth furthering.

"More than likely," he said, settling his black Stetson lower. With a parting wave to Duke and another drop-dead smile at the redhead, he started for the door. He'd put off the inevitable as long as he could.

GABE PULLED the truck into the circular driveway of his mother's home and stopped at the back. Through the glass panes that made up the outside wall of the chalet-style cedar house Joel Butler had built his wife the previous year, Gabe watched his mother bustling around in the kitchen. He smiled. It seemed fitting that after so long, Hannah Marshall Butler, who still owned a small restaurant in town and used to run the café at the weekly cattle auction, should finally have been given a kitchen she'd designed herself, one with every conceivable culinary convenience.

The farmhouse where the Butlers had lived when Hannah and Joel first married twenty-some years ago had been empty since Gabe's Grandma Marshall passed away last year. The old house, situated on the back corner of Joel's two hundred acres of prime hay fields and pasture, was where Gabe stayed when he came to town, presumably so he wouldn't disturb anyone with his comings and goings.

Though he and Joel got along okay—and considerably better as adults than they had when Gabe was a child—he wasn't comfortable around his stepfather. Deep inside, he knew that every time Joel looked at him, he was reminded of Hannah's youthful affair with Jesse Calloway. Not that he'd ever mentioned it except that once. God knew that once had been enough.

Someone turned on the floodlights that illuminated the massive deck spanning the back of the house. The sudden brilliance penetrated Gabe's musings. He reached for the stack of Christmas presents lying on the seat next to him and headed for the house.

Hannah met him at the doorway, pulling him out of the rain-chilled night and into the warmth of the house and the love he knew she felt for him. That love was one of the few certainties in his life.

"We were getting worried about you." Joel spoke from his place at the head of the oak table, while Gabe set down the gifts on the opposite end.

Gabe met Joel's gaze and shrugged out of his long black duster. In Gabe's mind, the look in his step-dad's dark eyes and the seemingly innocuous statement translated to "How dare you cause your mother any more grief?"

The last thing Gabe had ever wanted was to cause Hannah undue worry, but as a kid, he'd seldom thought about the repercussions of his actions, and as a man, he was past the age he felt he should explain them.

"Sorry," he said, offering the brief apology to Hannah. "I stopped by the Midnight Hour for a minute to see Duke."

Joel's lips tightened around the pipe clamped between his teeth, and Hannah's gaze slid from her son to her husband's set countenance.

She scurried around the bar that separated the dining area from the kitchen. "It's no problem," she said in an overbright voice. "I still have to make the gravy, anyway."

The clatter of footsteps coming down the stairs saved the trio from any further awkwardness. Wearing the smile she always brought to his lips, Gabe braced himself as Jody, his eighteen-year-old half sister, flung herself into his arms with a squeal of pure pleasure.

Gabe hugged her tightly, then set her away from him so that he could give her a thorough once-over. She was medium height, curvy in all the right places, a younger, slimmer version of Hannah. With her blond hair and dark-fringed blue eyes, she was a knockout, a fact that both pleased him and brought him no small amount of concern.

"I swear, girl, you get prettier every day," he told her in a husky voice. "And you've grown a foot since Thanksgiving."

Jody rolled her eyes. "You know I reached my full height by the time I was fourteen, Goob—I mean, Gabe." The correction was accompanied by a teasing, dimpled smile and a poke in the ribs with an elbow.

"Brat!" he said, holding her in a hard grip while he rubbed the top of her head with his knuckles.

Jody squealed an anguished, "Gabe, my hair!"

"You two stop that!"

"Yes, ma'am," Gabe said, releasing his sister and casting a glance at his mother. The sternness of Hannah's voice was contradicted by the twinkle in her eyes. Smiling the smile that set female hearts aflutter wherever he went, he winked at her.

Hannah shook her head and went back to stirring the gravy, charging him to hang up his things.

"Yes, ma'am," he said, hanging his hat and coat on the hall tree next to the door while Jody went to peer over her mother's shoulder.

"Is it about ready? Jason's supposed to be here in twenty minutes."

"It won't be long," Hannah said.

Jody pinned a mock-angry look on Gabe, who pulled out a chair at the kitchen table and sat down. "I guess I can go fix my hair while I'm waiting."

"You could set the table," Hannah suggested.

"Mama!"

"If you aren't ready when Jason gets here, he can wait," Hannah said with typical motherly logic.

Jody sighed, but set about doing what her mother asked. She was putting ice in the glasses when she turned to Gabe and asked, "Did that woman ever get hold of you?"

Gabe tipped his chair on its two back legs. "What woman?"

"Gretchen West from Westways Productions."

Gabe's heart took a nosedive. "Gretchen called?"

Jody nodded. "The day you left—the day after Thanksgiving. Isn't Westways the company you did the music video for?"

"Yeah."

There were times, like now, when Gabe wished he'd never agreed to perform in the country-music video of the remake of the old Everly Brothers hit, "Cathy's Clown." People on the circuit were always stopping him, telling him they'd seen him on TV and asking him if he was planning to give up bullfighting for acting. Being in the limelight made him uncomfortable. He preferred the anonymity of baggy, rope-tied jeans, patched shirts and greasepaint.

There were also times he regretted meeting Gretchen. Times he got so tangled up in the memories of the weekend they'd spent together that he could

think of little else. In his line of work that was tantamount to signing a death warrant.

"Maybe she wants to use you in another video."

Gabe stroked his dark blond mustache with a callused forefinger, an absent look in his blue eyes. That
was exactly what he was afraid of: being used by a
woman like Gretchen.

"It's really good, Gabe."

Hearing the seriousness in Jody's voice, he looked
up. "What's good?"

"The video. Don't tell me you haven't seen it," she
said incredulously. "It's been the Viewer's Choice
video ever since it first aired."

"Sorry, sweetcheeks," he said. "Don't forget that
I'm on the road almost every day, and when I do find
a motel room, I'm so pooped all I can think about is
getting a shower and crashing."

Jody shook her head in disbelief. "It's a wonderful
video, Gabe, and you're great." Her lips curved in a
sly smile. "Why, there isn't a girl in school who
doesn't have the hots for you."

"Joelle Deanne!" Hannah said.

Jody gave her mother a look that said she might as
well face facts. "It's true, Mama."

Jody and Gabe exchanged smiles. "So did she ever
get hold of you when you got back home?"

Gabe thought of all the hang-ups on his answering
machine and wondered if they'd been calls from
Gretchen. He thought of the times he'd tried to reach
her after she'd stormed out on him, wanting to make
her understand the futility of her hope that they could
forge a meaningful relationship.

They were poles apart in upbringing and life-style.
Gretchen was a people person, and, for the most part,

he was content with his own company. Or had been until she'd sashayed into his life.

"I haven't talked to her."

"What do you think she wants?"

Gabe arched an eyebrow at his sister. "Do I look psychic to you?"

Jody harrumphed, then crossed her arms and shifted her weight to one leg, tapping her toe in a gesture of impatience she'd learned from Hannah. "Well?"

"Well what?" Gabe asked with pseudo-innocence.

"Are you going to call her?"

"If she wants to talk to me, she knows my number."

"Men!" Jody said in disgust.

Outside, headlights pierced the gloom. Jason, no doubt, Gabe thought as an undeniable feeling of gratitude swept through him. "Speaking of men, here comes yours."

Jason was Seth Taylor's son. Seth was Tess Calloway's husband. The tall, friendly young man with the wide smile didn't much resemble the angry boy he'd been five years before. That young man wouldn't have been welcome in the Butler home, but as a college-bound A student with a spotless reputation, Jason didn't have much for Joel to criticize now.

Jason came in, was greeted and, without too much arm twisting, was persuaded to join the family for supper, which eased the tension considerably. Forty-five minutes later, Jason and Jody went to the living room to study. Hannah insisted that she'd clear the table so Gabe and Joel could drink their coffee in the den. Gabe and Joel complied, settling down in front of the fire that burned with a cheerful exuberance both men had a hard time matching.

They talked about the National Finals and the hectic pace of the holidays, and Joel told Gabe about his new young bull, a Brahman-Angus cross that, according to Joel, was "meaner'n a junkyard dog."

Gabe was glad when ten o'clock came and he could legitimately claim weariness and head to the old farmhouse. He gave a mighty yawn and stretched. "I'm bushed. I think I'll turn in."

"I was wondering how you held your eyes open this long," Hannah said, rising. "You must be exhausted from all that traveling."

"It is starting to catch up with me," he told her with a smile.

"Sleep in tomorrow, then. Joel turned on the heat this afternoon, and Jody put fresh sheets on your bed."

Gabe put his hands on his mother's shoulders. "I'm sure the place is immaculate. Thanks."

For an instant, her palm lingered against his cheek, and she whispered, "I'm glad you're home."

"Me, too." He kissed her still-smooth cheek, gave her shoulders a squeeze and smiled at his stepfather. In one more attempt to bridge the chasm separating them, he said, "I want to see that new bull of yours in the morning."

"Sure!" Joel said, a smile of genuine pleasure creasing his leathery cheeks. Like any cattleman, he was proud to show off his latest acquisition, especially one as well-bred and showy as this one was.

"See you tomorrow, then."

"Sure thing. Good night."

Gabe bade his mother good-night and let himself out the back door. In a matter of minutes, he'd driven the short distance to the old Butler place and entered. The house greeted him with the mingled scents of lemon oil and the spicy Christmas potpourri his mother had placed throughout the house. It wasn't long before he was lying between the sheets in the upstairs bedroom he'd slept in as a child.

He closed his eyes, able at last to surrender to the weariness that invaded him; conversely, Gretchen's face appeared the instant his eyes closed. The image was accompanied by the sound of Jody's voice asking if he was going to call her.

Damn it, he'd tried to reach her after the weekend they'd spent together. When he'd met with no success, he'd finally acknowledged that her refusal to talk about the way they'd parted was best for them both.

All that mattered was that he'd done the job she hired him to do, and by all accounts they made a helluva team. The video was a success. End of story, Gabe thought, rolling onto his side and giving his pillow a punch.

But if the story had ended—and it had—why had she called him after Thanksgiving? He thought of and rejected half a dozen reasons. Mumbling a curse, he wrapped his arms around his pillow and flopped onto his stomach.

Instantly his mind was filled with the memory of waking, his cheek resting against Gretchen's smooth belly, the nebulous scent of her perfume tickling his senses. He remembered lifting his head and finding her gaze on him, passion slumbering in the sapphire blue eyes that also held a wealth of satisfaction and a soft smile.

*Forget her, Butler!*

Easier said than done. He couldn't shake the troubling fact that somehow, without meaning to, he'd stepped in over his head. Meeting Gretchen was like drawing a certain bull and knowing immediately that his ride would be a series of ups and downs and twists—and that he'd probably get thrown long before the eight-second buzzer went off.

A love-'em-and-leave-'em kind of guy—at least on the surface—Gabe made it a point to shy away from serious entanglements. Until Gretchen, he'd never met a woman whose memory he couldn't shake, something that troubled him more than he cared to admit. The admission implied a depth of feeling he wasn't prepared to recognize, much less accept. But ready to admit it or not, one thing was undeniable: if it was over, why couldn't he forget her?

## CHAPTER TWO

WHILE GABE LAY wooing sleep in Calloway Corners, Gretchen was doing the same in the master bedroom of her house on Fort Worth's Elizabeth Avenue. The area had been *the* place for Fort Worth's wealthy to live during the twenties, but in recent years its popularity had given way to the fast-growing city of Westover.

As usual, when exhaustion forced her to stop for the day, Gretchen's memories of Gabe Butler crept into her weary mind—more specifically, memories of the weekend they'd spent together after they'd wrapped up the "Cathy's Clown" video.

Her legs moved restlessly against the floral, lace-trimmed sheets. Had she misread Gabe Butler? Had the doctor's warning colored her way of looking at a man? Dear God, had she been desperate when she'd given in to the longings of her body that spur-of-the-moment weekend?

She could still see her gynecologist's face when, in August, he'd told her bluntly that after battling a persistent case of endometriosis and ovarian cysts, a hysterectomy was in her near future. He'd stunned her by saying that if she hoped to have a child, she needed to find either a husband or a sperm donor...the sooner the better.

She'd left his office weighed down with depression, knowing how slim her options were. Though she could afford it, taking advantage of the anonymity of a sperm bank was distasteful at best, frightening at worst. She didn't relish the idea of someday telling her son or daughter that his or her father was a tall/short/ athletic/high-IQ/blond/brunet/attorney/doctor— "Sorry, honey, that's all I know about him." The truth was, she was most concerned with finding a man who was unselfish, kind and gentle while still being undeniably and unmistakably male. In short, she was looking for a man like her grandfather. Her heart told her that any woman would find these qualities important and that these things were programmed into a person's genes, like hair and eye color. Her heart also told her that the sperm bank had no way of determining the character of the men who were so willing to propagate the species by donating their sperm. As callous as her attitude might be, something told her many of these men were desperate for money or, worse, so high on themselves and their capabilities that they thought the world would be a better place with their offspring running around.

She was left with no other option but to find a husband. Her bitter smile was wasted in the darkness of the room. God knew she'd been trying to find the right man all her adult life, but marrying a man—any man—just because it was expedient to do so was the height of foolishness.

At thirty-three and with one failed marriage behind her, she knew firsthand how hard it was to find a compatible mate. Her ex-husband, Paul Brady, a fellow film student at UCLA who'd shared her dreams and her ambition, had been more interested in the fact that Gretchen was the daughter of wealthy oilman Tyrell West than in twenty-one-year-old Gretchen herself. It had taken her three years to figure it out and another year to get Paul out of her life when she'd learned he was sleeping with one of her "friends" while she was teaching at the Art Institute in L.A.

After that, she'd shied away from any long-term, possibly serious entanglements until she met Jim Pittman, a much-sought-after entertainment lawyer. Forty-four to her twenty-eight, Jim had been good company, pleasant and without a jealous bone in his well-maintained, California-tanned body. He'd treated her like a queen, lavishing her with expensive gifts and surprises that ranged from dinner at quaint places in the desert to a stolen weekend in Paris. The only problem in their relationship had been that he was content with the status quo. While words of love had flowed freely, marriage, the word she longed to hear, had never passed his lips.

Discontent set in almost simultaneously with her thirtieth birthday. A milestone of sorts, thirty seemed a prime time to take stock of where she was and decide if that place was anywhere near where she wanted to be. A close inspection of her life made her realize she was deeply dissatisfied. She despised living in L.A. After ten years, she was past ready to get out of the big city and back to the relatively small town of Fort Worth.

She was tired of teaching other people how to develop their artistic talents while keeping her own locked away. She couldn't do it any longer. Wouldn't. Her own talent was clamoring for a chance to break out and do something.

Increasingly, over the past couple of years, she had been plagued by the dream of starting her own video production company, one specializing in music videos—more specifically, country-music videos, since country music had been an integral part of her formative years.

More important than her dissatisfaction with her career, she faced the fact that, after almost two years, she was unhappy with the direction her relationship with Jim was headed. She wanted a home. A husband. A couple of kids and a dog.

After careful deliberation, she decided to use the trust fund she'd received from her grandfather on her thirtieth birthday to start her own music-video production company back in Texas. It was a gamble, but she was determined to do something to make herself happy, and she hoped that her absence in Jim's life would make him realize how much she meant to him.

Part of the plan had worked; the other part failed. Though Jim called often and they each made the trip between Texas and California at least once a month, he never offered marriage.

After two years of living in this particular limbo, she reached the end of her patience, and on New Year's Eve she confronted Jim about where he saw their relationship going. Sadly, he told her he was more than satisfied with things as they were; in fact, one of the things he liked about their relationship was the distance between them. When they did take time from their busy schedules to see each other, everything was so new, so fresh. He didn't want to get married, and, with kids in college, he certainly didn't want to start a second family.

Though Gretchen had suspected as much for more
than three long years, she hadn't been willing to face
the truth. She hated the dating game, and Jim was
such a good man in so many ways that she'd been
loath to end their relationship, but after his confession, it was impossible to pretend they had a future
together. She had broken off with him that night almost a year ago, and had never returned another of his
phone calls, preferring to make the break as clean and
painless as possible.

During the months that followed, she had thrown
herself into her work, tackling new and exciting projects that challenged her and her crew. Her professional success was gratifying, but her personal life was
as dull as day-old dishwater.

Then, almost four months ago, she'd met Gabriel
Butler. She'd been looking for a rodeo clown to use in
the video she was doing for Tandy McGillis's release
of an old Everly Brothers hit.

Her best friend, Nicole Logan, had been responsible for taking her to the Fort Worth stock show and
introducing her to Gabe. Gretchen still didn't know
whether to thank Nicole or strangle her.

"A rodeo clown, huh? Do I have the man for you!"
Nicole Logan's ebony eyes had sparkled with a
naughty pleasure.

The sole owner of Nicole's, a trendy Dallas boutique, Nicole was also making her mark as an up-and-
coming clothing designer on the Dallas/Fort Worth
fashion scene. She had moved her business from Little Rock, Arkansas, four years earlier when the rekin-
dling of an old romance failed to burn. Her move
preceded Gretchen's by less than a year. The two had
struck up a conversation on Gretchen's first visit to the

shop; each had sensed she'd found a soulmate, and their friendship had deepened daily ever since.

"You actually know a real rodeo clown?"

"Uh-huh."

"For such a classy lady, you've got some real strange friends," Gretchen told her.

Nicole chortled. "*I* have strange friends? This comes from the socialite who went to her cleaning lady's daughter's graduation and lunches with her librarian."

"Touché," Gretchen said. "So how do you know this guy, anyway?"

"Remember my calendar?"

"You gave me one, and I glanced through it, but one of the girls at the studio snitched it before I could get a good look," Gretchen said.

The previous year, Nicole had been looking for a way to showcase her night-wear designs and, seeing the popularity of the Chippendale and Fabio calendars, had opted to use both male and female models in hers. Though she was promoting women's night wear, she thought that having a man somewhere in every photo, someone who was obviously appreciative of the gowns, might appeal to women.

"The cost of hiring professional models was, and is, exorbitant," Nicole told Gretchen, "and I knew I couldn't afford big names, so I went to the modeling agencies in town. I found some great women, but all the men were either too old, too young or looked too much like professional models, if you know what I mean."

Gretchen nodded and Nicole continued, "I started thinking about how to get good-looking guys cheap. I asked Nick if he'd do it, and he said yes—but only under duress.''

Gretchen had met Nicole's twin brother, Nick, once or twice and liked him a lot. As an only child, she envied anyone with siblings, especially if they were as personable and handsome as Nick Logan.

''It was Nick's idea to talk to his brothers-in-law about helping me out. Since one of them is E. Z. Ellis, I'd have been a fool not to let him try.''

Gretchen had heard a lot about the four Calloway sisters and their husbands. According to Nicole, Calloway Corners, where they all lived, had cornered the market on handsome men.

''I needed at least six men, so they could do two months each. Nick's wife, Eden, said she had three cousins who might be willing to help out.'' Nicole sighed and her lips twisted into a wry smile. ''They all agreed to talk to me, but the trouble was that when I saw these guys, I couldn't decide which two to choose! Then Ford, Mariah's husband, backed out of the project. Some of his church members were offended by the night-wear aspect, so I was able to use all three cousins, after all.''

''And one of these guys is a rodeo clown?''

Nicole nodded. ''Jericho is an outdoor photographer, Daniel is a smoke jumper—he parachutes close to forest fires—and Gabe is a rodeo clown.''

''And he's good-looking?''

''Honey, you've definitely not seen the calendar, or you'd remember. All of these men are h-o-t.''

Nicole crossed the room and pulled open a drawer. She drew out her calendar, thumbed through the pages until she found the month she was looking for and handed it to Gretchen.

Gabe Butler had posed for the July spot. He sat in a porch swing, one bent, denim-clad leg resting on the swing, the other booted foot poised to set the swing in motion.

A gorgeous blonde sat between his legs, leaning against his bare chest. Her head was thrown back against his shoulder, exposing the graceful line of her throat and the swell of her breasts left bare by the filmy gown she wore, a gown as red as the sunset blazing behind them. One of her legs was stretched out the length of the swing; the other was bare and, like his, bent at the knee, the whiteness of her skin a startling contrast to the darkness of his jeans. One of his hands rested on her abdomen in a gesture that spoke of tenderness and intimacy; the other lay along the back of the swing.

Noting the look of adoration on the model's perfect features and the warmth of his gaze, Gretchen wondered if there was more to their relationship than posing together for a calendar picture. She started to ask Nicole, but her friend must have read her mind.

"I know what you're thinking. They never set eyes on each other before the day of the shoot."

"You're kidding!"

"Nope. Obviously he's a man of many talents, not to mention an outrageous flirt. Take a look at December."

While Gretchen was finding the next photo, Nicole explained, "I tried to have at least one shot with the men doing what they really do. Daniel is rescuing a woman from a fire, Jericho is photographing a model, and Gabe is in his clown getup—sort of."

Gretchen found December. The female model was different, but the look on her face was familiar. She wore a green velvet dressing gown that nipped in at the waist and flared out over her hips. She was shown only as a hazy, ephemeral reflection in a cheval mirror—Nicole's version of the ghost of Christmas past.

Gabe Butler lay on a bed, a sheet drawn up over his lower body, a photograph—no doubt of the woman—resting on his abdomen. His handsome face was melancholy in repose. The surprise was in his reflected image. The side of his face next to the mirror was painted with his clown face. White greasepaint served as a background for a heavy eyebrow with a triangle above. Deep wrinkles were drawn at the corners of his eyes, and a wide red smile all but obliterated his mustache. The triumph of the picture's concept was a solitary tear on his cheek, proof of the depth of his loss.

"This is wonderful," Gretchen said, that wonder evident in her voice. "He's certainly good-looking. But more importantly, he conveys a lot of emotion."

"He's a heck of a nice guy. So do you want me to arrange a meeting with him?"

"Sure," Gretchen said with a nonchalant lift of her shoulders. "Why not?" What did she care about his reputation? She didn't want to marry the man; she just wanted to hire him for the video.

Several days later they drove up to the arena just in time for the rodeo to begin. As they made their way to the designated meeting place behind the chutes, Gretchen was swept up in a barrage of memories and sensations. She'd always loved rodeo, and the smell of horses and cattle—"Cow chips smell like money, sugar"—brought back a dozen recollections from the summers she'd spent following her granddad around his ranch.

"There he is," Nicole said as they made their way toward a knot of people clustered around a man in clown costume who, with legs bowed and left arm aloft and right hand gripping an imaginary rigging, shifted his hips in mimicry of the moves of a bareback rider. Gretchen's stomach clenched at the unconsciously erotic motion of those lean, thrusting hips.

"How do you know that's him?" Gretchen asked, seeing another clown nearby.

"Look at all the women and kids. Wherever he goes, Gabe has a slew of women following him around, hoping he'll drop them a smile or ask them out. And he always takes time to sign autographs and help the kids with their form."

Gretchen tucked away those tidbits of information. If what Nicole said was true, the man was a true dichotomy: a terrible flirt, but someone who was willing to give his time to help young people. Will the real Gabe Butler please stand up?

As they approached the group, she heard Gabe say, "You've got to practice and practice. Honing your moves is the secret to success." Just then, he looked up and recognized Nicole. His teeth flashed against the red smile painted on his face, the same smile she'd seen in the photograph.

"Hey, Nicole!" he said, his deep voice sounding like the throaty purr of some big jungle cat.

"Hey yourself!" Nicole said.

As the two exchanged hugs, Gretchen gave Gabe Butler a thorough perusal. The physique that had been so outstanding in the calendar was disguised by his patched shirt and equally disreputable jeans. These jeans didn't fit him like the proverbial glove; they were so baggy he used gaudy Stars and Stripes suspenders to hold them up. The jeans were rolled up to his knees, revealing red-and-white-striped socks. His hat looked as if it had been stomped on by an angry bull, and a red bandanna hung from his back pocket; another was tied around his neck. Battered but expensive tennis shoes completed his attire. There was little to indicate he was the sexy man in the calendar, but Gretchen felt the pull of that magnetism nonetheless.

He and Nicole broke apart. "Gabe," Nicole said, "I want you to meet Gretchen West, president of Westways Productions."

Gretchen was tall, but she still had to look up to meet his eyes. The smile in them was warm, and the overwhelmingly blatant appreciation in the blue gaze set her heart racing in a totally unexpected and inappropriate way. She didn't want to fall under the spell of this man's practiced charm. She didn't have the time or inclination for a careless flirtation.

Grasping the crown of his hat with his left hand, Gabe swept it off, revealing a shock of sweat-soaked dishwater blond hair. "Pleased to meet you."

"It's a pleasure meeting you, too," she said, taking his outstretched hand and injecting a businesslike, impersonal tone into her voice. "I was impressed with your work in Nicole's calendar."

His face colored a little, but he managed a slight smile. "I'll never live it down, but thanks." He set the hat firmly back on his head. "I can't believe I'm actually considering doing a music video."

"It pays well."

"So Nicole said." He grinned that slow, sexy, devastating smile. "There isn't a cowboy alive opposed to making a few easy bucks."

"Making a video isn't as easy as the finished prod-uct makes it look," Gretchen warned. "There are a lot of long days involved."

"As long as it can be worked around the rodeos I have coming up, I guess I'm game."

"Good."

The public-address system crackled loudly, and the smooth voice of the announcer proclaimed the start of the grand entry. "I've got to go," Gabe said. "I'll treat you ladies to a Fritos pie and a Coke when the ro-deo's over."

"Last of the big spenders," Nicole quipped.

He grinned and favored her with a wink. "That's me." With a jaunty wave, he turned and walked away.

Gretchen was left feeling as if she'd been buffeted by a strong wind. Gabe Butler was larger than life, the kind of man it behooved unsuspecting women to be-ware of.

"Well?"

"Wow," had been Gretchen's response. "Wow" had also been her first coherent thought after they'd made love, and it still pretty much summed up her re-sponse to him.

His image rose now behind her closed eyes. Tall, broad shoulders, lean hips and a hard, muscular stomach made him a cliché of every good-looking man in the world, but on Gabe, the tried-and-true cliché took on new definition. He had those long, well-formed legs and the kind of tight masculine buttocks that did wonders for a pair of jeans, and dirty blond hair that grew a little too long in the back. His blue eyes were so pale they resembled ice chips, but the teasing laughter in their depths warmed them—and her heart. A mustache—darker than his hair—draped over a mouth shaped for just one purpose: to drive a woman crazy.

Crazy. That was what she'd been that weekend they spent together. Crazy from the weariness and euphoria that accompanied the finishing of a project well-done. Crazy with need. And crazy to have let him get close to her the way she had, especially since she knew better—

The phone rang, scattering her memories. Gretchen grappled in the dark for the receiver, grateful for the diversion from her troubled recollections, if only for a while.

"Hello."

"Hi!"

The low, pleasant voice belonged to Nicole. "Hi," Gretchen said.

"How are you feeling?"

"Tired, but wired, you know? It was a busy day."

"Did you do it?"

"Do what?" Gretchen asked, though she knew exactly what Nicole was talking about.

"Call Gabe."

"No." She heard Nicole's sigh.

"You have to tell him, Gretchen. He has a right to know."

Involuntarily, protectively, Gretchen's hand moved to her abdomen, where Gabe Butler's baby grew in its wet cocoon. Her eyes filled with tears, which plagued her often lately.

Finding the nerve to tell him about the baby that was the result of their passion-filled weekend was hard, considering he'd opted not to use protection after she told him her chances of conceiving were extremely slim. The fact that she'd walked out on him and refused to return his calls didn't help, either.

Nicole, on the other hand, was a big fan of truthfulness. Her own life had been shadowed by a series of life-altering lies that she'd only recently come to terms with. Thirty-four and unmarried, she longed for children. She thought it was wonderful that Gretchen was pregnant and felt sure Gabe would feel the same way.

Gretchen knew Nicole was right about telling him, but she was less sure about his reaction to the news. At the moment, she wasn't even sure how *she* felt.

"He isn't interested in a lasting relationship with me or anyone else, Nicole. He made that perfectly clear."

"He has a self-esteem problem."

"Gabe Butler?" Incredulity threaded Gretchen's voice.

"That's right," Nicole said. "He doesn't think he's good enough for a woman like you."

Gretchen blew out an irritated breath. Money. The universal panacea for all the world's ills. All it had ever done for her was raise barriers between her and the people she cared about.

"So he doesn't come from old money," she told Nicole, " and he doesn't have any big money himself. You know me well enough to know I have no problem with that."

"It's more than just the money or the lack of it," Nicole said.

"Then what is the problem?"

"There are a couple actually. I think he worries about his illegitimacy. His mother had an affair with a married man—Jesse Calloway. And though the whole town knows Gabe was the result, Jesse's never admitted to anyone that Gabe's his son."

The news surprised Gretchen, but she was too much a product of the times to be shocked. "Jesse Calloway? How's he related to the Calloway women?"

"He's their dad's brother. Ben was the good son, and his brother, Jesse, was the bad seed."

"Every family has their skeletons, don't they?" Gretchen said. "So his parents weren't married. Illegitimacy is no big deal anymore."

"Maybe not to movie stars or people who have enough money to thumb their noses at the world, but when you come from a small town where everyone knows everyone else, some folks are quick to judge," Nicole said. "And then there was that deal with his dad."

"What deal?"

"Jesse Calloway killed the local preacher nearly twenty years ago in what the courts called a crime of passion. He just got out of prison in September, a couple weeks after the two of you finished the video."

And after they'd shared a weekend together.

Suddenly Gretchen recalled a phone call Gabe received that weekend at the motel, where he'd told his family he'd be staying. It was his brother calling about an upcoming family reunion at Calloway Corners. Had that call been about Jesse's release? Up until then, the weekend had been perfect, but right after that, Gabe had begun to draw away from her in small, subtle ways she found baffling and hurtful.

"Sounds like a cop-out to me," Gretchen said. "None of us is responsible for our parents' behavior—thank God. Gabe has a lot going for him. He's handsome, successful at what he does—"

"—and a genuinely nice guy, in spite of a reputation that's totally undeserved."

"Why do you say that?"

"It's a front," Nicole told her. "Don't get me wrong. He's no saint, but he isn't the hellion he seems to be, either. He hides his real feelings by adopting this happy-go-lucky, hell-raising persona. By pretending to be something he isn't, he bypasses dealing with any deep emotions. That way no one can hurt him again. By acting footloose and flighty, he's trying to tell the world that what happened in the past doesn't hurt him anymore. Actually, I'm told he's as deep as the Atchafalaya River, but few people know it."

Gretchen frowned into the receiver. She was hearing things about Gabe that made her realize he was a far more complicated person than she'd believed. "Surely he's risen above what his dad did."

"For the most part, he has," Nicole replied. "Until something happens to remind him that we never leave our pasts completely behind."

Gretchen heard the note of pain in her friend's voice and knew that the statement was as much about her as it was about Gabe.

"How did you find all this out?"

"Nick," Nicole said. "Eden has told him all the Calloway family secrets, and he and Gabe go fishing sometimes when he's home."

"And how do the Calloway sisters feel about Gabe?"

"Accepting. They love their aunt Sarah and wouldn't hurt her for the world, and none of them is the type to throw stones. They all accept Gabe for who he is."

"What about his brothers?"

"Gabe was more or less brought up with Jericho and Daniel Calloway. Jesse owns the cattle sale barn between Haughton and Minden, and when the boys were young, they spent hours after school and all day during the summer hanging out there. By the time they were old enough to understand what the whispers were all about, they'd bonded in ways only boys understand."

"Tell me about the killing," Gretchen said.

Nicole related the tale about Daniel and Becca Harris's youthful romance and how Becca's father, the Baptist preacher, misconstrued a situation and assumed they'd slept together.

"Reverend Harris looked up Jesse at the Midnight Hour bar. There was a brawl, and somehow Jesse got his rifle out of his truck and shot him. He got twenty-five years for manslaughter."

"It must have been hard on his family."

"It was, but from what I hear, the boys took it harder than Sarah. Their dad was never a good role model—he was a real womanizer and a big drinker—and I think as a result the boys had always been pretty rambunctious. But Eden says that after the murder they spent the rest of their high-school days living up to the stigma of being Jesse Calloway's sons. His bad seed."

"No wonder Gabe has a poor opinion of himself."

"Which, I believe, brings this conversation full circle," Nicole said. "Are you sure you won't tell him?"

Gretchen's laugh was tinged with bitterness. "I'm not sure I can take another rejection."

"Okay then. What about your plans for Christmas? It's only five days away."

"I don't have any plans. My parents are going to Tahoe. What about you?"

"Eden and Nick are having my mom and dad down from Arkansas for a couple of days," Nicole said. "I'm going, too. There'll be a houseful on Christmas Eve."

Gretchen had heard nothing but praise for Nick's wife and her family. Thinking of her own parents' hit-and-miss approach to parenting, the closeness binding the Calloway clan was enviable. She wasn't aware of the craving in her voice as she said, "It sounds great."

"Come with me," Nicole said, surprising her with the sudden invitation. "Eden and Nick won't mind. You can stay in the garage apartment with me."

"Thanks, Nicole, but I can't impose on your family."

"You won't be imposing. Come on, Gretchen," Nicole wheedled. "It would be good for you to get away for a few days. If you're worried about seeing Gabe, don't be. Even if he is in town, he's not likely to come to Eden and Nick's."

"Thanks, but I think I'll just sit around here."

"And watch the video of Gabe over and over while you eat a turkey sandwich?"

"Maybe," Gretchen said, ignoring her friend's sarcasm.

"Well, at least think about it," Nicole urged. "If you decide to go at the last minute, just give me a call. Eden won't mind. Her attitude is the more the merrier, and she always cooks enough for a small army."

"I'll think about it."

"All right," Nicole said, as if the whole matter was settled. "Good grief! I didn't know it was so late. I'd better let you get some sleep."

"Wait a minute!" Gretchen said before Nicole could hang up. "You didn't call just to coerce me into going with you, did you?"

Nicole grew suddenly quiet. When she finally did speak, the lightness of her tone sounded forced. "Well, no. . . I called to see how you were feeling . . ."

"And to tell me something. What?"

There was a lengthy pause before Nicole said, "I talked to my mother this morning. She told me she heard through the grapevine that Lucas had gotten a divorce a few months ago."

Lucas Tanner was the man Nicole had been in love with at twenty-one. The man whose baby she'd carried before her mother arranged for an abortion.

"And how does that make you feel?"

"Curious, I guess," Nicole said. "I wonder why his marriage failed."

"You'll probably never know." Gretchen deliberately injected a light note to her voice. "You're seeing Steve, and he's a great guy who's crazy about you."

"Steve's okay, but he isn't Lucas."

"You and Lucas couldn't make it work, Nicole," Gretchen reminded her gently. "You've got to let go of the past."

"I know. And believe me, I've tried."

Gretchen heard the hopelessness in Nicole's voice. "I know you have." She drew a determined breath. "Look, we're both exhausted. Let's try to get some sleep. Things will look better in the morning. You'll forget all about Lucas Tanner and his divorce in a few days."

"You're right," Nicole said with a sniff, "as usual. I'll talk to you before I leave for Calloway Corners, okay?"

"Okay."

"And if you change your mind about going, just give me a call."

"I will."

Gretchen hung up, worried by Nicole's inability to let go of the past, even though it was clear that she and Lucas Tanner had no future together.

She rolled to her side and closed her eyes, thinking of Nicole's offer. The thought of going to the place Gabe had grown up held a certain appeal, even if it also held the danger of running into him again.

*As if you don't want to.*

*"I don't suppose you'd wanna marry me, would you, cowboy?"*

Without warning, the memory of her proposal skittered through her mind, and heat flooded her face. She'd said it jokingly, but even now, she couldn't deny that a part of her had been serious. Gabe's eyes had mirrored a strange combination of surprise and an emotion she couldn't quite put her finger on. His reply, though, had been clear enough.

"I'm not a marryin' kind of guy, darlin'. I'm more of a honeymoon kind of guy."

Joke or not, his answer hurt more than she'd been willing to admit. Furious—at herself more than him—she'd gotten out of bed, put on her clothes, gathered her things and left. She hadn't returned any of his calls, and finally, after a week, he'd stopped trying to contact her.

She'd done her best to put him out of her mind, which was hard since she'd been editing the video at the time. And after its release, she'd been inundated with calls about how good it was, along with dozens of favorable comments about the rodeo clown. The video's success made forgetting him even harder.

Then, a couple of weeks before Thanksgiving, two things had happened. Recurring dizzy spells had sent her to the doctor, where she'd learned she was pregnant. Still reeling from that unexpected news, she was stunned when Blake Adams, a hot Hollywood director, had called, looking for someone with Gabe's skills for a movie he was doing. Was she at liberty to pass out his phone number?

She had given the man Gabe's number, but he'd called back after a week, telling her there was no answer. She'd explained that Gabe was probably on the road and then committed herself to trying to get in touch with him through a mutual friend.

Getting his mother's phone number in Calloway Corners was easy. Getting up the nerve to dial it was not. When she'd finally found the courage to punch out the number the day after Thanksgiving, she'd learned from his sister that he'd already gone.

She was both relieved and disappointed at having missed him. What would she have said to him after relaying Blake's message? Would she have found the nerve to tell him about the baby? Even now, a month later, she was still working on the answer to that all-important question.

She pressed her palm to her stomach, hoping to feel something—some movement—anything to make the pregnancy more real, something to dispel the disbelief. But it was too soon. She hadn't even had morning sickness.

How had she gotten pregnant so easily after having one ovary removed earlier in the year? She had no answer, but it had happened, it was real, and come May she'd have one of the things she'd wanted for so long.

But a baby was just half the dream. She wanted a father for that baby and a husband to share her life. A man with old-fashioned values. A man who would put his woman first, who was kind to kids and animals and would cherish her and his child with every fiber of his being. For those few, brief hours they'd spent together, she'd believed that man was Gabe.

It didn't seem like a lot to ask, especially since she was willing to reciprocate those feelings.

Had her desperation colored her thinking? Had she deliberately and foolishly disregarded his reputation as a ladies' man because she'd wanted so much to believe there was more to him than that? Had she mistaken the attributes she'd seen in him, the ones Nicole maintained were a part of him?

She didn't think so. Never in her life had she experienced such a strong certainty that this was the man she'd been looking for. Not with Paul or with Jim.

Was Nicole right? Could Gabe's reluctance to continue their relationship come from the fear he wasn't good enough for her? She rolled to her side and tried to will the troubled thoughts away. She was so tired. Emotionally and physically.

She thought again of Nicole's invitation to spend Christmas with her at Calloway Corners. The prospect was very appealing. Far more so than spending Christmas alone.

*What if you run into Gabe? Will you tell him about the baby?*

She felt the sting of tears again. Would she be able to live with herself if she didn't tell him? Nicole was right. He should have the opportunity to decide for himself whether or not he wanted to be a part of their child's life.

Would telling him make him see just what they could have together? Would the baby be a link between them, or would the news of a child be like an anchor tied to the feet of the footloose cowboy clown?

Having a baby was potent stuff; earth-shattering, life-altering news—like Nicole finally telling Lucas about the abortion her mother had decided she'd have.

That news hadn't brought Nicole and Lucas closer when it had come to light five years before; it had been, in fact, the straw that broke the fragile back of their complicated and troubled relationship. Nicole wasn't over it, and Gretchen was beginning to think she never would be.

Even though she and Gabe hadn't spent much time together, she had a sneaking feeling that she was going to feel the same way about Gabe that Nicole did about Lucas.

Gabriel Butler would be hard to forget, especially with his child around to remind her of him.

# CHAPTER THREE

THE *WHOMP-WHOMP-WHOMP* of the chopper's blades beat against Gretchen's eardrums in time with the nervous beating of her heart. Was she really doing this? Was it really Friday, the twenty-third of December, and was she really on her way to Calloway Corners, Louisiana, to spend three days with people she didn't know? Was she really going to walk into a party without a proper invitation?

*"Very bad form, sugar."*

Mimi West's voice danced through Gretchen's mind. A veteran Texas socialite, Mimi was a stickler for correct behavior and expected the same of her daughter. Whenever Gretchen failed to meet those stringent standards, Mimi blamed her daughter's lapse on her ten-year stint in California.

Gretchen smiled to herself. Mimi would die of mortification if she knew that her only child had virtually invited herself to the Calloway Christmas. She'd said as much to Nicole and was reminded that she *had* been invited—by Nicole. And, even though Gretchen hadn't decided to accept the invitation until half an hour before Nicole closed the boutique's doors for the holidays, Gretchen was assured that everyone would be delighted she was coming.

A quick call to Eden verified Nicole's claim. "But Eden does have a favor," Nicole told Gretchen.

"Sure," Gretchen said.

"Tomorrow night is family night, but she's having a party for some friends and mill employees tonight, and I'd mentioned once that you had a company helicopter, and she wondered if you could fly us over, instead of us driving, so we can be there for the fun. She said she'd have everyone chip in for your fuel or whatever."

"Don't be ridiculous!" Gretchen had assured her. "Of course we can take the chopper, and I won't take a penny. It's the least I can do for barging in at the last minute."

So here they were, two hours later, aloft somewhere over East Texas. The lights of civilization scattered among the darkness below looked like a handful of precious stones flung onto a cloth of blackest velvet.

Gretchen glanced at Nicole. Her head was leaning against the headrest, and her eyes were closed. After a hectic month at the boutique, she was catching a much-needed catnap.

She worried about Nicole. There was far too much work and far too little play in her friend's life. Thank goodness she was taking a few days off. Though there was one more shopping day before Christmas, Nicole had said to heck with it, closed the doors of the boutique at five and given her employees Christmas Eve day and the Monday following the holiday off.

"That's Marshall below us," Dirk Bledsoe, the pilot, announced suddenly. "Shreveport's just ahead. It won't be long now."

The statement didn't do much to calm Gretchen's nerves, but it was too late to go back now. She reminded herself for maybe the hundredth time that going to Gabe's hometown didn't mean she had to see him.

"Almost there?" Nicole asked, opening her eyes and smiling sleepily at Gretchen.

"Almost."

In a matter of minutes, Dirk was setting the helicopter down. Since finding the field behind the Calloway house would be impossible in the dark, Gretchen's pilot had arranged to land at the small downtown airport in Shreveport. Eden had promised to have someone there to pick them up and take them to Calloway Corners, a thirty-minute drive away.

Dirk helped unload their luggage, while Gretchen rummaged in her bag for a small foil-wrapped gift and an envelope that contained a bonus check for his pleasant company and his uncomplaining service during the past year.

"Spend it on the riverboats," she told the fifty-seven-year-old Vietnam veteran. With no family to go to, he planned to gamble away the Christmas weekend.

"That's exactly what I'm going to do," Dirk said, sticking the envelope into his pocket. "Gamble and eat Cajun food." He looked around. "I thought someone was meeting you."

"They're supposed to be," Nicole said. As she spoke, a sheriff's car—lights flashing—came wheeling to a stop a few yards from them.

Dirk held up the Christmas present and grinned. "Did you heist this from under some poor soul's Christmas tree?"

Nicole exchanged a concerned look with Gretchen. "No." She was wondering if they'd violated some sort of flight regulation or something when a pint-size

brunette dressed in a sequined, sapphire-hued cock-
tail dress got out of the car. Gretchen and Nicole exchanged another look, this one puzzled.

"Nicole Logan and Gretchen West?" the woman
asked.

"I'm Nicole Logan," she said in a wary tone. "This
is Gretchen West."

"Thank goodness you're right on time!" the petite
woman said. "They were afraid you'd be late." Smiling, she held out her hand. "I'm Susan Calloway,
Jericho's wife and Webster Parish sheriff. I've come
to drive you to Calloway Corners."

"You're the sheriff?" Gretchen said as the three
women shook hands.

"For the last year and a half," Susan said breezily,
reaching for a bag.

Dirk was faster. "I'll get those. You get the trunk."

Susan Calloway took the keys from the ignition and
went to the back of the car.

"I hope they aren't waiting for us," Nicole said as
Dirk loaded the luggage.

"Are you kidding? People were just beginning to
arrive when I left, but I guarantee the party'll be in full
swing by the time we get back."

"Who all is Eden expecting?" Nicole asked.

"Some people from the mill. Friends of the family." She shrugged. "It'll be an eclectic, interesting
group. Oh, and Mariah, Tess and Jo—all sans kids."
She tipped backed her head of glorious sable hair and
looked up at Dirk. "Where are you headed?"

"To the downtown Holiday Inn and then the riverboats."

"Load your suitcase," she commanded with a grin.
"We'll drop you off."

Dirk took the seat next to Susan, and Gretchen and Nicole climbed in the back. Susan negotiated the car the short distance to the hotel and, after depositing Dirk and his bag outside the entrance, pulled onto the interstate. Once they crossed the river into Bossier City, she hit the gas and flipped on the cruiser's lights. Immediately cars began to get out of her way. She cast a brief, unrepentant smile over the back of the seat.

"One of the perks of the job," she said, maneuvering the car through the traffic with deft efficiency.

Gretchen couldn't help smiling back. Her stay in Louisiana looked as if it was going to be interesting.

Calloway Corners, which was just a crossroads on the map and not an actual town at all, was situated just across the Webster Parish County line, between the small city of Haughton and the smaller town of Doyline. Calloway Corners consisted of nothing but the Calloway lumber mill, a general store and the old Calloway homestead, now occupied by Eden Calloway Logan, her husband, Nick, and their four kids: Ben, age four; Katherine Nicole, more often called Kat, age three; and the eighteen-month-old twins, James Nicholas and Jennifer Marie, better known as Cole and Jenni.

Though Susan shut off the siren and the lights as they turned off Highway 80, she didn't let up on the gas until they turned into the winding dirt lane leading to the house. The car bumped over the railroad tracks. The big two-story house at the end of the lane was ablaze with white Christmas lights. Cars littered the circular driveway.

As they neared the house, Gretchen saw that the porch was draped with pine boughs and red bows. An ancient oak towered over the entrance of the front gate, and two magnificent magnolia trees stood sentinel at each side of the house. Gretchen could only imagine what the yard must look like in spring when everything was green and flowering.

Susan parked the car, and the three women got out. "I'll send Jericho to get the luggage later," she told them as the front door burst open.

Susan ushered them up the steps, where a handsome, dark-haired man and a pretty strawberry blond woman waited. Nick and Eden, the host and hostess. Nicole was soon in her brother's arms, receiving a hard hug and a kiss on the cheek, which was repeated by Eden. Gretchen had met the couple before when they'd visited Nicole in Texas, and they welcomed her with hugs as well. Susan was thanked for getting back with the guests so quickly, a comment that elicited a sly smile.

The interior of the house looked like something from a Victorian Christmas, all lace and ribbon and chubby cherubs. The scents of cinnamon and pine filled Gretchen's nostrils. Christmas music provided a muted background for a dozen conversations. The old house overflowed with people wearing their party best and wide smiles.

Gretchen and Nicole were escorted from room to room—the party was strung out through the spacious living and dining rooms, as well as the large den/kitchen/breakfast area—and introduced to more people than they could possibly keep straight. Gretchen especially enjoyed meeting the other Calloway sisters and their husbands, all of whom were much handsomer in person than they were in Nicole's calendar.

Gretchen experienced a moment of blind panic when the bubbly Mariah went to fetch her male cousins, and then went limp with relief when Mariah came back arm in arm with only two men: Susan's husband, Jericho, and Daniel, who was marrying pretty Becca Harris, "the one over there by the fireplace wearing the green velvet dress.

"Gabe couldn't make it," Mariah added, genuine regret in her voice. "His sister, Jody, and her boyfriend, Tess's stepson, broke up, and Gabe said he needed to try and bring her out of the doldrums." She gave a reminiscent sigh. "Ah, young love. There's nothing more painful."

Except grown-up love, Gretchen thought, torn between sorrow that Gabe's sister was suffering and thankfulness that he hadn't been able to make the party.

As the evening progressed, she was caught up in the warmth that emanated from the Calloway family and friends. The happy, casual Christmas at Calloway Corners was far different from the elaborate, stuffy Christmas parties she'd attended at her parents' Fort Worth home. The Calloway sisters, their husbands and cousins were bound by an intangible bond of love that was evident in every laughing glance, every teasing gibe.

Gretchen couldn't help feeling a little sorry for herself. She wished she'd grown up in that same kind of loving atmosphere, instead of being shunted off to an exclusive girls' school so she wouldn't interfere in her parents' globe-trotting life-style. She vowed that somehow—though she didn't know how—the child she carried would have the benefits of a close-knit family.

The only hint of disharmony was the slight but un-
derstandable anxiety in Becca Harris's eyes whenever
Jesse and Sarah Calloway came near, and the brief but
quickly masked lull in a conversation whenever Jesse
approached a group.

Gretchen could only imagine what he must be feeling to be among old friends and family after so many
years in prison. Standing by the doorway that led from
the kitchen to a brick patio, she sipped her eggnog and
studied Gabe's father with brooding fascination.

Jesse Calloway was still a handsome man. His body
looked lean and relatively fit. Age had added gray to
his hair, and the groove in his right cheek that he'd
passed on to Gabe was more crease than dimple now.
His angular jaw, inherited by both Gabe and Daniel,
had lost some of its firmness, but the thick eyelashes
that must have driven women wild back in his youth
were still as attractive as ever.

Yet despite the years of hell he must have suffered
and the weary wariness in his eyes, there was an undeniable assurance in the way he carried himself. Life
might have knocked Jesse Calloway down, but it
hadn't beaten him. Gretchen liked that. She only
hoped that he'd learned to rein in his temper and that
the things he'd gone through had mellowed him and
taught him self-control.

She saw him smile down at his wife, saw the way the
small gesture brightened Sarah Calloway's face, noticed the startled but pleased glance that passed between Jericho and Daniel. Maybe time did heal
wounds. Maybe love did cover a multitude of sins.

Jericho glanced Gretchen's way, caught her watching his parents and smiled. She smiled back. She liked
Gabe's brothers and found herself wondering what

they would think if they knew she was pregnant with Gabe's child. And what would Jesse think about his bastard son making him a grandfather?

Gretchen paused, the eggnog en route to her mouth. For the first time, she really faced the fact that Jesse Calloway, a man who'd been convicted of manslaughter, a man who had spent the past eighteen years in prison, was going to be her child's grandfather. That situation warranted some thought.

Mimi and Tyrell West were fairly liberal in their views about life, and Gretchen was smart enough to know that a few of her father's business dealings trod the fine line of legality. While she suspected they would be only marginally upset about her giving birth outside of marriage, they—especially Mimi—would be livid because her baby's father was illegitimate and even more so that Gabe's father had done time. It made little sense, but there it was.

She could hear her mother as clearly as if she was standing next to her.

*"Background is important, sugar. You can't raise thoroughbreds if you breed grade stock."*

Gretchen didn't agree with her mother's beliefs. What was important to her was how Gabe felt about the past and how it had affected his life. What kind of scars had Jesse's transgressions left on Gabe? Had his father's sins influenced his formative years for the good or bad?

Pressed for an answer, she would say that the teasing, gentle man she'd spent the weekend with had risen above the circumstances of his conception and the fact that the father who had never acknowledged him had served a prison term for killing a man. But when she recalled the way he'd distanced himself after that

phone call with Daniel, she wasn't so sure that con-
clusion held water.

The chiming of the doorbell in the other room
jarred her from her troubled thoughts. Cries of "So
glad you could make it!" and "Hey, everybody, look
who's here!" wafted back to the kitchen. Whoever
had come must be special, indeed.

"Gretchen!"

She turned at the sound of Nicole's voice. Her
friend approached with a smile, her arm linked with
that of the husband of one of the Calloway sisters. But
which one? Keeping all the sisters and their husbands
straight after only one meeting was mind-boggling.

"Seth, right?" Gretchen said, pointing a finger at
him. "Tess's husband. A son, Jason, almost nine-
teen, and another, Richie, four."

Seth Taylor laughed. "You must have an incredible
mind for detail if you can remember all that after being introduced to half the local population."

"Actually I made a special effort to remember the
people I thought I'd see a lot of during my stay,"
Gretchen confessed with a wry smile.

"Seth is a country-music fan, and he loves what you
did with 'Cathy's Clown,'" Nicole told her. "He
wanted to know how you came up with your ideas."

"Everything you always wanted to know about
making videos but were afraid to ask, huh?"

"Sort of," Seth said.

Just then, Nicole's brother stepped up behind her
and put his hands on her shoulders. She tilted her head
back and smiled at him.

"I hate to interrupt," Nick said, "but I need to talk
to Nicci a moment."

"Oh, sounds ominous," Nicole said, patting Nick's hand. Her smile encompassed both Seth and Gretchen. "Excuse us a minute."

"Sure," Seth said.

Frowning, Gretchen watched as Nick draped his arm over his sister's shoulders and guided her toward a corner of the kitchen. Though Nicole hadn't seen it, there'd been a strained look on Nick Logan's face—an ominous look. She wondered what had come up.

"Well, sur-prise, sur-prise, sur-prise."

Seth Taylor's Gomer Pyle impersonation shifted Gretchen's attention back. Seth was grinning and waving at someone across the room. She glanced in that direction and felt her knees grow weak.

No more than fifteen feet from her stood two men. One was a tall, dark stranger. The other was equally tall, with dark blond hair and a mustache adorning his upper lip. There was nothing strange about him. This man she knew well. Intimately. From the way the hair crinkled on his long, muscular legs to the way his tanned skin tasted, salty with sweat.

Her heart sank. The earth shifted on its axis.

Gabe.

SEEING GRETCHEN standing next to Seth Taylor in Eden's kitchen was like taking a blow to the gut. Gabe's ears rang and his heart slammed against his rib cage. His knees had that weak feeling he got when he was in the middle of a rodeo arena doing the do-si-do with a particularly ornery bull. What on earth was she doing here? he wondered as he and Lucas Tanner made their way through the guests.

She looked gorgeous. Even beneath the harshness of the fluorescent lights her complexion was flawless.

Red highlights glimmered in the depths of her brown hair. He thought he'd memorized every detail of her face, but he was surprised anew by the delicate arch of her eyebrows, the unique shape of her eyes, the fullness of her mouth. And he'd forgotten how she could put you in your place with a look down her patrician nose.

Seth stretched out his hand, and Gabe took it. "Hey, you old rodeo bum! What are you doing here? I thought you were on the road."

Gabe answered Seth, but his gaze was fixed on Gretchen. "National Finals were over Sunday."

"That's right!" Noting Gabe's interest in Gretchen, Seth said, "Gabe, I'd like you to meet Gretchen West."

"Gabe and I met making the video," Gretchen reminded an embarrassed Seth in a voice as chilly as the drink in her hand. She raised her chin a millimeter. "Hello, Gabe."

Apparently, he thought, she was still ticked off at him. "Gretchen."

"Good grief! Is that Nicole over there with Nick?" Lucas Tanner's stunned voice snapped the building tension.

"Yes, it is," Seth said.

Lucas had the distressed look of a man about to crawl across a mine field. Obviously more concerned with the appearance of Nicole Logan than he was with the disaster unfolding before him, he excused himself and started toward her.

Gretchen made a move to follow, but Gabe stopped her with a hand on her arm. "Whatever it is, it doesn't concern you."

His voice was quiet, firm. She looked to Nicole and then back up at him again, and he released his hold on her.

"I hate to leave good company, but I'd better go see if Tess wants help with anything," Seth said suddenly. The look on his face betrayed his desire to get out of the middle of a potentially dangerous situation.

Gabe bit back a wry smile. "By all means," he said. "Gretchen and I have a lot of catching up to do. We'll see you later."

Seth left them alone, or as alone as they could be in a room full of people. Gretchen set her cup on the counter and turned toward Nicole and Lucas. Gabe followed her gaze, noting the looks of passionate intensity on his friends' faces. If he'd been a betting man, he'd have said their conversation was headed along the same lines as his and Gretchen's.

He crossed his arms over his chest. "So what brings you to this neck of the woods?"

Gretchen cast him a cool look. "Nicole invited me. I figured you'd be on the road somewhere."

"So you wouldn't have come if you'd known I'd show up, huh?"

"I don't waste my time pursuing things with no future."

Outwardly, her attitude skirted boredom, but there was something else going on he couldn't quite pin down. Wariness? Frustration? Anger? His own frustration and anger and a ridiculous happiness at seeing her again waged a battle in him. "So you did mean that crazy proposal?" he said with a grin, wanting desperately to rattle her out of her seeming complacency.

"I was joking," she said, her voice filled with a steel he hadn't heard before. "On the other hand, I'm not a one-night-stand kind of a woman, either."

This time, there was no mistaking the look in her eyes. He'd seen enough pain in his own eyes to recognize it. For some reason he couldn't fathom, his refusal to let their weekend develop into a more lasting relationship had hurt her.

He took her arm again. He had a lot to say, and this time she wasn't going to stop him.

"Let's go someplace we can talk."

"You got what you wanted from me. I don't think we have anything to say to each other."

"No?" he drawled. "Then why did you call for me at my mother's house the day after Thanksgiving?"

Her brief glance was cutting, sharp. "Don't flatter yourself that it was personal. I was trying to get in touch with you about some business."

"What kind of business?" he asked, deftly steering her through the throng and into a bedroom off the living area. He didn't shut the door, but he guided her to a spot where they would be out of sight to anyone casually passing by.

"Blake Adams, a film director, saw you in the video. He wanted to talk to you about a part for some film he's doing. I gave him your number, but he couldn't reach you. I told him I'd try. I got your mother's number from Nicole, who got it from Nick." She relayed the information to him in a clipped, impersonal voice.

His heart took a nosedive. So all those hang-ups on his answering machine hadn't been her. "He wants me to act?"

"Why not?" She pinned him with another barbed look. "You do it so well."

"What the hell is that supposed to mean?"

"Nothing."

He counted to ten and forced himself to stay calm. "If you're referring to the weekend we spent together, I—"

"Look," she cut in, facing him with the full force of her anger. "I really don't want to discuss it. You made your feelings perfectly clear. I'm slow, but I get the picture. You don't want any strings. You aren't interested in things going any further between us."

"I have my reasons."

"Men always do," she said with a bitterness that surprised him. "Don't worry about me, Gabe. Getting dumped hurt, but I'm a big girl. I'll get over it."

"Maybe you will," he said, "but I'm not so sure about me."

His confession undermined her anger and sent confusion rushing to her eyes. "Don't," she begged.

"There are things about me you don't know."

"You're Jesse Calloway's illegitimate son," she said almost breezily.

This time it was Gabe who was shocked. "Who told you that?"

"Nicole."

His soft curse hung between them. "Nicole's a nice person, but she needs to keep her mouth shut," he said, his anger on the rise.

"Nicole is my friend. Yours, too. She was trying to help me understand you better."

"And did telling you about Jesse and my mother help?" he asked with barely veiled sarcasm.

The eyes that met his held a disturbing bleakness. "Not much."

"Then you don't know everything."

"I know about your dad . . . and Becca's."

"Damn!" Gabe turned away, scraping his fingers through his slightly wavy hair. He wasn't the kind to try to gain a woman's—or anyone's—sympathy by revealing the darker side of his past, and he didn't need anyone else doing that, either. It seemed to him that when people heard his history they either judged him harshly because of it or felt sorry for him.

He didn't want or deserve either.

What he deserved was to be judged on his own merit—good or bad. Jesse and his mother's affair had nothing to do with him, just as Reverend Harris's senseless slaying was Jesse's sin, not any of his sons'.

*But you've paid for those sins, haven't you, Gabe. Not just you. Jericho and Daniel, too. All of you. And you'll pay till the day they put you six feet under.*

He felt Gretchen's hand on his arm. He looked down at her, unaware that his pale blue eyes revealed his torment. The pain of his memories had almost made him forget she was standing next to him.

"It doesn't matter," she told him, softness in her eyes and apology in her voice.

"It matters to me," he told her. And without another word or a backward glance, he turned and walked out of the bedroom and straight to the front door.

There wasn't much Gretchen could do but watch him go. The set of his wide shoulders in the Western-style sports coat was stiff and unyielding. She blinked to hold back a rush of tears. What was it about him that managed to move her from uncertainty to anger to frustrated tears all in the space of minutes?

The answer was quick, unexpected.

*Love.*

The tiny inner voice brought her up short. Love? Oh, she'd been intrigued by him and thought he was the right man for her, or she'd never have agreed to stay the weekend with him. Had she suspected it was love, even back then?

Of course she had. But she'd discounted the notion, telling herself that rightness she felt in his arms, that heady feeling, was infatuation, the thrill of a new romance; after all, she'd believed Paul and Jim were right for her, too.

Maybe she didn't know what love really was. Maybe, she thought, swallowing hard, she was a bad judge of character, one of those pitiful women doomed to give herself to men who had no desire to commit to a lasting relationship.

*Maybe you will, but I'm not so sure about me.*

Gabe's words sprang into her mind and kindled the tiniest spark of hope. Had he meant that he was having a hard time forgetting her, too? Did he mean that his heart was more involved than he wanted to admit, or did he mean that the lovemaking they'd shared was hard to forget?

It was difficult to say, but any way she looked at it, the statement seemed to be a positive thing. Maybe there was a chance that whatever his feelings were, they could be tended and cared for until they grew into something lasting.

"Gretchen? Are you in there?"

Nicole's softly voiced query brought Gretchen back to the present. How long had she stood staring after

Gabe Butler's retreating back? Shaking off her be-
musement, she left the comparative anonymity of the
bedroom. Nicole stood just outside the door, her face
pale, her eyes awash in unshed tears.

"Nicole! What's wrong?"

Nicole shook her head. "Can we get out of here?"
she asked in a trembling voice.

Her friend's desperation frightened Gretchen. "Of
course we can, but where?"

"The garage apartment," Nicole said.

Pleading weariness to Eden, who pretended not to
notice the impending tears and said she understood,
Nicole led the way to the apartment above Eden's garage, which served as a stopover for anyone who
needed a place to stay.

While Nicole pulled the blinds, Gretchen took a
quick survey of the place. The apartment consisted of
a large living/sleeping/kitchen area all done in yellow
and white with touches of wisteria. Gretchen noticed
that, good to her word, Susan Calloway had seen to it
that their bags were brought up.

When the last blind was pulled, Nicole turned, her
still-trembling hands clasped tightly together.

"What is it?" Gretchen asked. "I know that whatever is bothering you has something to do with that
man, doesn't it?"

Nicole nodded. "That man," she said, "is Lucas
Tanner."

## CHAPTER FOUR

"LUCAS TANNER!" Gretchen exclaimed.

Nicole nodded. "He's the new mill manager."

"Isn't it a little coincidental that he's working for your brother?"

Nicole threaded her fingers through her glossy chocolate-hued hair. "Not really. Nick heard about Lucas's divorce and figured he might be interested in making a change, so he contacted him. Gil Tanner worked in my father's lumber business for years, and he raised Lucas. So Lucas knows lumber inside and out."

Gretchen saw the torment on her friend's face and knew she was hurting—badly. "Didn't Nick stop to think about how seeing Lucas might upset you?"

"I'm sure he did. Nick's always been sensitive to my feelings, but I don't come here often or stay long, and I never go to the mill. Chances of my running into Lucas were pretty slim."

Gretchen's mouth twisted in a wry smile. "So what happened tonight?"

"'The best laid plans...'" Nicole quoted with mild sarcasm. She went to the window and peered through the slats in the blinds. "Nick said that Lucas told him he wasn't coming over tonight because he had to unpack. I guess Eden thought it would be safe for us to join the party."

"Seeing him still hurts." Gretchen's statement echoed the misery on Nicole's face.

Nicole pursed her full lips, swallowed and nodded. Tears glittered in her eyes.

"How long has it been since you last saw him?"

"Around five years. That was when I told him about the baby..." She shrugged. "It was just too much."

"Do you want to talk about it?" Gretchen asked. "I'll be glad to listen."

"I don't know," Nicole said, misery lurking in the depths of her dark eyes. "Maybe it would help." She gave a harsh laugh. "But it isn't pretty."

Gretchen's voice held a world of gentleness. "All of us have our dirty laundry, or skeletons or ghosts or whatever you want to call it. None of us has lived the perfect life."

"I suppose not." Nicole sighed and slumped onto the sofa, staring at the fingers she knotted together. "Lucas and I were in love when I was in college. We were... pretty hot and heavy, and we wanted to get married, but my mother seemed to hate him, so we sneaked around to be with each other."

"Been there, done that," Gretchen said with a smile. Hadn't every girl dated a boy her family hated?

"I didn't understand why Mom was so dead set against him. He was a nice guy, and Ellie and Gil Tanner were the best. In fact, Gil taught Luke and Nick everything they know about the lumber industry.

"Anyway, one day my stepbrother, Keith, caught me and Lucas together." Nicole's eyes filled and ran over. She clamped her teeth down on her bottom lip so hard it started to bleed.

With a cry of dismay, Gretchen grabbed a tissue from a nearby box and thrust it into Nicole's hand.

"Thanks," she whispered, pressing it to her lip. She took a shaky breath. "Keith beat Lucas to a pulp. I tried to make him stop..." Her voice trailed away, and her eyes held a faraway look. "I don't remember much after that. When I finally regained consciousness, I was in a fancy sanatorium and had been there for several months. My memory of that night was gone. Mom told me Lucas had raped me and that Keith had caught him in the act. All I remembered was getting in Lucas's truck earlier that day."

Nicole sniffed, blotted her eyes and took up her tale again. "My mother also told me that while I was in my...comatose state I'd had an abortion. It was her call. Neither she nor the doctors thought I should go through a pregnancy considering my emotional state. The baby would just be a reminder of what Lucas had done, and I was in no condition to mother a child."

The grief on Nicole's face was almost more than Gretchen could bear. She felt tears slide down her own cheeks.

"It didn't make sense to me, Gretchen. I didn't remember what happened that night, but I remembered loving Lucas and I had occasional flashes of us together. I kept asking myself why he would rape me if we were already sleeping together."

"What happened to Lucas?"

"Dad ran the Tanners out of the county."

Gretchen had no reply. Nicole brushed at her eyes.

"So I spent almost two years at this exclusive sanatorium, and when I did get out I was...what did they call it?" She closed her eyes and then said caustically, "Oh, yeah. Fragile. I was fragile emotionally."

"Obviously you've come a long way."

"I have. But it was hard. I borrowed the money from Dad to start a boutique in Little Rock, but I paid him back every penny. I was successful but miserable. Nick was the only thing that kept me going, but I didn't get to see much of him because he and our dad had a major falling-out over Dad letting Keith take the position that should have been Nick's in the family business.

"The autumn that Nick first came here, our family was pretty torn up. Then my dad got some pretty shocking news and had a stroke. He was under a lot of stress—he was already being investigated for some of his business dealings. Keith found him in his study. It was pretty bad.

"Anyway, Dad realized he'd better get his life straight." Nicole smiled grimly. "Staring death in the eye does that to you, they say. So he and Mom decided to tell me and Nick the truth about our parentage."

"Were you adopted or something?"

"If only it was that simple." Nicole got up and paced the width of the large room. "Stuart—Dad—has always been the kind of man who got what he wanted one way or the other. And it seems he wanted Ellie Tanner. This was before I was born."

"Lucas's mother?" Gretchen asked, aghast.

"Yes. Ever the gentleman," she said sarcastically, "he blackmailed her into agreeing to an affair. It didn't last long, and when Gil came home from serving overseas, Ellie's conscience got the best of her and she confessed. Naturally Gil was devastated, but in true macho fashion, he decided to get back at Ellie and

Stuart by coaxing my mother, Theresa, into an affair."

Gretchen's mouth fell open. "So they had, like, double affairs?"

Nicole nodded. "I can't put all the blame on Gil. It couldn't have been hard talking Mom into it. She cared about him a great deal."

"You're kidding, right?"

"I only wish," Nicole said. "After a while, Mom learned she was pregnant, and it seems she had no doubt that Gil was responsible for her pregnancy. Ellie was pregnant, too, but a little farther along than Mom."

"Wait a minute," Gretchen said, hoping she wasn't hearing what she thought she was. "Are you saying that Gil Tanner—Lucas's father—is your and Nick's father, too?"

Nicole nodded again. "Mom never told Dad— Stuart—the truth, but he found out later."

Full comprehension leeched the color from Gretchen's face. "Oh, God, Nicole. Lucas is your half brother?"

Nicole blew out a deep breath. "That's what Mom thought, which is why she didn't want me dating Lucas and why she made me have the abortion. We didn't find out until five years ago that it wasn't so."

"Wait a minute!" Gretchen said, clutching her head. "I'm lost."

"Well, hold on to your hat, honey, because it gets weirder. Remember my telling you that Stuart's stroke was partially brought on by some news he received?"

Frowning, Gretchen nodded.

"Well, the news was that *he's* Lucas's father—not Gil. Because Gil was overseas when Lucas was conceived and when Ellie found out she was pregnant, she had no choice but to tell him about her affair with Stuart. So, Gil always knew that Lucas wasn't his, but Stuart didn't find out about Lucas until the day of the stroke.''

"Are you sure you didn't see this during soap-opera sweeps week?''

In spite of herself, Nicole was able to smile. "Truth really is stranger than fiction.''

"So you and Lucas aren't related.''

"No. Which brings me to the end of this nasty little story. When Dad told me all this, it was like the opening of Pandora's box. I suddenly remembered what really happened the day Keith beat up Luke.'' The look she gave Gretchen was filled with sorrow and shame. "It wasn't Lucas who'd raped me. It was Keith.''

Gretchen's mouth fell open.

"He raped me and told Mama and Dad that Lucas had done it and he'd caught him in the act, which excused his beating up Lucas. That's what sent me over the edge and caused my breakdown. That's what I was blocking out. When I got out of the sanatorium, I think I knew the truth on some level, because I couldn't stand being around Keith.''

"Nicole . . . I don't know what to say.''

Her smile was wan, tentative. "There's nothing to say, but thanks for listening.''

Gretchen smiled back. "What about Gil Tanner?''

"Nick and I have established a relationship with him, and it's nice, you know? He was always a nice man.''

"But you and Lucas couldn't work it out?''

Nicole shook her head. "We gave it our best shot. We spent months trying to get back on some sort of solid ground, but with all the lies and the accusation that he'd raped me...and the abortion—" she shrugged "—we couldn't overcome it all."

"Well, he sure was anxious to see you tonight. What did he say?"

"Nothing much. How had I been? What was I doing here? He asked about Stuart. I asked about Gil. Banalities. He seems different. Sad. Maybe even bitter."

"I'm sorry."

Nicole met Gretchen's sympathetic gaze. "Yeah. So am I." Then she squared her shoulders and shook her head as if to shake off the whole episode. "Do you love Gabe?" she asked, abruptly shifting the conversation away from herself and her problems.

"What can I say? I really don't know him very well, but I'm very attracted to him."

"Come on, Gretchen," Nicole chided. "When it's right, you know it. Time isn't a factor."

"I know what I think I feel, but I've been hurt so many times I'm afraid to trust my heart."

"Don't be. If you care for him, go after him. I was looking at you two from across the room. He looked as if he'd like to drag you off to his lair and ravish you."

The observation surprised Gretchen. "Really?"

"Really. Maybe all he needs is a little jolt. Tell him about the baby."

Gretchen shook her head. "I want him to want me for who I am, for what I can give him, not because of the baby."

"He still has a right to be told."

"What if he doesn't want anything to do with me or the baby? I don't think I could stand it if he turned his back on us."

"You'll stand it." Nicole smiled sadly. "Look at it this way. At least you'll have his child as a reminder of him. I don't even have that."

Gretchen was overwhelmed with empathy for her friend's loss. She had to concede that Nicole had a point. Even if Gabe walked out of her life, she had a lot to be thankful for.

"Maybe you and Lucas can work out your differences in time," she said, wanting to offer Nicole some small comfort.

Nicole shook her head. "I don't think so. And it seems like such a shame, you know? I still love him, and deep down, I think he still cares for me."

Long after the lights were off, Nicole lay next to Gretchen on the king-size bed thinking about her conversation with Lucas. When Nick had told her that Lucas was there, she'd been furious at her brother until Nick explained that he'd had no idea Lucas would show up. Evidently Gabe had stopped by Lucas's place after he'd taken Jody home, and the two had made quick work of unboxing Lucas's belongings.

Knowing the truth didn't make facing Lucas any easier. If she'd known he was coming to the party, she'd never have asked Gretchen to have Dirk fly them over. But they were here now, and all she could hope for was that she'd get through the rest of the weekend without any more unexpected encounters.

Her lips quirked wryly in the darkness. She was certain Gretchen, running so unexpectedly into Gabe, felt the same way. Recalling how Gabe had left the party in a huff, Nicole tossed restlessly onto her side. Maybe she shouldn't have told Gretchen about his past, but she felt strongly that her friend had a right to know what motivated Gabe. How else could Gretchen make a decision about her future or the child she and Gabe had conceived?

Nicole's hand moved to her abdomen, where Lucas's baby had once lain. Empty. But the emptiness went far deeper than her womb. It had permeated her very soul and infiltrated the deepest places of her heart. There were times she was certain the aching void would never be filled, times she was certain she would never love and be loved again—and never again shelter the precious gift of life in her needy body.

Then, just when she was at her lowest, something would happen to give her a bit of hope. She'd meet someone new, someone like Steve, someone who claimed to be crazy about her, and for a while she would cherish the notion that it would all be okay. But she'd never met a man who was able to fan that spark into a flame, and she would break off the faltering relationship, throw herself back into her work and fall back on reliving her lonely, bittersweet memories.

The problem wasn't with the men she met. The problem was she still loved Lucas Tanner. There were times, such as when she'd heard about his divorce, she entertained dreams of working things out, but she knew they were just that—dreams. Impossible dreams.

Nights like tonight proved it.

Lucas had been as shocked to see her as she was him. When she'd explained how she happened to be there, he actually apologized for showing up without warning. They'd talked about inconsequential things.

Gil's health. How Lucas liked his new job. How he
was settling into Calloway Corners.

The conversation had been strained, but he'd
been . . . polite. That was the problem, she thought.
They'd both been through so much pain that they were
extremely sensitive to the prospect of inflicting more.
Even five years ago, when they'd acknowledged that
their relationship didn't stand a chance of going anywhere, they'd been excruciatingly civilized.

Sometimes Nicole thought that things might have
been better if they'd screamed and yelled at each other
so they could rid themselves of their frustrations and
anger once and for all. But now, chances of that happening were slim, and life had to go on. She was getting older, and at times the ticking of her biological
clock approached a deafening decibel.

Times like now.

Gretchen's pregnancy was both joy and agony. Like
Nicole, Gretchen wasn't getting any younger, and
she'd had her share of bad experiences with men. She
was due for some happiness, and Nicole knew that,
despite Gretchen's uncertainty over the unplanned
pregnancy and her fear that Gabe might not want to
be part of her and the baby's life, she'd find a tre-
mendous amount of joy in mothering this child.

Gretchen, however, didn't see it that way. She
wanted it all. The complete family triangle: man,
woman and child. It was Nicole's fervent prayer that
she get it.

GRETCHEN AWOKE from what little sleep she'd gotten, feeling as if the weight of the world were pressing
her down. As she'd lain rigidly in the unfamiliar bed,
she suspected that her friend wasn't having any better

luck finding sleep than she was. Her own mind danced from her disturbing conversation with Gabe to the strange tale Nicole had told her and then back again. Nicole's story was almost too bizarre to be believable, but as she'd said, truth was stranger than fiction.

Finally her weariness had overcome her active mind, and she'd succumbed to a restless sleep. Now it was barely daylight, but a yawn from the other side of the bed told her Nicole was awake, too.

Nicole told Gretchen to take the first shower, which she did. Minutes later she pulled on a pair of faded jeans and a bulky forest green sweater while Nicole took her turn. According to Nicole, today was the day Eden and her family took Christmas goodies to the shut-ins. The elder Logans would arrive from Arkansas at midmorning, and tonight would be spent with the immediate family. The kids would be hustled off to bed early to sleep away the hours till Santa came.

"Don't we have to fix the last-minute things for dinner tomorrow?" Gretchen asked.

"Eden doesn't do a traditional Christmas dinner with turkey and all the trimmings. She does that for Thanksgiving. For Christmas she fixes brunch about ten, after the kids have opened their presents and played a while. Then she has a pot of gumbo on the stove so that everyone can eat when they get hungry.

"Mariah, Tess, Jo and their husbands will probably show up sometime tomorrow afternoon with their kids, but basically they just play games and visit and watch ball games. Very low-key."

"It sounds nice," Gretchen said, thinking of the elaborate dinner her mother's chef always prepared and how the whole Christmas holiday was a study in formality. She wondered how Gabe and his family spent the holiday, then pushed the thought away. She refused to let musings of what Gabe Butler might be doing ruin her weekend.

"UP AND AT 'EM, stud muffin, or I'm comin' to roust you out!"

The throaty warning roused Gabe from a light sleep. With a groan, he rolled onto his back and flung one arm over his face. Jody. Sounding disgustingly cheerful. He wondered what had happened to the brokenhearted woman-child whose tears had drenched his shirt the night before. If only his emotions were so resilient.

He'd brooded half the night over his conversation with Gretchen, part of him wishing he'd kissed the stubborn pout from her lips, part of him wishing he'd shaken some sense into her and another part of him wishing he could have crawled into a hole somewhere. Instead, he'd done the next best macho thing that came to mind: he left the party.

The sound of Jody's boots on the stairs scattered his thoughts and sent him bolting to a sitting position. Clad in jeans, sneakers and a red plaid flannel shirt that looked like a castoff of Joel's, Jody burst into the room with a look of mock-disgust on her pretty face.

She planted her hands on her hips. "Sun's gonna warp your ribs," she said, using the phrase their mother had always taunted them with whenever they slept late.

He crossed his arms over his bare chest. "So?" The query came out a husky croak.

"So get up and come on over to the house. Jericho wants you to call him. Something about meeting him and Daniel at Shoney's in Bossier City for break-fast."

"I'll get up in a minute."

Jody started to leave.

"Sis!"

"Yeah?" she said, turning back to face him.

"How come you're so cheerful? I thought you left old Jason standing at the edge of goodbye," he said, using the title of a country song to describe the breakup of the day before. "What happened after I brought you home?"

"He called me this morning and told me he was sorry for talking to that trashy Cindy Lou Harper. He said she didn't mean anything to him."

Gabe grinned. "And you fell for that old line?"

"Ga-abe!" Jody cried, putting her fists on her hips again.

His chuckle was unrepentant. "I'm glad you're feeling better, sweetcheeks."

Suddenly serious, Jody said, "Thanks for caring, big brother."

"My pleasure. Comforting cowgirls in distress is what cowboys do best."

She smiled. "You're pretty cool—for an old man of thirty-four."

"Thanks—I think," Gabe said. "Now get out of here so I can jump in the shower."

"I'm gone. See you later." She flashed him another smile and disappeared through the doorway. The sound of her cheerful voice lingered in his mind long after the thump of her footsteps and the slam of the front door faded.

Gabe's heart ached with a familiar heaviness. He couldn't remember his teenage years being filled with such normal things as having a fight with his girl-friend. All he remembered was ignoring the whispers and either working three times as hard as anyone else or fighting for what little respect he got.

He didn't feel as if he'd ever really been young. He and his brothers had been forced to grow up fast. Pain and heartache had a way of making a person old before his time....

GABE PULLED into a parking place at Shoney's just two minutes before the time Jericho had appointed. The impromptu breakfast would be the brothers' only chance to get together before Christmas. It occurred to Gabe—not for the first time—that they'd never spent a Christmas together as brothers and probably never would.

He spotted Jericho's van and wondered if he and Daniel had ridden to town together.

As usual, Shoney's was filled. Last-minute shoppers lined up to gorge from the breakfast buffet, fortifying themselves before confronting the frenzy of the nearby mall. Gabe spotted his brothers at a corner table. He was surprised to see Jesse with them. Thank goodness he had his dad's Christmas gift in the truck.

As he neared the table, he saw the easy smiles on the trio's faces. A part of him was glad that his brothers and Jesse were working through their differences. Families should be close and supportive. But as happy as he was for his brothers, another part of him still resented the fact that he was on the outside, where he'd always been—Jesse Calloway's misbegotten son.

Jesse hadn't even said hello to him at the party the night before. Maybe, Gabe reasoned, it was because he'd approached Gretchen almost as soon as he got there, but he suspected that even if she hadn't been in attendance, Jesse would have stayed clear of him as a courtesy to Sarah. Gabe understood Jesse's behavior, understood that his very existence was a thorn in Sarah Calloway's side, a constant reminder of her husband's infidelity. The deliberate snub hurt nonetheless.

Gabe used to dream that one day his dad would own up to his past and claim him, but he'd long ago realized it would never happen. Jesse would never say the words, and maybe that was the way it should be. It would only cause Sarah more pain, and Gabe didn't figure it would change the world's perception of him. Still, it would have satisfied some need inside him, some inner hunger to know that his dad loved him enough to tell the world, "This is my son and I'm damn proud of it!"

And yet, looking at Jesse now, Gabe couldn't deny that the pleased expression in his dad's eyes was genuine. Smiling, Gabe exchanged greetings with the three men who'd played major roles in his life.

They discussed the party as they went through the buffet, but it wasn't until they were seated again that Jesse asked, "Who was that woman you were talking to in the kitchen last night?"

Suddenly Gabe felt the impact of three pairs of eyes. He wasn't sure, but he might have blushed for the first time since junior-high school when Amy Gordon told him his fly was unzipped. He did know that the simple question was not cause for the sudden flurry of butterflies assaulting his stomach. "That was Gretchen West. She owns the company that did the video."

Fortunately, the explanation came out with just the right amount of nonchalance, at least to his ears.

"Classy-looking lady," Daniel said. "What's she doing here? Don't tell me she hunted down an old rodeo bum like you."

"She's a friend of Nicole's," Gabe said. "Nicole asked her to come here for the holidays."

"I can't believe a woman who looks like that doesn't have somebody to curl up next to on a cold winter night," Jericho said.

Gabe recalled the feel of her body curved next to his. He discreetly kept his mouth shut.

"I saw the two of you go into the bedroom to talk," Jesse said. "What'd she say to make you storm off like that?"

Gabe's jaw tightened. He countered Jesse's curious question with anger. "That's really none of your business, is it, Jesse?"

Jesse's face flushed, but before he could say anything, Jericho intervened. "Come on, Pop, give him a break. You know how rocky the road to romance can be."

"Gretchen and I aren't romantically involved."

"Aha! He calls her Gretchen. Methinks the dude doth protest too loudly," Daniel misquoted with a smirk.

"Yeah?" Gabe said. "Well, I think you've got a big mouth."

"Undeniably," Jericho said with a lift of his eyebrows and a smile, "but it's Christmas Eve, so we're gonna be nice to him, right?"

"Right," Gabe grumbled, ashamed that he'd let Jesse get a rise out of him. He looked from one companion to the other and said, "The woman is Tyrell West's daughter." Which should explain everything.

Jericho whistled. There wasn't a Texan alive who didn't know that Tyrell West was one of the few oil barons who'd emerged from the oil bust as one of the wealthiest men in the state.

"If she's interested, you better latch on to her," Daniel said. "You can't fight off the buckle bunnies forever."

Gabe shook his head. "I never thought I'd see the day you and Jericho would play matchmaker. Just because the two of you have fallen head over heels doesn't mean I will. Besides," he said, shrugging with feigned indifference, "even if I was interested, she's way out of my league."

"Love can bridge those kinds of gaps," Daniel said, suddenly serious.

Love? The very mention of the word brought on a suffocating panic. "Love! What's love got to do with it?"

"Isn't that the title of an old Tina Turner song?" Jericho asked, pointing at Daniel with a forkful of gravy slathered biscuit.

"I believe so," Daniel said, humming a couple of bars.

Gabe swore softly and shook his head. "Trying to carry on a conversation with the two of you is like trying to talk to Abbott and Costello in the middle of one of their routines."

"The problem with you is you have no sense of humor," Jericho said. "Right, squirt?"

"Right," Daniel, who as a child had been dubbed "squirt" by his older brother, agreed.

"And the problem with the two of you is that love has made you soft in the head."

Jesse, who'd been out of the familial loop for too many years, looked from one son to the other, uncertain how to take either the good-natured ribbing or Gabe's acerbic replies.

Seeing the look on his dad's face, Gabe said, "Don't look so worried, Jesse. We haven't come to blows in years."

Jesse's brow smoothed. "That's nice to know."

They finished the meal with more conversation about the party: what a great job Eden had done, as usual; how happy Tess looked; how mellow Jo seemed to have grown; how settled Mariah appeared. They even discussed Lucas Tanner's new position as manager of the Calloway lumber mill and speculated about what was going on between him and Nicole Logan.

When both breakfast and conversation were exhausted, Jesse picked up the tab for the meal and they all trekked outside to exchange their gifts. Gabe got a pair of hand-tooled Rocketbuster boots from Jericho and a new Browning rifle from Daniel. Jesse, obviously getting sentimental since he'd left prison, gave all the boys something that had belonged to his father. Jericho got Ben, Sr.'s, watch. Daniel got his ruby tie tack.

Gabe was feeling decidedly uncomfortable when Jesse drew another package from his coat pocket. "This is for you," he said, handing it to Gabe. Shocked into silence, Gabe unwrapped the slender gift slowly. A hunting knife lay nestled in white tissue paper. The carbon blade had been honed to razor sharpness. The wooden handle held the patina of more than fifty years of use. Gabe knew that Jesse's dad had handmade the knife when Jesse himself was a boy.

Gabe's throat tightened. His gaze climbed to Jesse's. They both swallowed visibly.

"Thanks, Jesse," Gabe murmured. "I'll take good care of it."

Jesse gave a single sharp nod. The quartet grew quiet. Finally Jesse spoke. "I'd better be gettin' back home. Sarah's made me promise I'd help her wrap gifts for the kids in her Sunday-school class."

"I've got to go, too," Jericho said. "I promised Susan I'd help her decorate cookies to take to her dad."

"I suppose Becca has something equally emasculating for you to do," Gabe said to Daniel with a show of faux chauvinism. Deep inside, he wished he was going to help Gretchen with some silly Christmas task.

"Sticks and stones—" Daniel began, then broke off with a sheepish grin. "I'm helping Becca wrap stocking stuffers for her kids."

Gabe shook his head. "You know what I think of all you henpecked suckers?"

"No," Jericho said, "but I have a sneaking suspicion you're going to tell us."

Gabe grinned. "I think you're all a bunch of lucky stiffs." Jericho laughed, and Gabe and he exchanged a hug. The action was repeated with Daniel and even perfunctorily with Jesse before the Calloway men climbed into Jericho's van and pulled into the mid-morning traffic.

Gabe watched them go, fighting a feeling of incredible sorrow. He looked down at the knife in his hand.

He knew that by giving him a family possession, Jesse was saying what he couldn't—or wouldn't—put into words.

It should have been enough. But it wasn't.

# CHAPTER FIVE

As GABE LEFT SHONEY'S and drove back to the farm, his thoughts were far from joyful and shockingly lacking in goodwill for a Christmas Eve. Instead, his mind was focused on the past and the pain he'd suffered as a child unknowingly bearing the brunt of his parents' sin.

There had been whispers and sidelong looks, especially when he tagged along with his "friends" Jericho and Daniel into nearby Doyline or Haughton. The murmurs and secretive glances were worse when Jesse was with them. Jesse ignored the whispers, going about his business with his charismatic hail-fellow-well-met routine, and they tried to disregard the townsfolk's behavior, too, but that proved impossible. The few times they'd asked Jesse what was going on, he'd just cursed and muttered something about "self-righteous hypocrites."

The nonanswer wasn't enough for three sensitive little boys. Uncomfortably aware of the talk, they had done the only thing they could: turned it into a joke. Had one of them sat in a cow patty? Were their flies unzipped? What the heck had Jesse done, anyway—robbed a bank?

But deep inside, Gabe had known—even back then—that the whispers had something to do with him. He had no idea that the real fault was Jesse's; he just knew it had something to do with his being a bastard, a word he'd heard often enough when someone didn't think he was listening. When he was nine he'd asked his mother what it meant. White-faced, Hannah had told him in her sternest voice never to say that word in her presence.

Hurt and confused by his mother's unaccustomed anger, Gabe had gotten out the dictionary. *Webster's* said a bastard was a disagreeable or offensive person, or someone who was illegitimate. He thought about that for a while and decided he was no more obnoxious or disagreeable than Jericho and Daniel—or a lot of boys his age, for that matter—and no one called them bastards. If it wasn't that, it must be the illegitimate thing. When he looked up that word, he learned that it meant someone who was an illegal offspring, born of parents not married to each other.

Gabe had known all along that Joel wasn't his "real" father; he recalled meeting him for the first time just before his fifth birthday. But prior to that, when Gabe had asked his mother where his daddy was, she'd simply said that he'd gone away when Gabe was a baby and he wasn't coming back. Gabe had accepted this unquestioningly, as only a child can, and had never even considered the possibility that his mother and this man had never married.

When he'd told Jericho and Daniel what the dictionary said, they were surprised, too. Jericho even suggested that Joel probably treated Gabe the way he did because Gabe's illegitimacy was embarrassing for him.

He and his dad had never been close. Joel Butler was a tough taskmaster, demanding more from Gabe than he sometimes thought he could bear. Joel sel-

dom laid a hand on him, but he was hard and unyielding and expected perfection. The tongue-lashings
Gabe got were as hurtful as any whipping might have
been.

Not understanding what he'd done to deserve the
older man's anger but feeling that if he was out of the
picture things would be better for his mom, Gabe, at
the age of seven, had begun cutting through the fields
to the highway and hitchhiking to the cattle auction
barn, seeking refuge with Jericho, Daniel and Jesse.

The forays to the barn brought relief for a while, but
they also brought a new set of problems. His mother
worried about his "traipsing off to God knows
where—don't you know that someone could come
along and steal you away from us?" His dad just got
angrier, telling him he was "selfish and insensitive"
and causing his mother a lot of grief.

Still, Gabe was driven by a need even he didn't understand. He tried to ease his mother's mind by telling her that he was careful, that he knew not to ride
with strangers. His maturity didn't impress her, and
the lectures and cruel tongue-lashings continued.

He didn't stop going. Couldn't. He'd found his
peace, or at least an oblivion of sorts, in the hours he
was on the back of a horse working with the lowing
cattle in the pastures, or with the heifers, steers and
bulls that clustered in the small pens on sale day. He
loved the smell of the barn, the hay, manure and even
the sweat of the workers who praised him for his hard
work and smiled at him as if they really liked him.
They *did* like him.

It was there, at the age of eight, that he met a
busted-up, wisecracking rodeo rider named Dizzy
Crenshaw. Dizzy worked at half a dozen part-time

jobs to earn his entry fees, or as he jokingly put it, "to support his habit"—rodeo riding. Jesse was happy to have an employee of Dizzy's knowledge, and as a former amateur bronc rider himself, he understood Dizzy's obsession.

It was Dizzy's talk of rodeo that filled Gabe's head with dreams of someday winning the National Finals. It was Dizzy who patiently tutored him in the finer points of bronco and bull riding, Dizzy who put him on his first bucking horse and later his first bull.

Dizzy introduced him and Daniel and Jericho to snuff, Bud Light and "girlie" magazines. Grinning, charismatic fast-talking Dizzy Crenshaw was Gabe's idol, his friend, his mentor and his stand-in father. And he was only twenty-three the year Gabe met him.

Hannah saw the changes in her son and, at her wits' end, tried calling Jesse at the barn; but if she'd hoped for an ally there, she was disappointed. Once, Gabe stepped into the office and overheard Jesse telling Hannah that Gabe was just fine. He was no trouble, Jesse assured her, winking at Gabe. He liked having him around—if Hannah knew what he meant.

Jesse's stance pleased Gabe. Unfortunately Hannah knew exactly what he meant, even if, at that time, Gabe didn't. All he knew was that the phone calls continued and so did his bad behavior. His mom and dad argued even more. Joel demanded that he stop running off to that godforsaken place so that his mother wouldn't have to call the barn and talk to that sorry SOB. His mother cried a lot.

Realizing that his actions were causing trouble for her but not fully understanding why, Gabe tried to stay away from the forbidden lure of Jesse and Dizzy and the feeling of oneness he felt with the animals, but loneliness and boredom soon got the best of him.

His life settled into a pattern. He sneaked off several times a week and caught hell at home for shirking his duties on the farm. The arguments between Hannah and Joel increased in number and heat. By the time he was ten, Joel had stopped trying to keep him at home, stopped asking him to do any chores. Instead, he more or less ignored Gabe, contenting himself with coldness and an occasional hard look, which brought a perpetual frown to Hannah's eyes whenever her husband and son were in the same room. The good part was that his parents stopped arguing.

Gabe was eleven when he learned the truth. Confined to his room without dinner after he'd been expelled from school for spray-painting graffiti on the gym walls, he'd overheard—via a floor vent—an argument Hannah and Joel were having in the kitchen. Gabe had long before discovered that the duct was a perfect conduit for any conversation held in the kitchen.

"That boy is just like his father. Irresponsible and a troublemaker!"

Joel's angry voice overrode the sound of Hannah's crying. There was little doubt in Gabe's mind that the boy his dad was talking about was him.

"He's a good boy!" Hannah defended Gabe in a trembling, tear-filled voice. "All he needs is a little praise and a father he can look up to, not one who's constantly looking for fault and expecting him to come up short."

"I guess you think Jesse Calloway is a better father than I am." Joel's voice dripped sarcasm.

Gabe heard his mother's gasp. "Leave Jesse out of this!"

"How can I," Joel railed, "when every time I look at that boy's face I see Jesse Calloway and am reminded that you slept with a married man! And every time I meet sweet Sarah Calloway on the street I think of how the two of you must've hurt her."

"I know she was hurt, but dear God, Joel, I was seventeen!" Hannah cried. "Jesse was older, smoother—"

"And that excuses what you did?"

"No! It doesn't make it right, but everyone makes mistakes." There was quiet for a long moment, and then Gabe heard her say, "Obviously Gabe and I will both have to live with the fallout of what I did for the rest of our lives—at least with you."

"You don't understand," Joel said in a broken, tortured voice. "I love you, Hannah!"

"And I love you, Joel. Surely you know that. What happened between me and Jesse happened years ago. Let it go!"

"God help me, I can't." Even eleven-year-old Gabe recognized the despair in Joel Butler's voice.

Hannah's tone was a perfect match. "Then God help us all."

Gabe heard the kitchen door slam shut and his mother's renewed sobbing. He reached down and closed the vent to shut out the sound and then flung himself facedown on his bed. He'd listened to enough talk at the barn to understand most of what he'd just overheard.

He pretty much knew what the "sleeping with" part meant. That was sex. He'd learned all about that at the barn from Dizzy's and the other workers' conversations. He'd snickered along with Jericho and Daniel as they'd watched cows and dogs "do it." He couldn't imagine doing it himself, but if the guys at the barn could be believed, it was great, and evidently some people liked it. His mom and Jesse had liked it.

Suddenly everything became as clear as the crystal bell on his mother's bookcase. He felt exactly like a character in a comic book when an idea hit and the lightbulb came on: he was Jesse Calloway's son.

Now he understood why Joel hated him, why Hannah's calls to the barn were such a touchy issue. And he understood the whispers and the looks he received when he went somewhere with Jesse and Jericho and Daniel. They were talking about Jesse and him because Jesse and his mom had done something bad. Illegal. And they'd hurt Sarah Calloway when they'd done it.

Gabe rolled onto his back, filled with a sudden sadness for Sarah Calloway. He liked Jericho and Daniel's mother. Though he seldom saw her—he wasn't allowed to go into the Calloway house, and now the reason for that was clear—he was always struck by the sweetness of her smile and the kindness in her eyes. How could anyone hurt nice Mrs. Calloway?

Gabe felt a rush of anger at his mother and Jesse. That emotion hardly registered before another troubling thought invaded him. Did Jericho and Daniel know? Gabe squeezed his eyes shut against a sudden surge of moisture. Surely not, or they wouldn't be so nice to him. They were his best friends. The three of them were like brothers.

The lightbulb flashed again and his eyes flew open. They weren't like brothers; they *were* brothers. He

knew now why he felt so close to them, why he understood their secret thoughts and feelings and why they
understood his. And he knew why Jesse let him trail
around after him, why he encouraged him to come to
the barn and hang out with his boys. Jesse wanted
them to be together, to like each other.

He understood, too, why Jesse always let him off at
the end of the lane, instead of driving him to the door,
and why Hannah's face always wore that pained look
when she asked where he'd been or who he'd been
with.

The realization that Jesse cared for him brought a
sudden burst of joy to eleven-year-old Gabe's heart.
Jesse Calloway—his real dad—loved him and wanted
to be with him. To hell with Joel Butler. As soon as the
curse word entered his thoughts, Gabe was filled with
shame.

*God knows your every feeling and hears your every
thought.*

His Grandma Marshall's words rang in his mind.
Imagining the fury on Joel's face, Gabe clenched his
teeth together and muttered the defiant curse aloud.
"To hell with him."

He didn't care if God heard him. He hoped He did
and wished Joel had, too.

As soon as he'd indulged in a good cry, Gabe
stormed downstairs and confronted his mother about
the conversation he'd overheard. Hannah shed more
tears, told him she was sorry and begged him to forgive her. He told her he never would.

When he told Joel he'd heard everything he said,
something had moved in the depth of his stepfather's
eyes. Compassion? Sorrow? Regret?

Whatever it was, it was too late. Though Joel had never legally adopted Gabe, he'd given him a name and a place to call home. Security. Three meals a day. Clothes for his back. Gabe vowed he wouldn't be beholden to Joel Butler for anything. From that day, Gabe's attitude toward his stepfather changed. He treated Joel with the respect his mother expected of him and did whatever he knew needed to be done without Joel ever asking him to do it.

Gabe stopped calling Joel Dad. He became Joel, something that brought a flash of pain to Hannah's eyes for years to come. Gabe didn't care. He stayed mad at her for a long time, too. She was his mother and he loved her, but she'd fallen from her pedestal, and he didn't fully forgive her until sometime in his twenties when he'd learned a little more about life and adult relationships.

The day following the revelation that changed his life, Gabe took Jericho and Daniel aside and told them what he'd overheard. His voice had shaken with tears when he ended his tale with the statement, ''That's why you guys don't come into my house and why I'm not allowed to go inside yours. I'll remind your mom of...you know...my mom and Jesse uh, having well, you know...sex. If you guys don't want anything to do with me, I'll understand. Honest.''

''What do you mean, not have anything to do with you?'' thirteen-year-old Jericho had said. ''You're our *brother*. Nothing's going to make us feel any different, is it, squirt?'' The last was asked of Daniel, who was just one month older than Gabe.

''Nope,'' Daniel said with a shake of his head. ''I can't imagine them having sex, can you, Jericho? Him and Mom, either.''

"I don't want to talk about it," Gabe said, turning away. "The thought of it makes me sick to my stomach."

"Then we won't talk about it anymore after today," Jericho said. "Grown-ups are all screwed up. Whatever happened, they did it. It has nothin' to do with us. We're friends—brothers. I say we make a pact that nothing—*nothing*—will ever change the way we feel about each other."

"Pax," Daniel said, holding out his hand. The others laid theirs on top of his and said solemnly, "Pax."

Nothing ever had come between them. If anything, Gabe's news brought them closer together.

As they grew older, their dad stopped being their idol, the man they looked up to. Their eyes opened, and they began to see Jesse's faults: his quick, often violent temper, which was more and more frequently directed at them as their hormones started raging and the need for independence ate at them. His drinking. The women. They saw that while Jesse had a lot of rowdy friends, he'd also made a lot of enemies. He was feared by many, respected by few.

They saw how he put his needs and wants before anyone else's and how easily he hurt the other people in his life, especially Sarah. Witnessing Jesse's self-indulgence, he and his brothers came to see that Jesse didn't really care who his actions hurt. Disillusionment turned to resentment, and resentment mutated naturally into rebellion.

By the time Daniel and Gabe were sixteen and Jericho eighteen, the Calloway brothers escapades' were legend. They wore the tightest jeans, drank the hardest liquor, drove the fastest cars, rode the roughest stock and dated the wildest women.

Indisputably the best-looking guys in town, they held the female population of Webster Parish in thrall. To receive a smile from one of them was enough to set feminine hearts aflutter. To be asked out by any of them was both exciting and scary. Every girl thought she'd be the one to "tame" the wild heart of the one she dated, but none of them ever did.

Mothers of the town's "nice" girls cringed to find out their daughters were interested in any of the three. Fathers who could afford it threatened convents or boarding schools. Others threatened whippings and prayed a lot.

In the throes of their youthful passions and an accumulation of pain none of them could admit, much less deal with, the boys sought to dissociate themselves from their dad. It was years before they realized that by taking the road of rowdies and roughnecks they were inadvertently following in his footsteps.

When Jesse slew the Baptist preacher outside the Midnight Hour and was sentenced to twenty-five years for manslaughter, the bond between Gabe and his brothers grew even stronger. Though the community was divided, Jesse's boys stood together against the gossip and the censure, holding their heads high, laughing the loudest, drinking the hardest and hurting more than they ever let on. This time, Gabe set the pace. He'd had the most experience at pretending to be what he wasn't.

Jericho, who graduated that year, left town almost immediately, wanting, needing to get away, fleeing Jesse's legacy in a variety of jobs until he stumbled upon photography. By walking into violent storms and among wild animals to photograph the untainted world of nature, he hoped to brighten the planet with pictures that showed the world's intrinsic, inalienable beauty.

Daniel and Gabe understood his need to leave and vowed to follow as soon as their diplomas were in hand. There was nothing for them in Calloway Corners but heartache, and each knew that if he was ever to overcome the stigma of being Jesse Calloway's son, it would have to be someplace besides Webster Parish, Louisiana.

Follow they did.

Daring Daniel, a devotee of his cousin Mariah, soon learned to tempt fate and death by jumping close to blazing forest fires. Strangely, Gabe was more like Jesse than any of them. Even more strangely, he took up his dad's persona and became the flirt, the tease, the cowboy all the cowgirls wanted. He gained quite a reputation among the rodeo crowd, and only a few knew it was a lie. Later, when Dizzy was killed, he donned the clothes of another personality: Rowdy, the rodeo clown.

The first night he put on the clown getup he knew he'd finally found his niche. What he didn't realize was that a clown's costume was the ultimate hiding place. Beneath Rowdy's ragged, baggy clothes and greasepaint smile, no one could possibly guess he was laughing on the outside and crying on the inside.

They had all accomplished what they wanted. Jericho had made a name for himself as a photographer. Daniel had become a hero and the recipient of an honor from the president, and Gabe was the highest paid, most sought-after bull fighter in the country.

In the beginning, none of them had understood that they were chasing danger as certainly as their father had, or that they were running from their heritage as Jesse Calloway's sons. But that was in the past now. At least for Jericho and Daniel.

Though Gabe still resented his dad for hurting a good woman and leading another astray, it seemed his brothers had made their peace with Jesse since he'd paid his debt to society and come back home. Gabe hadn't yet granted his father forgiveness. He and his mother were still paying. He suspected they always would.

He told himself it was Christmas Eve and he was just feeling sorry for himself, and that was true. It was also true that no matter how far he ran or how much greasepaint he put on, when he looked in the mirror, he saw Jesse Calloway's face. He was still Jesse Calloway's bastard, the son he had never publicly or even verbally acknowledged.

FROM THE UPSTAIRS WINDOW of the garage apartment, Gretchen watched Nick and Eden Logan load their kids into their Voyager minivan. Nicole climbed in behind them, and Nick slid the door shut. In a few seconds, the taillights of the van disappeared down the lane and across the railroad tracks. Gretchen turned away from the window and sank onto the floral sofa.

The Logans, including Nick and Nicole's parents, were all headed to a Christmas Eve service at the small church where Mariah's husband, Ford, preached, but a queasy stomach had kept Gretchen from joining them. She hadn't had a sick moment so far during the pregnancy, but she supposed there had to be a first time.

Eden laughingly said the upset stomach might have something to do with three slices of fruitcake—non-alcoholic, of course—several different kinds of cookies and a taste of three different fudges, divinity and peanut-brittle, all topped off with a bowl of spicy chili.

Gretchen groaned at the thought. It wasn't like her to be such a pig when it came to food, but she usually didn't have a smorgasbord of goodies at her finger-tips, either. She stretched out on the sofa and reached for the TV remote control, letting the songs of a Christmas special roll over her senses like a gentle wave.

The day had been revealing in many ways, not the least of which was experiencing the generosity and love that radiated from Eden Logan. Nicole's sister-in-law seemed to know everyone in the Haughton, Doyline and Sibley area, and, from the amount of cookies she delivered to the old people and shut-ins, it seemed she took an active interest in the life of each and every one of them.

When they'd all finished dispensing Christmas cheer to Eden's friends and acquaintances, they stopped by the Calloway sisters' homes to deliver elaborately decorated Santa cookies to each niece and nephew. With a combination of pleasure and envy, Gretchen had witnessed the expressions of love among the family members. An only child, she couldn't imagine having that sort of easy camaraderie. For years, she'd suspected that her upbringing had denied her some vital inner need, but she'd never felt the denial of that need as keenly as she did this Christmas Eve. Maybe it had something to do with her pregnancy and the desire to fill that need in the life of her child.

Thoughts of the baby led to thoughts of Gabe and the unexpected meeting at Tess and Seth's place that morning when Gretchen had been introduced to Jason's girlfriend, Jody. As Gretchen was trying to figure out why the girl's name sounded so familiar, the pretty blonde had exclaimed, "Gretchen West! Are you with Westways Productions?"

"Yes, I am."

"Then you're the one who called my brother the day after Thanksgiving."

Of course. Jody Butler—Gabe's sister. The resemblance was undeniable. Both she and Gabe had the same wavy blond hair, ice-blue eyes, dimples and chin shape.

As she'd cataloged Jody's physical attributes, Gretchen had agreed that it was indeed a small world, all the time wondering whether the baby she carried was a girl, and if so, if she'd inherit any of the physical traits she saw in Gabe's sister.

The chance meeting made her realize just how easy it was to run into people in an area where everyone knew everyone else—and everyone else's business. Small-town life had many blessings, but she could imagine what it must have been like for the Calloway boys and Gabe trying to live down their dad's misdeeds in a place where gossip was as common as a friendly greeting.

When they left Tess Taylor's home, Eden had made a final stop to drop off a basket of homemade jam and bread to her aunt and uncle, Sarah and Jesse Calloway. Uncomfortable with the thought of looking Gabe's biological father in the eye, Gretchen opted to stay in the van. Meeting Gabe's sister was enough for one day.

Now, Gretchen closed her eyes and pictured Jesse Calloway's home on the highway. Even though it was winter and the trees and flower beds were bare, it was evident that Sarah Calloway had kept her home and yard well tended during her husband's absence. The modest pale blue house shone like a jewel between yards that held rusting cars, old appliances and waist-high grass that had turned brown with the first frost.

Gretchen wondered what Gabe's mother's house looked like. What did Hannah Butler herself look like? More importantly, what kind of woman had she grown into after falling for an older married man and bearing his child? What traits would she pass on to the child Gretchen and Gabe had created together?

Heavy footsteps, indisputably masculine, pounded up the stairs, prompting Gretchen to sit up. She frowned. She hadn't heard anyone drive up. Had Nick and Eden forgotten something? she wondered as the screen door rattled with an insistent knocking.

"It's open!"

The doorknob turned and the door swung wide, but it wasn't Nick who stood framed in the opening. It was Gabe.

Panic brought her to her feet. "What are you doing here?"

"Unfinished business, I guess."

His deep voice and the look of determination in his eyes sent a shiver down her spine. Apprehension or desire? Her stomach did a slow roll. She folded her arms over her middle and squeezed tightly, as if the gesture would hold everything in place.

"Jody said she met you at Tess's."

The unexpected, innocuous statement contradicted the intensity in his eyes and knocked Gretchen off guard. Speechless, she nodded.

"Jody said you were a classy lady."

"That was sweet of her," Gretchen replied. "She's a beautiful young woman. She'll be devastating in a few years."

A familiar crooked grin lifted a corner of Gabe's mustache. "Now there's a scary thought. Mom hardly sleeps nights now."

"Jason Taylor seems like a nice boy," Gretchen said.

"Eighteen-year-old boys' minds are directly controlled by another portion of their anatomy. They're master manipulators. Smooth talkers. Hell at laying on guilt trips. You know, 'If you love me, you'll do it,' that sort of thing—remember?"

"I remember," Gretchen said, meeting his smiling gaze and wondering what Jody's love life had to do with them. "But I never fell for manipulators myself."

The smile in Gabe's eyes faded. "The smooth talkers got you, huh?"

Memories darted through Gretchen's mind.

*I've never met a woman like you—smart, beautiful, warm and giving. God, so giving.... You're a great kisser, Ms. West. I could kiss you all night. As a matter of fact, I think maybe I will.... Your skin is like satin. And it tastes like peaches. Did anyone ever tell you that?*

Smooth talking went a long way, but Gretchen knew now that it was more than what Gabe had said. Fledgling feelings of love—born in the way he'd been willing to work with her ideas for the video, the way he'd captured the hearts of everyone working on the project, the way he'd pitched in with anything that needed to be done—had been the source of her capitulation, but there was no way she could tell him that.

"A little flattery never hurt," she admitted, giving him that much. Before he could reply, she said, "Look, you didn't come here to talk about your sister's love life. Why did you come?"

"Like I said, unfinished business. You never told me the details about that movie director."

"Beyond the fact that he liked what he saw in the video and wants to use you in a movie he's making, I really don't know what he has in mind. You should call him and find out for yourself."

"If you'll give me his number, I'll be glad to."

Gretchen grabbed her purse and drew out a piece of paper with Blake Adams's name and number on it, and handed it to Gabe. "Thanks," he said, reaching beneath his jacket and putting it in his shirt pocket.

"You're welcome." Gretchen suppressed the impulse to laugh at the mundane tone of their conversation, not that there was anything humorous about the situation. Actually she felt like crying. As a matter of fact, she wished he would go so that she could.

"Look, it's Christmas Eve. Peace on earth, goodwill to men and all that. Do you think we could bury the hatchet?" he asked, his gaze holding hers. "Preferably somewhere besides my back?"

Surprise held her speechless. She nodded.

He smiled. "Would you like to go get a hamburger or something to seal the bargain? There's a place that makes these big greasy taco burgers with everything on them. Chili, cheese, grilled onions, hot peppers—the works."

Bile rose in her throat, and her already queasy stomach lurched at the vision that came to mind.

"Uh, no thanks," she managed to get out before she clamped her hand over her mouth and raced past him to the small bathroom. Slamming the door shut, she knelt beside the white porcelain commode and gave in to her nausea, the image of Gabe's stunned expression imprinted forever in her mind.

# CHAPTER SIX

As GRETCHEN BOLTED from the room, an unaccountable feeling of panic bombarded Gabe. Did she have that flu bug going around? he wondered as the sounds of her retching filtered through the bathroom door. He shifted from one booted foot to the other, his anxiety shifting naturally to helplessness. He didn't deal with sickness well. It was his understanding that men never did, at least, not according to women.

But women were very good with illnesses. He recalled himself being sick as a kid and Hannah slipping into the bathroom and offering him what comfort she could—the refreshment of a cool washcloth, the gentleness of her touch, soothing words and the certainty that even though she couldn't do anything about the situation, she cared.

Gabe pushed open the bathroom door. Gretchen was too sick to notice, much less object. One of her hands gripped the cold porcelain of the commode; the other held her hair out of the way. He wasn't sure which upset him the most: the fact that she was so sick or the way her retching made his heart ache.

He reached for a hand towel, wet the corner and squatted beside her, gathering the hair from her hand and using the edge of the towel to brush some maverick strands away from her cheeks.

Finally, thankfully, she finished. Without a word, Gabe stood and drew her to her feet. Red, mascara-smudged eyes stared up at him with a combination of wariness and embarrassment.

"You okay?" he asked, skimming the damp cloth over her pale face.

Her eyes flooded, and she clamped her teeth onto her bottom lip with a brief nod.

"That flu bug's nasty," he said as he continued to carry out his gentle ministrations. "Mom and Jody both had it."

Tears spilled over her bottom eyelashes and down her cheeks.

He tried to concentrate on his task, but the look in her eyes was ripping his heart to minuscule shreds. "It doesn't last but a day or so," he said, putting down the towel and filling a paper cup with water. "'Course, you won't feel too great for Christmas morning."

He offered her the water, but she refused it with a shake of her head. Misery ousted the apprehension in her eyes.

"Still queasy, huh? I'll see if I can rustle up a cup of hot tea and some crackers. My mom swears by hot tea and soda crackers for an upset stomach."

He started to turn away, but she grabbed his arm.

"I don't have the flu," she said, her voice trembling and uncertain, the look in her eyes defiant. "I'm pregnant."

His stunned gaze locked with hers. The room spun and the floor dipped, a sensation not unlike what he experienced on the backs of ill-tempered bulls and broncs. The memory of her body pressed close to his and her voice murmuring, "Marry me," leapt into his mind like a mugger jumping out of the dark. Had she been pregnant when he'd met her in September? Had she fallen into his bed so easily because she was looking for a scapegoat?

That scenario vanished as another memory surfaced: the two of them making love in the shower—without protection. It had only happened once, but he'd known when he did it that he was taking a potentially life-altering risk. Hadn't Hannah preached abstinence all his life? Hadn't she made it clear that if abstinence was impossible he should use protection—for his sake and the woman's? Hadn't he always been careful to heed her warnings?

Every time except that time.

He'd known better than to engage in unprotected sex, and he had no excuse other than the flimsy assumption that, when he got into the small cubicle with her, their hunger for each other had been temporarily sated. But it hadn't been sated at all, and now she was pregnant with his baby.

He brushed his palm over his forehead as if the action would wipe away the taunting images. Instead, he felt the cold, clammy sweat that had popped out the instant he realized the depth of his culpability.

He stifled a sigh of remorse. Now he was in more or less the same fix his mama had once been in, only this time the roles were reversed.

"It's your baby," she said, sensing he was looking for a way out, asking himself if she was telling the truth.

"I know that," he told her at last.

"I can't believe it happened," she said, her voice growing stronger. "I mean, I've had so many problems and the doctor said it was going to be hard but if

I was going to have a baby I needed to do it pretty fast—but I didn't really mean for this to happen."

The garbled explanation came out in a breathless rush, as if unburdening herself would somehow ease not only his mind but hers.

"What problems?" Gabe asked in sudden concern.

"Female problems."

"What kind of female problems?"

"Do you have a couple of hours?" she asked with a wry twist of her lips.

"As a matter of fact, I do. Why don't I go find that tea while you—" he waved his hand in a vague way "—fix your makeup...or something."

Gretchen glanced over her shoulder and grimaced at the image reflected in the mirror. "Good idea."

Trying to maintain a semblance of calm while his mind reeled drunkenly with the news she'd just broken to him, Gabe took off his jacket and hat and went into the small kitchen area that was set apart from the living room by a Formica-topped bar. He found a tea kettle and set the water to boiling. The teabags were where they should be—in the cabinet above the stove.

A baby, he thought again. Gretchen was going to have a baby. His baby. Babies meant diapers. Nighttime feedings. Colic. Yet having them seemed to be a goal most people aspired to. God alone knew why.

Bawling babies grew into mischievous toddlers and from there into snotty little girls like Jody had been and obnoxious little boys who sneaked off so they could look at girlie magazines and smoke stolen cigarettes. He ought to know; he'd done all of those things himself.

And after these coveted offspring left childhood,
they dragged their parents into that unfortunate seven-
year sentence called adolescence when the girls got
snottier and tried to look like the girls in the magazines, and the boys stopped being satisfied with looking at the pictures and graduated directly into the
"hands on" phase. Girls got pregnant, and the cycle
started all over again. Gabe knew his reasoning was
cynical, but by golly, he felt cynical at the moment.

*That isn't cynicism you're feeling, Gabe old buddy.
It's downright terror. You're scared spitless about being responsible for someone else's welfare, someone
else's happiness.*

It was the truth. How could this have happened?
What had made him so careless that one time with
Gretchen? What did she want from him? Marriage?

"It isn't the end of the world."

At the sound of Gretchen's voice, he turned away
from the stove, where he'd been watching the steam
roiling from the kettle's spout. She'd freshened her
makeup and combed her dark hair back, securing it
with a band at the nape of her neck. She still looked
tired, but a little color was coming back to her cheeks.

He added hot water to the cups holding the teabags
and set them to steep, then said, "It's the end of life
as we know it." Their eyes met. The shock of that bit
of truth startled them both.

"I guess it is," she agreed with a nod. "I hadn't
thought of it that way." She sat down at the bar and
reached for the cup of steaming tea he set in front of
her. "You don't look like the hot-tea type," she said
as he reached for the sugar bowl.

"What type do I look like?" he countered.

"The beer-drinking, womanizing, love-'em-and-leave-'em type."

One corner of his mustache inched up in a slow, mocking smile. "You been readin' my diary?" When Gretchen didn't smile back, he said, "Guess that wasn't funny under the circumstances, was it?"

She shook her head. He sighed.

"I'm sorry. For everything." He wasn't sure whom the simple statement surprised most.

Recovering quickly, Gretchen gave a shaky laugh. "Please! No apologies."

"But I am sorry. A baby will mess up your life. You're a successful career woman with a lot of responsibilities. Motherhood will make a lot of extra demands, unless you decide to—"

"Don't!" She stopped the upcoming suggestion with her harsh command. "Don't suggest an abortion. It isn't an option for me. I wanted a baby. Badly. And in case you don't know it, children do more than make demands. They give a lot of happiness and they love unconditionally."

Her unexpected comment surprised him. Even more revealing was the glimpse of a need he'd never recognized in her before. Was that really wistfulness he'd seen in her eyes? Had her voice trembled with emotion? Was it possible that wealthy, raised-with-a-silver-spoon-in-her-mouth Gretchen West had been given everything except what a child needed most? Had her life been filled with things and deficient in love?

Another thought nipped at the heels of that one. She said she wanted a baby badly. Had she planned that weekend together in the hope she'd get pregnant? He poured milk into his cup.

"No," she said, seemingly reading his mind. "I didn't sleep with you to deliberately get pregnant, as much as I wanted a child. Like I said before, I can't believe it happened so easily."

"Because of the female problems?"

She nodded. "I've had cysts and endometriosis since my early twenties. The cysts got so bad about a year ago that I had to have an ovary removed, which is supposed to make getting pregnant harder."

"Obviously that's a fallacy," he said with an attempt at levity.

"Obviously."

"So is everything okay with your...female problems now?"

"For the time being. Not long before I got pr—I mean, before the weekend we spent together, my gynecologist told me that the endometriosis was getting worse. We've tried a dozen remedies including simulating a pregnancy, faking the change of life and laser surgery. Nothing worked for long. My doctor said I was going to have to have a hysterectomy in a few months, and if I wanted to have a baby, I should either find a husband or go to a sperm bank."

He watched her mouth quirk in a humorless smile.

"Both options were easier to suggest than to carry out." The look in the eyes that met his was frank, uncompromising. "I'm thirty-three, Gabe. Obviously I've been looking for a husband—without luck—for several years now, so that wasn't a viable option. Neither was going to a sperm bank. Picking out a father for my child from a dossier and vials of frozen sperm left me cold—no pun intended."

Gabe couldn't find the heart to smile.

"I want you to believe me when I say I didn't plan our weekend together so I'd get pregnant. First of all, I'm so irregular I couldn't figure out the right time if my life depended on it. And secondly, I wouldn't deliberately do that to you or any man."

Her slender shoulders lifted in a slight shrug. "Nicole says the pregnancy was meant to be. That God planned it. Maybe she's right."

Gabe crossed his arms over his chest. "And what does God want us to do now?"

Uncertainty darkened her eyes. "I don't know," she said, shaking her head.

"I'll be glad to help financially."

Her cheeks colored. "I don't mean to sound ungrateful, but the last thing I need is your money," she said, her voice as stiff as the set of her shoulders.

He felt the slow heat that rose to his own face. "If you don't want my money, what *do* you want?"

"Marriage," she said, looking into his eyes with a steady, unfaltering gaze.

"Marriage?" His deep voice echoed the simple request.

"Is the idea of marriage to me so distasteful?"

"How can I answer that? I'd say no, but we hardly know each other, so how can I be sure? To tell the truth, I never planned on marrying anyone."

"Why?"

"You said it yourself. I'm a love-'em-and-leave-'em kind of guy. My reputation stands for itself."

"Your reputation is a smoke screen," she said.

"Says who?"

"The people who know you. Your cousins. Your brothers."

"You can't believe everything you're told."

"My point exactly."

Seeing that he couldn't get that one past her, he pinned her with an angry gaze. "All right. You want the truth? My grandmother told me I'd never have a name to offer a woman."

Gretchen gasped. "Oh, Gabe, this isn't the nineteenth century, and thanks to Joel, you have the Butler name to offer."

"Yeah," he said, barely hiding his bitterness, "he did give me that."

"As for being sure whether a marriage will work, no one is ever sure about that," she said. "Is there someone else?"

"No!" He leapt to his feet, his denial quick, definite. He went to the sink and gripped the edge of the countertop.

Neither spoke for long moments. Finally he turned and leaned against the cabinets, crossing his arms over his chest. "Why is getting married so important to you? You don't seem like the kind of woman who'd care what people said about her."

"I don't care what *people* say," she told him. "Just my mother." He watched as she rested her elbow on the bar and propped her chin in her palm. "That's a pretty scary confession for a woman my age, don't you think?"

"Surprising, anyway."

She sighed. "I want to get married because I want my child to have a father, since I never did."

"What are you talking about? I thought Tyrell West was still alive and well and wheeling and dealing all over the country—if not the world."

"Oh, he is," she said. "That's the problem. He was always too busy making money to be a parent. And

Mama was always right there by his side. I was left at home with a series of housekeepers who took very good care of my physical needs.''

"Come on, Gretchen. It couldn't have been that bad."

"Yeah, I know. Poor little rich girl," she said in a whiny voice. "You're right. It wasn't bad. It just wasn't enough. I had lessons in everything imaginable, every advantage money could buy, but there was never anyone to come to my dance recitals or my fencing tournaments or to appreciate my artwork. I want this baby to have more than that. More than either of us had.''

"What? A father whose own father won't even acknowledge him? A grandfather who spent eighteen years in prison? Your mother will love that."

"I want this baby to have a father and a grandfather with a capacity for love. Maybe Jesse never told the world the truth, but he loved you enough that he made you a part of his life, which is more than my father did.''

Gabe thought about the times Jesse had come to his school functions, not as his dad, but as Daniel's. He remembered Hannah dragging Joel—under duress— and the way the Calloways and the Butlers steered clear of each other. Either way, he hadn't really had a father, either. Still, Gretchen had a point.

"I think a child should be nurtured by his or her own father if humanly possible," she told him. "That's why I want us to be married and raise the child we made together. I want us to be better parents than either of us had. I know we can do it, and I believe that even if we don't—" she paused "—love each other, we can deal with each other in a decent, fair way.''

He had no reply. The look in her eyes begged him to understand, to think carefully about what she was saying. Inadvertently she'd hit the right buttons. Decency and fairness were two things that had always been important in his life.

''I'd like to have found a husband who would love me more than life itself, but since that doesn't seem to be in my future, I'll settle for a husband who likes and respects me enough to share in all the ups and downs of bringing up a child.''

He thought about that. He did like her, and he respected her for many reasons, among them the fact that she'd had the courage to build a successful business without relying on her father's largesse.

''The fact that Jesse Calloway didn't marry your mother doesn't matter to me, Gabe,'' she told him. ''Neither does the fact that he did time in prison. What matters is who you are and what you've done. I believe you're a good and decent man who tries to do the right thing. So it seems logical you'd want to do the right thing for your baby, especially since you know firsthand how hard it is to grow up without a real father.''

Gabe rested his weight on one foot, planted one hand on his hip and raked the other through his hair. How did she know how hard it had been on him? Ah, yes. Nicole. Nicole must have filled her in.

''You play dirty, lady,'' he said, his gaze narrowing as he stared at her.

She shook her head. ''Not really. I just believe in playing the hand I was dealt to the best of my ability and laying all my cards on the table.''

Gabe couldn't think of a snappy reply to that. In fact, he couldn't think of anything else to say at all. He blew out a harsh breath and strode into the living area. "I've got to get out of here. I need to think."

"I understand," Gretchen said. "I know it's a shock. I forget that I've had a month to get used to the idea."

"It's gonna take me more than a month," he told her, sliding his arms into his sheepskin-lined suede jacket.

"For what it's worth, I think you'd make a great father."

The compliment made him pause in the act of settling his black felt Charlie One Horse hat on his head. "Why do you say that?"

"I watched you with kids at the rodeo. No question is too stupid to answer. You're never too tired to sign one more autograph. No kid is too green that you don't take time to give him a lesson in form and execution."

"My mother taught me to be polite, that's all," he said gruffly.

"Then you should thank your mother. A lot of kids aren't taught much about courtesy anymore."

He had no answer for that. He was halfway out the door when he heard her say, "Merry Christmas, Gabe."

He paused and turned. She was still sitting at the bar, one hand cradled around the mug of tea. There was nothing merry about her pale, determined face or her sorrow-shadowed eyes. There was certainly no happiness for the holidays in his heart.

Instead of wishing her the same, he said simply, "I'll call you tomorrow."

She nodded. He closed the door and almost ran down the steps. His boots thudded against the wood, and the sound echoed hollowly in the empty chambers of his heart.

Gretchen watched him go, her own heart beating painfully. With a groan of dismay, she rested her head in her palm. Had her insistence on marriage just driven him out of her life? Should she have played the modern woman and told him that she could make it on her own but would love to have him be a part of their child's life whenever he felt like it or it was convenient for him to do so?

Maybe. But that wasn't what she wanted. It wasn't right for her, and it wouldn't be the best for any of them in the long run, which was all that interested her.

Short-term arrangements held no appeal. What kind of life would her child have if Gabe waltzed in and out according to his convenience or his whim? What would that teach her son or daughter about responsibility and stability? What could he or she possibly learn about love? No, something in Gretchen's makeup demanded commitment, in business, as well as her personal life. Nothing less would do.

But what would do for Gabe?

Because of his background and Jesse's lawlessness, Gabe claimed he didn't want marriage, not to her or anyone else. Evidently his grandmother had preached tenets to him that had gone by the wayside with bra-burning and women's rights. She didn't think she'd ever run into any man born outside of marriage who still clung to the old-fashioned belief that he had no right to marry because he had no name to give a wife and child. The fact that Gabe respected his grandmother so much was touching, though, and fit the overall picture of Gabe Butler that was forming in her mind. Still, if anyone had asked her, she believed his real shame was rooted in Jesse's conviction and incarceration.

She sipped at her cooling tea. Gabe was right about one thing: her mother would have a fit when she found out about Jesse Calloway killing another man. To Mimi, self-defense, heat of passion or manslaughter were all the same and deserved no place in the life of Tyrell West's daughter, who, according to Mimi, could have any man she wanted.

Which wasn't exactly true, Gretchen thought on a wave of sadness. She wanted Gabe, but it was beginning to look as if that was one wish that might not be realized.

GABE ROLLED out of bed at five-thirty. Troubled by Gretchen's announcement and even more troubled by what to do about it, he hadn't slept much. As soon as he perceived the slightest lightening of the room, he threw back the covers and headed for the shower. He emerged a few minutes later, feeling somewhat revived from his sleepless night.

After donning fresh jeans and a clean shirt, he pulled on his boots, went to the window and pushed aside the curtain. Lights blazed in the house across the winter-brown pasture. After thirty-four Christmases he knew his mother had already put the turkey in the oven and was finishing the last of the Christmas-feast preparations. He also knew Joel wouldn't be up for another hour or so. Now was a good time to catch his mother alone.

Feeling the same regret he'd felt at ten when he'd been caught smoking in his room, Gabe squared his shoulders and, grabbing his coat, headed down the stairs and out onto the porch.

The thermometer on the porch said it was below freezing. Plunging his hands into the pockets of his jacket, he filled his lungs with the icy air and blew out a plume of warm breath. He stepped into the yard and lifted his face to the sky, which was still sprinkled with stars. The moments just before daybreak were his favorites, filled with promise. A new day meant another chance. A fresh start.

Opting to walk, instead of driving the truck, Gabe started down the driveway that was little more than a narrow trail between two barbed-wire fences. Gravel crunched beneath his boots, and the chill air blew the remainder of sleepiness from his mind.

He was halfway to the new house when he heard a snort and turned to see the silhouette of Joel's new bull in the semidarkness. Warm air from the bull's nostrils wreathed its massive head as he pawed at the ground, ready to charge.

"Get a life, Toro," Gabe said, and kept walking. The sound of his voice must have triggered something in the bull, because he lowered his head and charged the fence.

Instinctively Gabe swung around to meet his adversary face-to-face, but the bull was obviously just throwing his weight around. He skidded to a stop just short of the five strands of barbed wire.

From somewhere across the pasture a heifer lowed. Deciding to answer the call of his lady love, the bull gave a final snort, turned and trotted away.

Gabe released a pent-up sigh and picked up his pace again. No matter how often he faced the ornery critters, he always came away with a renewed sense of relief. He knew only too well what damage they could do to an unwary or unlucky adversary.

The back door to his mother's house was unlocked, and he let himself quietly into the mudroom. Hannah must have heard him, because she was smiling when he stepped into the kitchen.

"Merry Christmas," she said, crossing the room with a smile as she dried her hands on her apron. Standing on tiptoe, she pressed her lips to his cheek.

Gabe gave her a squeeze and murmured, "Merry Christmas, Mom."

Hannah patted his cheek, the way she had when he was a little boy. "What are you doing up at such an early hour?"

"I couldn't sleep."

Her eyes twinkled with undeniable mischief. "I'd have thought you'd outgrown that Christmas Eve excitement by now."

"I only wish it was the thought of Santa's coming that kept me awake," he told her, taking off his coat and hanging it on the back of a chair. "I'm afraid it's a little more serious than that."

Hannah's smile vanished. She pressed a hand against her heart. "What's wrong, son?"

"I met a woman."

Relief erased the furrows from her forehead. She smiled again, a pleased smile it seemed to Gabe. "You're in love."

"I don't know if I'm in love or not," he said with a shake of his head. "I just know that I met her in September and I haven't been able to get her off my mind."

"Well, it sounds like love." Hannah went to the coffeepot and filled a mug with the hot, steaming brew. "It's certainly nothing to make you so solemn."

He knew there was no point in prolonging the news and blurted out the truth. "She's pregnant, Mom. It's mine."

Twice in a matter of minutes, Gabe watched the smile drain from his mother's eyes. This time he saw them fill with tears. "Oh, Gabe!"

He felt that little-boy shame again, that little-boy guilt. It was even more uncomfortable at thirty-four than it had been at ten.

"Don't start, Mom," he cautioned, raising a hand in protest. "You've been preachin' to me for years, and I'll just say that I'm usually not careless."

"I'm not saying anything," she said, brushing at her eyes. "I'm certainly not one to cast stones."

She took a deep breath and reached for a dishrag to wipe up a drop of coffee she'd spilled. Keeping busy was Hannah Butler's way, her mantra against worry, even though he'd never known the ploy to work. Worry was as much a part of her as her dimples and blond hair.

"Who is she?" He accepted the cup of coffee she offered and sat down at the table.

"Gretchen West."

"Isn't that the woman who called here? The one who did that video you were in?"

"One and the same. She's Tyrell West's daughter."

"Oh, Gabe!" his mother cried again. "What are you going to do?"

"She wants me to marry her."

Surprise widened Hannah's eyes. "She does?"

His smile was slow and mocking. "It sort of surprised me, too."

"Oh, honey, you know I didn't mean that in a bad way. It's just that people who move in those circles don't usually marry beneath them."

Gabe's grin grew wider. "You're digging a mighty deep hole, there, Hannah Butler."

His teasing reddened her cheeks. "You know what I mean."

"Yeah, I do, and I tried my best to make her see that not only are we worlds apart, I don't have a name to give her or her baby."

A familiar look of sorrow entered Hannah's eyes. Gabe knew she was thinking of her own mistake and how it had affected him.

"Of course you have a name to give them. You have the Butler name."

"I *use* the Butler name. But we both know Joel never made it mine legally."

"Well, you've used it since you were a child. It's legal as far as I'm concerned."

Gabe shrugged, dismissing the subject. "Then there's Jesse." His mother's gaze shifted from his. "I know you don't like to talk about him, but we have to sometimes, Mom. I thought it was only fair that I tell Gretchen about Jesse, but she already knew. She's friends with Nicole Logan—Nick's sister."

"What did she say?"

"That it didn't make any difference, that what mattered was the kind of man I am."

"She sounds like a sensible girl," Hannah observed. "So what do you plan to do?"

Gabe scrubbed a hand over his just-shaved cheek. "I couldn't sleep for trying to figure it out. I don't think a marriage between us would stand a snowball's chance in hell of working."

"It can work if you want it to. Lots of people have married for reasons besides love, and it's worked. Joel and I are living proof."

"You didn't love Joel when you married him?"

Hannah shook her head. "I married him for respectability and because I finally realized that Jesse would never leave Sarah—that he shouldn't leave Sarah. I married Joel so you'd have a name and a father to love you." Her lips tightened and an unfamiliar look of hardness crept into her eyes. "But Jesse saw to it that never happened."

"What do you mean?"

"I mean that Jesse's attitude back then was like the dog in the manger. He wouldn't claim you, but he saw to it that Joel couldn't, either."

"I don't get it."

"It's very simple. Joel couldn't compete. Jesse Calloway is larger than life. You know that. He always was. He was the handsomest guy in the parish, the best cowboy, the best rodeo rider, the best lover." Hannah's face turned crimson with the admission, but there was defiance in her eyes.

"Joel felt outclassed from the first. When you were little, things weren't so bad." She must have seen the look on Gabe's face and added, "I know he was too hard on you, but it might still have worked out." She shook her head. "But when you turned seven and started slipping off to the sale barn to be with Jesse, it all fell apart. Joel knew he couldn't measure up, so he quit trying, and he started resenting Jesse. After a while, that resentment crept over into his feelings for you. He couldn't help it, I guess."

"Are you saying Jesse took me with him, let me be a part of his life, just to cause trouble?"

"No," Hannah denied quickly. "I'm not saying anything of the kind. Jesse loves you as much as he does his other boys. I know that. What I'm saying is that even though he did what he did out of love, a part of him did it out of a need to hurt me."

"Why would he want to hurt you? He loved you."

Hannah shook her head. "He never loved me. He's always loved Sarah. He wanted me, and he didn't want me to break off with him, and later, he didn't want me to marry Joel. Jesse Calloway wanted to have his cake and eat it, too. If he'd had his way, we'd still be sleeping together behind Sarah's back. Luckily, as I got older, I got smarter. By the time you were four, I'd had enough."

Gabe's mind churned with the implications attached to Hannah's story. Joel Butler and Jesse Calloway were cast into a new light. Was it possible that Joel had wanted to be a father to him—at least at first?

"If it hadn't been for the hardheadedness you got from Jesse, you and Joel might have built a relationship," Hannah said thoughtfully, as if she could read his mind or had considered the possibility often in the past. "I suppose that the older you got, the more like Jesse you became and the less Joel cared to try."

"I'm not like Jesse!" Gabe said, fury thrumming in the deep denial.

"Yes, you are," she said with a wan smile. "You're so much like him in some ways it's downright frightening. But mostly in the good ways, thank God."

Neither spoke for long seconds. Finally Hannah said, "So. You never said. Are you going to marry her, not sure of your feelings and already believing the marriage is doomed?"

Gabe was thankful to leave the conversation about Jesse behind. He nodded. "I'm going to marry her and give it my best shot. I thought about it all night, and I have to do it. At least if it all falls apart, I'll know I did what I could." He met his mother's sorrowful gaze. "I thought about me and Jesse. And me and Joel. And I realized I don't want my baby to grow up the way I did. Never knowing who I was. Never knowing where I belonged. Hearing the whispers and thinking it was something I did."

He saw the stricken look on Hannah's face and was instantly contrite for opening his heart and his mouth. "I'm sorry, Mama," he said. "I didn't mean to hurt you."

Her lips quivered; tears chased down her plump cheeks. "I didn't mean to hurt you, either, son."

"I know," he said, getting to his feet and taking her into his arms. "I know."

And he did. There was no doubt in his mind that she loved him and would have taken his pain if she could.

As usual, she got her emotions under control in a matter of moments—at least on the surface. Stepping out of his embrace, she ripped a paper towel from the roll, dabbed at her tears and blew her nose.

"When are you bringing her home?"

"Anytime, I suppose. She's in town for a few days."

"My stars!" Hannah said, obviously discomfited by the news that the meeting was so close at hand. "What's she doing in Calloway Corners?"

"Nicole invited her to stay at Nick and Eden's."

"Well, then," Hannah said decisively, "if she's here, you may as well ask her over today."

"You want to have her here for Christmas dinner?"

"Why not? There's no sense putting it off."

"If I do that, we'll have to tell everyone why."

Hannah shrugged. "There's no sense putting that off, either."

## CHAPTER SEVEN

THE RINGING OF THE PHONE roused Gretchen from the sleep she'd succumbed to just before morning. With a sigh, she lifted a corner of the pillow and stuck her head underneath. At last the ringing stopped.

"Gretchen?" Nicole's voice was soft, tentative.

"Hmm?" Gretchen mumbled, unwilling to break the tenuous bonds of slumber.

"It's Gabe. He wants to talk to you."

*Gabe!* Gretchen was out from under the pillow in a flash, shoving back the covers and grabbing the phone from Nicole's hand.

"Hello." Her voice sounded breathless, excited. It was. She was.

"Hey."

Gabe's voice sounded warm and low, the way it had when he'd nuzzled her neck while they were making love. The resonance of the deep, sexy timbre reverberated through her very soul and tickled the base of her spine. She suppressed a shiver.

"Are you up?"

She pushed herself to her elbows. "I am now."

"My mom wanted me to call and invite you to Christmas dinner."

"What!" Did this mean he intended to tell his family he was going to marry her?

"I thought it was a bit out of the blue, too, but then, once Mom makes up her mind about something, she doesn't let any grass grow under her feet."

"You told them about the baby." It was a statement, not a question.

"I told my mother," he said. "No one else is up yet, but no matter what we decide, she has a right to know she's going to be a grandmother."

"Yes." Gretchen heard the catch in her voice. "What did she say?"

"What could she say?" he asked her in a dry tone. "She was surprised. Disappointed. Her little boy let her down. But don't worry about Mom. She isn't judgmental, believe me. She just asked who you were and what we were going to do."

A small gasp escaped Gretchen's lips, and her hand went to her throat in an involuntary gesture. "And...have you decided?"

"I don't want to talk about it over the phone."

Her heart sank. If he didn't want to talk about it, it must be bad news.

"I know you probably planned to eat with the Logans, but I don't think they'd mind if you came here, instead. We eat at straight-up noon. What do you think?"

"I don't know." Gretchen was filled with a sudden panic at the thought of meeting his family—especially under the circumstances. "It should be okay."

"Good. I'll be there about eleven, then. That'll give you time to be with Eden and her family this morning and time to visit with everyone here for a while before we eat."

Her stomach churned with nervous apprehension. "Fine." She strove to make her voice even and self-

assured, something she usually had no problem doing. "I'll see you then."

They said their goodbyes and Gretchen recradled
the receiver.

"Well?"

The question came from Nicole, who was sitting on
the edge of the bed, an expectant look vying with the
weariness on her face.

Gretchen had kept her up until the wee hours, telling her the details of Gabe's visit, pacing and wondering what she should do. Nicole hadn't been—and
still wasn't—the least worried about Gabe's decision.
He would do the right thing. He was that kind of man.

"He told his mother."

"And?"

"She wants me to have Christmas dinner with
them."

Nicole's smile was beatific. "What did I tell you?"

"He hasn't agreed to marry me, Nicole. I think he's
made a decision, but he didn't want to talk about it
over the phone." Gretchen's voice quavered with uncertainty. "It doesn't sound good to me."

Nicole got up, rounded the bed, took Gretchen by
the shoulders and gave her a little shake. "Wake up,
woman! I don't think you'd be having Christmas dinner with them if he didn't plan to marry you. Have a
little faith, here. It's the season of miracles, for cryin'
out loud!"

Someone banged on the door before Gretchen could
acknowledge that Nicole might be right.

"Come in!" Nicole called.

Wearing a white terry-cloth robe and furry house
slippers, Eden pushed through the doorway, a wide
smile on her face. "Merry Christmas!"

"Merry Christmas," Nicole and Gretchen chimed together.

"I know it's early, and I'm so glad you're both awake. The kids are chomping at the bit to open their gifts, but I wouldn't let them start without you two."

"Meany," Nicole teased.

"Meany nothing," Eden said, raking a hand through her tousled strawberry blond hair. "The stuff Santa Claus brought should keep them busy for a few minutes."

Nicole looked at Gretchen. "I'm ready if you are."

"I haven't even washed the sleep from my eyes!" Gretchen wailed.

"Well, go do that, grab your robe and come on," Eden said, backing through the doorway. "I'll tell the kids you'll just be a minute."

Less than five minutes later, Gretchen found herself in front of a blazing fire in the Logan den, a mug of coffee between her palms while she watched Eden and Nick's children unwrap their Christmas presents.

Four-year-old Ben had it down pat, ripping the bright-colored paper from the boxes with an economy of motion, glancing at the present and tossing it aside in favor of another. Kat, who was just three, was more reserved, taking the time to comment on each gift and listen while Eden told her who bought it. Cole and Jenni, the twins, weren't sure what was going on. They sat in their red pajamas, thumbs in their mouths, watching the whole procedure with wide green eyes, content to let the adults do the opening for them.

They were all adorable, Gretchen thought. Just the way children were supposed to be. And Eden and Nick were great parents, patient and loving, but stern when the situation called for it.

What kind of parent would she be? Gretchen wondered. Just because she felt her parents had done a lousy job bringing her up, there was no guarantee she'd do any better. Would she have Eden's patience or Nick's sense of humor when things went wrong?

She envisioned Christmas a year from now. Her baby would be nearly seven months old. Old enough to be fascinated by the lights and gnaw on a cookie. Maybe even old enough to say, "Da-da." Would Gabe be around to hear it?

"Okay, gang!" Eden called, clapping to get the children's attention. "Let's pick this mess up. Honey, will you take care of it while I go start breakfast?" she asked Nick.

He smiled. "Only if you put lots of butter and syrup on my waffles."

"Deal." Turning to her in-laws, and Gretchen and Nicole, Eden said, "Come on, ladies. Let's adjourn to the kitchen, where there's just a little less noise."

Gretchen followed the women from the room, dreading the next half hour when she would break the news of her pregnancy to Gabe's cousin. Still, she knew it was something that had to be done, and the sooner the better. Eleven o'clock was just four short hours away.

"AND YOU TOLD ME you didn't even kiss girls."

Before he was to leave to pick up Gretchen, Gabe had decided to break the news to his sister. He'd found her outside putting sunflower seeds in the squirrel feeder. He'd sat her down in the glider on the deck and told her about the baby.

She'd listened to his story without interrupting. Her teasing comment was made with a smile, but Gabe saw the disappointment in her eyes. He had no snappy comeback, no defense. All he could do was rub his mustache, tip his head back to look at the sky and sigh.

"I know this is the nineties and all that, but I thought—"

"That I was above that sort of thing?" he interrupted. His sorrow-filled eyes met hers. "I never meant to disappoint you, sweetcheeks, but I'm human. That's my only excuse—not that it's a good one." He sighed again. "I've never been a bed hopper, if that makes any difference."

"I know that. You're a flirt. So am I, but I know you're much too fastidious to sleep around."

Gabe arched an eyebrow at her. "A thousand-dollar word for a ten-dollar cowboy?"

"Stop putting yourself down."

"I'm not putting myself down. I just see myself for what I am."

"Bull. You see yourself as Jesse Calloway's bastard."

"You know about that?" The surprise in Gabe's eyes was echoed in the question.

"Of course I do. Mama told me so I wouldn't make the same mistakes she did."

"She's a pretty savvy lady."

"Yes, she is. And so are you—savvy, that is," she added with a grin. She took his hand and squeezed it. "Your self-esteem could use some serious bolstering, big brother. You've got a lot going for you, a lot to offer the right woman. Everybody knows it but you."

He didn't answer. Arguing with her would get him nowhere. Jody perceived him differently, that was all.

He'd always been her hero, and despite her disappointment now, he still was.

"End of discussion, right?" she asked with a wry smile.

"Right."

She rose from the glider and turned to leave, but his voice stopped her.

"Mom was right, Jody. It's best to wait."

"You don't want to marry Gretchen?"

"I didn't want to marry anybody."

"You don't think you can be what she needs, do you?" Jody asked with more insight than he'd have given her credit for. "You're wrong about that, Gabe. When people look at you, they see a rough-and-tumble cowboy who's the biggest flirt in town. But that isn't you. That's the you that you want the world to see. When people look at Gretchen, they see a rich man's daughter with all the usual trappings. But on the inside, I think she's looking to belong to someone just like you. And I think you belong with each other."

As PLANNED, Gabe left his mother's house early enough to stop by and see his brothers. He'd called to let them know he was coming, and Jericho and Daniel were waiting for him just inside the door when he pulled into the driveway and honked, something he'd gotten into a habit of doing when they were teenagers.

In seconds, Jericho and Daniel were squeezed into the front seat, and Gabe pulled out onto the highway.

"What's got you so torn up you had to have a little comfort from your big brother on Christmas Day?" Jericho asked in a taunting tone. "Didn't Santa leave any goodies in your stocking?"

"I got something, all right," Gabe said. "but it wasn't from Santa, and it isn't exactly a goodie."

From the corner of his eye, Gabe saw his brothers exchange a questioning look. "What's up, bro?" Daniel asked.

"I'm going to be a father."

The blunt announcement exploded in the close confines of the truck's cab. No one spoke for several long seconds.

"Who?" Daniel asked.

Gabe shot him a sideways look. "Who? Gretchen, of course."

"Gretchen? You mean Gretchen West?" Jericho asked, a stunned look on his face.

"Turn up your hearing aid. That's what I said."

"How did that happen?" Jericho asked. Seeing the scathing look Gabe shot him, he held up a hand and said, "Let me rephrase that. What I meant to say is that I didn't know you and Gretchen had gotten that...close."

"Well, it wasn't planned, and it was only briefly— a day and a half—but we did and it did."

Daniel whistled. "This is pretty heavy for Christmas morning. What are you going to do?"

"What do you think I'm going to do? What any man who's worth his salt does. I'm going to marry her."

"Crazy."

"Stupid."

"There you go, ganging up on me again," Gabe said, hoping the attempt at humor would drive away the sudden pain his brothers' opinions caused.

"We're not ganging up on you, are we, squirt?"

"Not at all," Daniel said. "What Jericho and I mean is that you ought to give a decision like this some serious thought. We're talking about a big life-style change. Having a baby outside of marriage isn't as big a deal as it used to be."

"It is to me," Gabe said. "I know my life is going to be different, believe me, but thinking about it more won't change things. I'm Jesse Calloway's bastard." Jericho started to speak, but Gabe waved him into silence. "I know he cares for me, but not enough to claim me. It hurts. It's always hurt. I don't want my child growing up with that kind of pain."

"I understand," Jericho and Daniel chorused.

"No," Gabe said, his voice firm with conviction, his eyes filled with thirty years of pain. "You don't."

GABE'S TRUCK pulled into the driveway at precisely 11:00 a.m. Gretchen smoothed her palms down her sides, more to wipe away the perspiration than to adjust her baggy cranberry red cable-knit sweater. The sweater topped an ankle-length, winter white skirt that buttoned down the front and a pair of soft cranberry leather boots. Pearl and diamond drops, a birthday gift from her mother, dangled from her ears, her only jewelry besides the no-nonsense Timex strapped to her wrist.

Fighting the impulse to watch Gabe get out of the truck, she stepped away from the window and turned toward the door. Her heart thudded in time with each thump of his boots on the wooden steps. He rapped smartly, and she called a breathless "Come in."

The door swung wide and he stepped inside, letting in a cold blast of air. He looked tall and rugged and so handsome it hurt. In honor of the holiday, he'd swapped his usual blue denim for black. The fabric clung to his muscular thighs and molded his narrow hips, accenting his masculinity in a way that reminded her of all sorts of things she was better off forgetting.

His hip-length leather jacket hung open, revealing a forest green shirt. Beneath the shadow of his black Charlie One Horse hat, his eyes were unreadable. Beneath the swath of his mustache, his mouth was firm, unsmiling.

"You look very handsome," she said truthfully. If nothing else, the occasion demanded truth.

"Thanks." His gaze moved over her from head to toe. "You look pretty good yourself."

Gretchen felt the tension at the base of her neck ease a bit. She smiled, pleased by the compliment.

"All I have to do is get my coat and a couple of packages," she said. "I didn't want to go empty-handed, so I—"

"Whoa!" Gabe said, catching her arm as she swept past him.

Forced to a stop mere inches from him, Gretchen looked up into his crystalline blue eyes. For the first time this weekend, she thought she saw the hint of a smile there. That tiny bit of softening was her undoing. Her nervous heart melted into a puddle of longing.

"Did I ever tell you that it makes me tired just watching you?" he said.

Gretchen shook her head.

"You go at everything you do like you're killing snakes," he told her, draping an arm across her shoulders and guiding her toward the sofa. "I remember how you were when we were doing that video.

Even when everyone around you was working at top speed, you made them look like they were standing still.''

"There's always so much to do and not enough time to do it," she said, almost as if she was apologizing. He indicated that she should sit. She did and he took a seat beside her. She turned toward him and their knees touched. Neither moved away.

His gaze was steady, concerned. "Maybe you'd better think about slowing down."

"Why?" Then, grasping his meaning, she added, "Oh." She shook her head. "I don't see how I can."

"You'd better learn to delegate, or else take on fewer projects."

She knew it was just a suggestion, and a suggestion based on concern, but it felt like an order. No one had told her what to do for years, and she wasn't sure she liked it—not even when Gabe was doing the telling. Still, his concern, like the compliment, was touching.

"Careful there, cowboy," she said with a flutter of her eyelashes and a coy smile. "I'll start to think you care about me and this baby."

"I do care about you and the baby. I'm scared spitless, but I care."

"What do you have to be scared of?" she asked, leaning toward him and crossing her arms on her knees.

"I'm responsible for putting another person in the world. An innocent, helpless person. That puts a mighty heavy burden on a man. Or a woman. Being responsible for someone else is frightening."

She knew exactly how he felt. It was something she still hadn't come to terms with.

"Being accountable to someone else is scary, too. I've been comin' and goin' without checking with anyone for as long as I can remember. I don't know how I'll do on a leash."

Gretchen held up a hand. "Wait a minute. Let me be sure I understand what you're saying. You said accountable to someone. Does that mean that you're considering—"

"Getting married," he interjected. "Yeah. Against my better judgment."

The negative comment filled her with a sudden fury. Gretchen leapt to her feet. Without thinking, she doubled up her fist and swung at him. Only Gabe's prompt reflexes saved him from catching the blow on the chin.

"Damn you!" she cried, trying to wrench free of the grip he still had on her wrist. "Don't do me any favors. I wouldn't want you putting yourself out on my account. Or the baby's!"

"Simmer down," Gabe said. He loosened his hold on her, but he didn't let her go. Using a gentle, inexorable tugging movement, he drew her back onto the sofa. His warm touch undermined her temper. Gretchen felt her anger dissolving and tried to drum up some backbone.

"What I said has nothing to do with you personally," he told her. "All I meant is that we come from different worlds, and I'm not sure we can ever overcome that, even though we might want to."

"Are we back to that?" she asked, exasperated.

"It'll always come back to that," he said. "I'm willing to marry you, with a few conditions, but I can tell you right now, I won't fit in with your life or your ways—"

"That's ridiculous," she scoffed, pulling her wrist free. "Of course you will."

"—and you won't like mine."

"What do you mean?"

"I'm gone a lot. More than I'm home sometimes," he told her. His jaw was set and resolution shadowed his cool blue eyes. "I'm not about to live off your money like some gigolo, and I'm not giving up rodeo until I'm ready. Not for you or anyone. It's the only way I know to make a living. Other than that, I'm willing to give marriage a try."

There it was. His conditions for marriage. His terms. Her eyes searched his, looking for something, not knowing what that might be, and finding nothing there but a steely determination and the deep-rooted pride that went hand in hand with a masculine ego.

"No one could ever mistake you for the kind of man who'd live off a woman, and I don't want you to give up rodeo," she said honestly. "I know you well enough to know that rodeo is who you are. What I don't know is why, but maybe in time I will."

"Does that mean you accept my conditions?"

She crossed her arms over her breasts and glared at him. "Yes, damn it!"

"Good." He reached into his shirt pocket. "I have something for you."

Her eyes widened in dismay. "I don't have a present for you."

"This isn't a Christmas present," he told her, and he held up a ring between his thumb and forefinger. "It was my grandmother's."

"An engagement ring?" she asked, taking the small circlet from him.

There was absolutely no emotion in Gabe's clear blue eyes. "If it suits you."

Gretchen's rapt gaze lingered on the sapphires and diamonds arranged in an old-fashioned filigree setting. It was just the kind of thing she scoured estate sales and pawnshops for, and the size looked about right, too. Considering that he had his doubts about the marriage working, she was more pleased than he would ever know that he wanted her to wear his grandmother's ring. She decided to take the gesture to mean that he wanted things to work out between them.

She looked from the ring up at him, her expression soft and wondering. "It's exquisite. Will you put it on for me?"

He looked surprised by the request. "Do you really want me to?"

"I do."

The simple statement sounded so much like a wedding promise that they were both caught off guard for a moment. Dragging his gaze from hers, he took the ring in one callused hand and her left hand in the other and slid the circle of gold and stones into place. She hoped he wouldn't notice the slight tremor in her hand—or the breathlessness his nearness invoked.

The ring fit so well it might have been sized for her finger. She lifted her hand to the light, turning it this way and that, the small but brilliant diamonds flashing in a way that seemed joyful somehow. The ring looked and felt as if it belonged there. A flicker of hope lightened the heaviness of her heart.

"If you'd rather have something more modern—'

"No!" she said quickly. "It's perfect. Thank you for offering it to me."

"I'm glad you like it." The pleasure in his eyes said far more than the stiffly voiced statement. "When Grandma Marshall left it to me, my Mom said one day I'd find the right woman to give it to."

Gretchen's eyes, full of hope and uncertainty, met his. "Am I the right woman?" Her voice was tremulous, questioning...expectant.

"You're going to be my wife. The mother of my child. You must be."

It wasn't what she wanted to hear, but she supposed it would have to do—for now. Something told her that even if she and Gabe were wildly in love, he wasn't the type to wax poetic about his feelings.

He glanced at the watch on his brawny wrist. "We'd better get cracking. If we're late, Mom will have my hide."

Gretchen preceded him out the door, her mind occupied with thoughts of her upcoming meeting with his mother. Hannah Butler, who'd had a lengthy affair with a married man. Hannah Butler, soon to be her mother-in-law.

"WOULD YOU LIKE some pecan pie, honey?"

The question came from Hannah Butler and was aimed at Gretchen. The fact that she called her by the endearment meant one of two things: either Hannah liked her, or she couldn't remember her name.

Just now, Gretchen didn't care which. Whatever she might feel inside, Gabe's mother hadn't acted the least bit hostile. Gretchen had been welcomed, told that Jody had gone to have dinner with Tess, Seth and Jason, and had engaged in polite conversation with Gabe and Joel while Hannah put the finishing touches on the meal. Then she'd been plied with so much of that delicious food she felt as stuffed as the magnificent bird, which was big enough to feed a small army.

Groaning in repletion, Gretchen looked from the last bite of cornbread dressing on her plate to Hannah's solicitous face. "I couldn't eat dessert if my life depended on it," she told her hostess truthfully. "It was delicious, Mrs. Butler. Thank you for having me."

Joel Butler's face glowed with a triumphant pleasure; Hannah's plump face turned a pretty pink. "I'm glad you enjoyed it," she said. "I confess I was a little worried. I'm just a plain country cook."

Though slight, it was the first reference to the difference between Gretchen's station in life and Gabe's.

"Well, I don't cook much at all," Gretchen said. Then, afraid that the Butlers would take the statement to mean that she had a cook, she added hastily, "Not that I don't like cooking, but I'm usually too tired when I get in to fix much."

Hannah tsked softly. "Missing meals isn't good for you, especially now."

The hand lifting the last bite of dressing to Gretchen's lips stilled. The first reference to the baby. "I know," she said. "I'll try to do better."

"Gabe, honey, you see to it she eats right."

"Okay, Mom." Gabe's voice held just the right mix of obedience, humor and tolerance his mother's directive required. His lazy, smiling gaze met Gretchen's. He winked.

Gretchen smiled back, the first real smile she'd been able to summon since arriving.

He reached across the table to the platter of turkey, plucking the wishbone from the remains. "Don't tell Jody," he said to his mom in a conspiratorial whisper. He held the V-shaped bone toward Gretchen.

"Jody has claimed all the wishbones since she was old enough to know what they were," he explained. "I guess she thinks no one else has wishes."

Gretchen looked at him questioningly. "What do I do?"

The stunned look on his face was comical. "You've never made a wish with a wishbone?"

She shook her head. Tyrell and Mimi West would never have allowed anything so crass at the dinner table. What was left of their holiday bird was whisked off to the kitchen and never seen again. Unlike other American homes, there were no turkey potpies or turkey sandwiches made from the leftovers. For the first time in her life, Gretchen wondered if the chef took the remains for himself.

"Take hold of your side," Gabe instructed. "Close your eyes and make a wish. Then we break the bone in half. Whoever winds up with the big side gets their wish."

"Okay." Gretchen took one side of the slender bone in her fingers and squeezed her eyes shut. She wished for a healthy baby and for Gabe to love her. When she opened her eyes, he was smiling at her.

"What?" she asked.

"It took you long enough."

"I've never done this before," she said with a lift of her eyebrows. "I had a lot to wish for."

He acknowledged the excuse with a smile. "Ready?"

Gretchen nodded and they began to pull. The fragile bone snapped, and with a cry of triumph Gretchen held the bigger side aloft. "I get my wish."

"Not so fast," he said, his fingers curling around her wrist.

She leveled a questioning look at him. "What?"

His dark blond mustache crawled up at one corner. "Some people say that whoever winds up with the little side is the winner."

Her smile faded.

"Gabriel Butler!" Hannah said. "You stop teasing that poor child right now." She looked at Gretchen. "What he says is true, honey. It's a debate as old as the custom." She pinned her son with a reproachful look. "But in this house, it's always been the big side."

"Beginner's luck," Gabe said. "What'd you wish for?"

Gretchen's heart sank. No way was she telling him her wish.

"Gabe!" Once again, Hannah's voice stopped him. "You are so bad." Shaking her head, she turned to Gretchen. "You can't tell your wish or it won't come true." She shot Gabe a disapproving look. "Of course, Gabe could tell us his wish, since it won't come true, anyway."

"It might," he said, "so I'm not telling. Not even if you bribe me with a piece of pecan pie. Not even for a piece of pecan and pumpkin pie."

"Are you trying to say you want dessert?" Hannah asked, smiling.

"Of course I want dessert."

"My stars!" Gabe's mother rose with a disbelieving shake of her head. "I don't know where you put all that food."

"Hey! I saved room by not having a third helping of dressing," he said, straight-faced.

Hannah's giggle sounded young and girlish. "Knowing how you love dressing, that is a sacrifice."

She turned to her husband. "Would you like dessert now, too, honey?"

"Just another cup of coffee, please."

"Sure thing. Do you mind coming to help?"

Gretchen's stomach churned in nervous apprehension at being called into Mama Bear's den, but there was no way she could refuse. She pushed back her chair and, with a last look at Gabe, followed her hostess from the room.

The encouraging look in his eyes was like a calming balm.

"We don't have long to talk," Hannah said when the door swung shut behind them, "but I wanted a couple of minutes with you."

Gretchen wasn't allowed time to say anything before Hannah blurted, "Gabe said you'd had some female problems. Is everything all right with you and the baby?"

Telling Hannah about her recent backaches and occasional cramps would serve no purpose except to worry Gabe's mother; besides, Dr. Mason said she'd have a lot of unusual aches and pains. "Everything seems to be fine," Gretchen assured her.

"That's wonderful." Hannah placed a piece of pecan pie on a plate and looked up at Gretchen apologetically. "I don't want to hurt your feelings or make you angry, but I do wish we'd met under different circumstances."

Gretchen wasn't about to explain her actions to Gabe's mother; neither was she going to defend herself. All she said was, "Believe me, Mrs. Butler, so do I."

The older woman's smile was tinged with sorrow, and her eyes were filled with the residue of painful remembrances. "Well, we can't change things. We have to pick up and go on."

"I agree."

"Has Gabe told you about *his* health problem?"

"What health problem?" Gretchen asked, uncertain if she was more shocked by the question or the fact that anything could be wrong with a man who looked as physically fit as Gabe.

"I didn't figure he'd said anything," Hannah said, slicing into the pumpkin pie and raising her candid gaze to Gretchen's. "Gabe was born with only one kidney."

"What!"

Hannah placed a reassuring hand on Gretchen's arm. "Oh, don't worry, honey. It's never given him a minute's trouble, and everyone tends to forget it. Even I forget sometimes. I don't know why it happened. Neither Jesse nor I have any history of it, but I thought I should tell you so you'd be prepared—you know, if it shows up in your baby."

Gretchen felt her growing apprehension subside at Gabe's mother's matter-of-fact attitude. "Thank you for telling me, Mrs. Butler. I'll be sure and pass the information on to my doctor."

She was still trying to come to grips with that startling piece of news when Hannah said, "You're getting a good man."

Gretchen felt the sudden sting of tears beneath her eyelids. "I know that. I've known that from the first moment I saw him."

It was clear that the admission pleased Hannah. "Do you love him?"

"Yes," Gretchen said, needing to make the confession as much as Hannah needed to hear it.

Hannah's eyes were filled with worry and sincerity. "He wants to do the right thing. He's made up his mind to, even though he's admitted he's not sure a marriage between the two of you will work."

"I understand his doubts," Gretchen said. "I have some myself."

"Maybe I shouldn't say this, but someone needs to..."

"Please," Gretchen urged, wondering what other surprises Hannah Butler could pull out of her bag. "It's important that we're honest with each other."

Hannah took Gretchen's hand in hers. "Two wrongs don't make a right, honey. As much as I'd like to be a part of this baby's life, you should understand that divorce can be just as painful to a child as finding out his parents weren't married."

"Believe me, Mrs. Butler, I've thought about all that. I know Gabe worries what my parents will say about...Jesse and the differences in our social standing and our pocketbooks, but none of that matters to me. I was never particularly enamored of my life-style growing up. I'd much rather have spent more time with my grandfather on his ranch. Money isn't my god. It's just a means to an end."

Hannah nodded. "Gabe's a proud man."

"I know that. We need time," Gretchen said. "Time will prove to each of us that we are what we say we are, and maybe show us what we really feel for each other. I love him, Mrs. Butler. I only hope he comes to realize that he loves me, too, and that what we are inside and what we feel inside is more important than outward appearances."

"What Gabe has inside is a lot of anger," Hannah Butler said. "At Jesse. Joel. Even me, though he'd never admit it."

"Gabe loves you," Gretchen said, squeezing the older woman's hand, and knowing instinctively it was true.

"I know he loves me, but sometimes when Jesse's done something to hurt him, I see the way he looks at me, and I know that even though he's an adult and understands what happened, he's blaming me for some of that pain." Hannah's eyes filled, and she dashed away the moisture with her fingertips. "How could he not?" she asked. "God only knows, I still blame myself."

## CHAPTER EIGHT

AFTER SPENDING the afternoon trying to carry on a conversation with Gabe and his parents while dealing with a mutual uneasiness, Gretchen announced that she was tired, and Gabe took her home. At the bottom of the garage apartment steps he plunged his hands into his coat pockets. She was poised on the step above him, which put them eye to eye.

"Why didn't you tell me about your kidney?"

The question took him by complete surprise. "I didn't think about it. I never do."

"It hasn't been a problem?"

"Never," he told her truthfully.

"Good," she said with a nod. "Your mom and Joel are very nice. Be sure and tell her again that I enjoyed the day."

"Thanks, I will." They stood looking at each other for a moment, not speaking. Finally Gabe cleared his throat. "When are you leaving?"

"Sometime after lunch tomorrow," she told him. "I don't go back to work until Tuesday morning."

"I'll call you first thing in the morning, then, so we can decide when I should meet you in Fort Worth to break the news to your parents."

"They won't be back until after the first of the year, which is a plus."

His brow furrowed. "Why?"

"I'll have plenty of time to get the wedding plans under way before Mother gets home and insists on doing things her way."

Gabe, who was still feeling a little punchy over the whole state of affairs, liked the idea of a week's postponement, too. Facing the Wests was more intimidating than squaring off against the meanest bull on the circuit; however, "wedding plans" sounded a little frightening, too.

He scowled. "I thought we'd just go to a justice of the peace or something."

Gretchen looked at him as if he'd just crawled out from under a rock. "Gabriel Butler, regardless of your doomsday opinion about how well our marriage is going to work, I want to do it right." A wave of color swept up over her cheeks. "Or as right as we can under the circumstances."

His frown deepened.

"Look," she said in a conciliatory tone, "I don't want a fancy church wedding with five hundred people, but I want a minister and family and friends and a reception—all the usual brouhaha."

"Sounds just peachy."

Reluctant amusement lifted the corners of her mouth. "Like looking a red-eyed, ornery bull in the eye, huh?"

"Worse."

To his surprise, Gretchen laughed. "This is going to be really interesting!"

"What?" he asked, not certain he liked being the brunt of her teasing.

"The next thirty years." When Gabe had no answer, she said, "I promise to keep everything simple and low-key. Believe me, I don't want it to turn into the Fort Worth social event of the season, either."

"Good."

She clutched her purse against her breasts and looked him straight in the eye. "You may not know it, but underneath all the external trappings that go with being a West, I'm a pretty normal woman with ordinary wants and needs."

How could she say that? To him, she was a rare and extraordinary woman. "You may be a lot of things, but a normal woman isn't one of them."

"Is that good or bad?" she asked, laughter dancing in her eyes again.

"It's...special."

"Why thank you, Gabe." She leaned forward and pressed a kiss to his lips.

The touch of her mouth against his sizzled along his nerve endings at the speed of light, sending desire throughout his body. She broke off the kiss and said simply, "As good as I remembered."

"Why did you do that?" he asked, torn between need and dismay and the pleasure her statement evoked.

"I don't know," she said with a shrug and an unrepentant smile. "It just seemed appropriate, somehow. After all, we're going to be married. Kisses are a part of marriage, aren't they?"

The expression on his face must have mirrored his bewilderment. Her eyes mirrored her incredulity.

"Oh, Gabe! Surely you didn't think we were going to have one of those old-fashioned marriages of convenience?"

In truth, he hadn't thought that far ahead. Trying to come to terms with the fact that he was going to be married and become a father had filled his mind to the exclusion of exactly what those new roles might entail.

"I guess I hadn't given it much thought," he told her. "Just what do you want from me and this marriage, anyway?"

"To share your bed, for starters," she told him, startling him with her honesty. "Because if you have separate bedrooms in mind, we'll just forget the whole thing. I have no intention of going into a marriage that doesn't aspire to be a real one in every way.

"I love you, cowboy," she said, putting her hand on his chest and tapping the place over his heart with a crimson-tipped fingernail. "I want it all, and that includes sharing every aspect of our lives—the work, the play, fighting and making love. The good and the bad. Take it or leave it."

Her confession of love stunned Gabe. Scared him. "Don't try to fool yourself about what you feel for me just because you're having my baby."

"I don't think I am," she said sincerely. "Maybe you don't want to hear it, but I think we owe it to each other to be honest."

Her tone held a determination that was growing familiar. As ultimatums went, hers was a dilly. The idea of her loving him blew his mind. It was unbelievable. It was both heaven and hell, and it added to the pressure he was already feeling. How could he ever live up to all she expected of him? He wasn't sure he could deal with the kind of closeness she demanded, even though he knew that if he married her, she had a right to expect it from him.

He felt an unaccountable ache in his heart. The real question wasn't so much whether or not he wanted to share his life with her, but if he was able to. Old habits were hard to break, and he'd played his cards so close to his chest all his life that he wasn't sure he'd be able to change. Rather than confess that uncertainty, he said, "You drive a hard bargain, lady."

"Wests usually do," she told him sweetly. "It's how we got where we are."

He nodded. "Yeah. On top. So where does that leave me?"

Gretchen's smile was slow and more than slightly naughty. "You can be on top, too—at least sometimes."

Her meaning was crystal clear. The image that came to mind was one that had plagued him often since their September weekend. It was one he'd like very much to repeat.

"Deal?" Her voice jolted him from the tantalizing memory.

He shook his head. "You're going too fast. I don't have time to get used to one thing before you throw something else at me."

"Damn it, Gabe!" Gretchen said, all pretense of teasing and patience vanished. "Do you want to marry me or not?"

"I gave you a ring, didn't I?" He heard the irritation and frustration in his voice. "Where I come from, that means I want to marry you. But I don't know if I can be what you want. Hell, I don't know if I *want* to be what you want," he told her with a candor that made her face go ashen. "All I know is that I've made all the promises I can for a while. I want to keep rodeoing and take our…relationship slow and easy and see what happens. Those are my conditions. Take it or leave it."

He tossed her ultimatum back in her white, worried face. Her gaze probed his for tortured seconds. He was afraid to speak, afraid to breathe. Dear God, he was so afraid....

He watched the surprise on her face turn to wry amusement, saw the slight crinkles fan out from the corners of her eyes. Damned if she wasn't laughing at him again. Or was she laughing at herself?

She sighed. "Blame it on Gramps, but I'm darned if I don't love all that macho bull."

"What does that mean?"

Her answer was spoken with a grudging respect. "I've never turned down a challenge yet. I'll take it."

"WELL?" GABE RUBBED his palms down his thighs and looked at his mother, waiting for her to voice an opinion of how the day had gone and how she and Joel felt about Gretchen.

"Joel liked her," Hannah said. "And I know Jody was impressed when she met her yesterday at Jason's."

"And what did you think?"

His mother's candid blue gaze met his. "I think she's hurting inside as much as you are."

"What do you mean?"

Hannah's shoulders lifted. "Pain. Loneliness. Maybe they're the same, but I know that look when I see it."

"She's Tyrell West's daughter. She's rich and successful and leads a very busy life. How can she be lonely?" he asked even as he recalled Gretchen's telling him about being left with a housekeeper as a child.

"Being surrounded by people is no guarantee against loneliness. You should know that."

Yeah, he should. Did. Even when he was surrounded by his rodeo buddies, he still felt as if there
was an invisible wall between them, something that
kept him separate from the group. Some intangible
something that made him different. He *was* different.
He was Jesse Calloway's bastard, and he'd never be
able to forget it. He didn't want to forget it.

Recalling the things Gretchen had told him about
her past, he pictured a young Gretchen sitting in a big
window watching a long white limo disappear down a
winding driveway. Saw an older version of that same
girl on a big stage dancing to an audience that didn't
include her parents. Imagined a grown-up Gretchen
sitting in a fancy condo unwrapping Christmas presents alone. His heart clenched in pain, and he admitted that his mom might be right. He also admitted that
he and Gretchen West had more in common than
anyone could imagine. More than he would ever have
believed.

Would it be possible for the two of them to do what
she thought they could even though their marriage was
starting with a less than auspicious beginning? Could
they give their child a better life than they'd had? Was
it possible to have the real marriage that Gretchen
wanted, possible to create something good and lasting out of this accident—or quirk of fate? The possibility that they could was both exciting and
frightening.

"She wants this marriage to work," Hannah said.
"I know that much."

Gabe met his mother's concerned gaze. He wanted
to tell her about Gretchen's confession of love, but
didn't. It was too unsettling. "So do I, Mom."

As he spoke the words, he realized they were the truth. The funny thing was, until that moment, he hadn't known just how true they were.

TO GRETCHEN'S never-ending gratitude, Eden volunteered her home for the wedding, citing that she was going to do the same for Daniel and Becca in the spring. She insisted that she and her sisters would love to help; besides, she didn't want Gabe to feel left out, something he'd felt all too often. Gretchen was only too happy to turn over the bulk of the work to someone with more time and energy than she had.

So, via fax and phone, and despite the hectic post-Christmas week, when Gretchen had to do the final edit of a new video and Nicole had to deal with returns and sales, not to mention the distance of almost two hundred miles, Gretchen, Nicole and the Calloway sisters arranged the wedding.

Gretchen didn't want a formal gown but planned on wearing winter white and carrying burgundy roses. She did want real flowers. Eden just happened to know someone in Haughton who did the "most gorgeous weddings in the state." Another friend—"she's better than any of the bakeries around"—would bake the cake. The Calloway sisters would take care of the rest of the reception themselves.

The ceremony was set for the fourteenth of January, a Saturday, and would be held in the Logan living room, a Victorian delight, complete with a huge fireplace and lots of lace-covered windows and huge ferns. By the time the Wests returned to Texas, the plans were well under way, which was exactly what Gretchen wanted.

Her mother reacted to the news of her pregnancy with the expected parental angst.

"I suppose terminatin' the pregnancy is out of the question," Mimi said during lunch at her favorite restaurant.

"You suppose right. You know how much I want a baby, Mother. I can't believe you'd even suggest it."

"I just don't know what people will say."

"As if I'm the first single person in the social register to get pregnant!" Gretchen said. "And I don't care what they say or think. What about you?"

Mimi raised her dark eyebrows. "Who am I to cast stones? God knows I haven't been an angel."

Gretchen knew her mother was referring to the brief, fiery affair she'd had with her college-age pool man when Gretchen was thirteen. That summer fling had almost cost Mimi her marriage and access to several million dollars. Gretchen had always believed it was the money Mimi would have missed, not her husband.

"Who's the father?"

"His name is Gabriel Butler. He's a friend of Nicole's."

Mimi looked surprised. And pleased. "I'm sure he's very suitable, then."

Gretchen knew Mimi approved of her friendship with Nicole. After all, the Logans were to Arkansas timber what the Wests were to Texas oil.

"He's a rodeo clown, Mother."

Mimi's mouth literally fell open. It was a full ten seconds before she could speak. "I beg your pardon?"

"Gabe is a rodeo clown."

"You mean he dresses up in old clothes and cracks corny jokes at rodeos?"

"And he keeps the bull riders safe."

Mimi's face flamed. "Good God, Gretchen!"

"Lower your voice, Mother."

"A rodeo clown!" Mimi reached for her martini and took a fortifying gulp.

"There's more."

Mimi set her glass on the table with a thud. "What do you mean, there's more? How could there be more?"

"He's illegitimate."

Obviously expecting something worse, Mimi looked decidedly relieved and gave that piece of news a dismissive wave. "That's no big deal. It happens all the time. Even in our circles, as you just pointed out—though we do manage to cover it up quite well, I think," she tacked on. She took another swallow of her drink. "What does his family do?"

"His stepfather raises cattle and grows hay," Gretchen said. "His mother is a homemaker, though she owns a small local restaurant. He has an eighteen-year-old sister." When Mimi just nodded in acceptance, Gretchen took a deep breath and plunged. "His biological father spent time in prison."

"What?"

"Jesse Calloway spent eighteen years in Angola for manslaughter." Mimi turned so white Gretchen thought she might faint. "Are you all right?" Gretchen asked.

Mimi squared her shoulders and lifted her glass again. Her eyes shot fire. "I'm fine, but I believe you've taken leave of your senses," she said in a low whisper.

"What Jesse did has nothing to do with the kind of person Gabe is."

"Blood will tell."

Gretchen snatched her napkin from her lap and slapped it onto the table. "Look, Mother, I'm not going to argue with you about this. I'm marrying him and that's final. His family may not have any blue blood, but his mother is a sweet and loving person, as, I might add, are the rest of his family. He cares enough for me and this baby that he wants to do the right thing."

"Gettin' you pregnant is pretty convenient, wouldn't you say?"

"What's that supposed to mean?"

"In the old days, a woman tried to make a man marry her by gettin' pregnant. Has it occurred to you that your rodeo clown got you pregnant in hopes that he'd be able to latch on to some of the West money?"

After the way she'd practically had to beg Gabe to marry her, the idea of his marrying her for her money was so ridiculous Gretchen broke into laughter. "Mother. If you knew Gabe, you'd know how ludicrous your idea is. I practically had to get down on my hands and knees and beg the man to marry me. It was a humbling experience, I assure you. Even then, he didn't want to do it. He offered to pay me money for the baby's care."

Mimi had no quick comeback for that.

Gretchen reached for her purse and laid some bills on the table. "Lunch is on me." She met her mother's cool blue gaze. "I'd like for you and Dad to be at the wedding. If you choose not to, I'll try to understand. I'd also like for you to be a part of this baby's life, but if you decide you can't handle that, either, all I can say is, it'll be your loss."

And with that, she'd left Mimi sitting at the table, a bemused look on her exquisitely made-up face.

TWO DAYS LATER Gabe guided his pickup through the gates of the West mansion in Westover, the elite town smack-dab in the middle of Fort Worth. After Gretchen had lunch with her mother, Mimi had called and asked her to bring Gabe for dinner. Knowing there was no way out, she'd agreed, and they were about to face the lions in their very ritzy den.

Gretchen, who was a bundle of nerves, had wanted to bring her car, but Gabe refused, saying that he had no intention of pretending to be something he wasn't. He drove a pickup, and he wore jeans and boots. Take him or leave him.

Hearing the familiar refrain, Gretchen just smiled and asked if he'd consider having half an inch cut off his hair. "It's called compromise," she'd told him.

So he'd compromised. He supposed it wasn't too much for her to ask, considering it was time for a haircut, anyway, and Gretchen had already been put through the wringer when she told her mother she was carrying a rodeo clown's baby.

"Are you sure you want to do this?" he asked as he drove the recently washed truck through the meticulously kept grounds.

Gretchen glanced at him. "What? Visit my parents?"

"Get married."

"Gramps used to say if you want to dance, you have to pay the fiddler. We danced. Now we're paying."

They'd danced, all right. And they'd been perfect together. He wanted to tell her that he really didn't mind paying, that the price wasn't too high at all, but the words couldn't get past the roadblock in his mind, the one that said he wasn't good enough for the likes of Gretchen West.

"What's the matter? Scared?" she asked as the truck came to a halt beneath the portico.

He turned off the ignition. "I'm not scared, but I'm not into unnecessary misery, either."

"Look," she said, her exasperation clear, "I know you don't feel for me what I feel for you, but will you do one thing for me?"

"Sure. What?"

"Will you at least pretend you care for me? My parents might just be willing to overlook..." Her voice trailed off and she pressed her lips together.

"They might be able to overlook my questionable parentage and the fact that Jesse did time for killing a man if I act like I'm crazy about you. Is that what you're trying to say?"

"I'm sorry." The contrition threading her voice matched the frown that drew her eyebrows together. "I didn't mean it that way."

"What other way is there?"

Gabe got out of the truck and slammed the door. He was angry at her, yet he knew the fury was misdirected. Her thoughtless comment had reminded him of the old hurts, and she was a convenient scapegoat for the resentment that should have been directed at Jesse.

He stalked around the hood of the truck and jerked open the passenger door. Gretchen stepped out. He started to turn away, but her hand on his arm stopped him.

"Pride," she said.

His eyes found hers. "Pride?"

"No self-respecting woman wants to admit to any-one—especially her parents—that the man she's marrying is only doing it out of a sense of duty. I'd feel a lot better, and I could deal with it a lot more easily, if my mother thought you felt something for me."

If he lived to be a thousand, Gabe thought, he'd never understand the female mind. "I'll try."

"Great," she said, but he could tell by her expression it wasn't what she wanted to hear. He sighed. He just wasn't good at gauging or dealing with feminine feelings. Or playing games. Maybe he'd get better in time.

The Wests were pretty much the way he'd imagined them, Gabe thought as he went through the ritual of introductions and followed the couple into the book-lined library. Tyrell's stern visage and steel gray hair were familiar; his face had graced the front page of Texas newspapers often.

Mimi West was an older version of her daughter, but where Gretchen's face was oval, Mimi's was somewhat round. Where Gretchen's blue eyes held animation, Mimi's held a cool aloofness. Their noses were identical, but Gretchen didn't look down hers often, the way her mother did. Gretchen had the be-ginnings of laugh lines around her eyes; a skilled sur-geon had eradicated those signs of character from Mimi's flawless face.

Gretchen had a soft natural beauty that went with the chocolate brown skirt and wheat-colored sweater she wore. While Mimi's makeup was applied perfectly, she looked as if she was about to step on stage. Everything about her was just...too much. At least in Gabe's opinion.

"You're late, darlin'." Mimi's slow Texas drawl was a direct contrast to the sharp look that swept over her daughter and then moved to Gabe.

"I'm sorry," Gretchen said. "Eden called with a question about the wedding just as we were about to walk out the door."

"Eden?" The query was accompanied by a lift of Mimi West's perfectly arched eyebrows.

"Nicole Logan's sister-in-law. I spent Christmas with Eden's family, remember?"

The explanation was made in an even tone, but it was accompanied by the slightest straightening of her shoulders. Gabe recognized the gesture. Gretchen was preparing for combat.

"Eden and Nick have a lovely old home in Louisiana," Gretchen said, sinking into the burgundy leather sofa. "She offered to have the ceremony there. I thought it was very gracious of her."

Gabe knew he was right in the middle of a clash of wills. He also knew it wasn't the first time these two had gone to battle and it wouldn't be the last. He shot a surreptitious look at Gretchen's dad, who was stirring a batch of martinis. His mouth was a lipless slash in his granite face, but he didn't say anything. As tough as the older man was by reputation, Gabe got the distinct feeling that he'd tried to come between these two before and had come away with his tail between his legs.

"But, sugar, I've already spoken to Reverend Lansing about usin' the church," Mimi said, brushing an imaginary hair from her forehead with the tip of a perfectly manicured nail. "And I checked with Gizella's about doin' the cake."

"I don't want a big church wedding, Mother," Gretchen said. "I just want a handful of people. You and Dad—if you want to come, and a couple of my closest friends." She patted the place beside her, and feeling a little weak in the knees, Gabe sat down next to his intended. "I want Gabe's family, of course, and whoever else he wants to ask."

Hearing Gabe's name seemed to remind Mimi that he was in the room. Her gaze moved from Gretchen to him. "And what do you want, Gabe?"

He reached for Gretchen's hand, which was a tightly curled fist in her lap. He rubbed his thumb over her white knuckles in what he hoped was a twofold gesture. First, he wanted to soothe the obvious tension binding Gretchen, and second, he hoped—for Gretchen's sake—to prove to Mimi West that he cared for her daughter.

"I want whatever Gretchen wants."

He felt her hand relax. She turned it until their palms met and their fingers meshed. He raised his gaze from their hands to her face. There was no mistaking the gratitude in her eyes. He winked at her—the eye that Mimi couldn't see. Gretchen smiled, and when she did, the weight that had been bearing down on his heart ever since he'd awakened that morning dissipated like a fog beneath the hot rays of the sun.

Gretchen beamed at her mother. "I want small and informal."

"Oh." Beyond that, there wasn't much for Mimi to say. She excused herself to go check with the cook about dinner.

"Why don't you go with your mother?" Tyrell suggested, his meaning obvious.

"You go on with your mama, sweetheart," Gabe said, the look in his eyes telling her he could handle her father.

Gretchen unwound her hand from his. "I won't be a minute."

As soon as the door closed behind the two women, Tyrell spoke. "You live in Fort Worth?"

"No, sir. I have twenty acres out near Aledo. I stay there when I'm not on the road."

"That's right. You travel a lot. Gretchen tells me you're a . . . rodeo clown." The smile on his face was a facsimile of friendliness, and his mouth formed the words as if they had a nasty taste.

"Yes, sir."

"And do you do . . . well?"

"Well enough." Gabe accompanied the laconic answer with a matching grin.

Tyrell rounded the bar. "Look, son, there's no use beating around the bush about this. What I mean is that being a clown seems rather lowly and, shall I say . . . unstable work."

Gabe fought to control his temper. He'd much rather do "lowly" work than be a part of some of the things Tyrell West had been a part of, all in the name of big business.

"Actually being a clown is rather dangerous and exciting work, and it isn't unstable at all. I travel a lot, but I work most of the year."

Gabe's challenging attitude wasn't what Tyrell wanted or expected. He took a swallow of his drink. "Can you maintain the life-style my daughter has come to expect?"

Gabe offered Gretchen's father a smile as fake as the one he'd received seconds before. He crossed one booted foot over the opposite knee with a lazy nonchalance. "I know my place won't be big enough for a wife and kid," he lied, "so I thought I'd move in with Gretchen. And as far as money gettin' tight, well, I figure she's got plenty to tide us over if things get slack."

Ty West's face turned fiery red. From the doorway, Mimi West gasped.

Gabe leapt to his feet, the temper he'd inherited from his father making one of its rare appearances. "Hell, I don't have to put up with this." He raked a hand through his hair. "Let's get to the point. You don't think I'm good enough to marry your daughter because, instead of being born with the proverbial silver spoon in my mouth, I'm the illegitimate son of a convicted felon, and I make my living by fighting bulls, not sitting in an office wearing a business suit."

"I'd say that pretty well sums it up," Tyrell said.

"Being illegitimate isn't my fault, and I've dealt with it the best I can. My mother is a good woman who made a mistake as a young girl. I figure you can understand that, because I imagine you've made a few mistakes yourself."

Something Gabe couldn't put a name to glimmered in Tyrell West's eyes.

"As for my dad going to prison, I didn't ask for that, either. I've tried to make Gretchen see that marrying me won't be a walk in the park. I'm not proud of that part of my life, but I can't change it. But I will say this. I'm damned proud of being a rodeo clown. My grandmother taught me that no work is lowly if it's honest. Fighting bulls may not have the status that being chairman of the board has, and I'll never make a fraction of what Gretchen makes, but I make an honest dollar and I'm tops in my field.''

Another noise came from the doorway. He turned toward the sound. Gretchen stood next to her mother, tears shining in her eyes. Though his next statement was directed at her father, he looked at her as he said it. ''God knows why, but Gretchen wants to marry me in spite of all that, so I'm going to do my best to be a good husband. I know for damn sure I can be a better father than you ever were.''

''Oh, Gabe!''

Gretchen's cry was both surprised and anguished. The look on her face said that she didn't want that particular wound ripped open. But Gabe had spent a lifetime disobeying orders and breaking the rules.

''Stay out of this, Gretchen,'' he advised at precisely the moment her father thundered, ''Exactly what do you mean?''

Gabe turned to Tyrell again. ''I mean, sir, that you were so busy trying to become Tyrell West, millionaire oil tycoon, that you forgot you were a little girl's father.''

''I've given my daughter the best this world has to offer,'' Tyrell said in a cold, hard voice. ''The best clothes, toys, schools, the freedom to pursue anything that piqued her interest. She's had every advantage and she's wanted for nothing.''

''She's wanted for plenty,'' Gabe said, his voice as controlled as the older man's. ''Things, Mr. West. You were so busy buying her *things* that you never bothered to find out what was really important to her.''

''And what do you think she really wanted?''

"What every kid wants. A father who wasn't too busy with his own life to be a part of hers. A father who showed her how much he loved her by spending time with her, by listening to her. A mother who read her bedtime stories, instead of reciting rules of etiquette and listing who's who from the Texas society pages."

He heard Mimi West's gasp and Gretchen's sob from behind him. The sounds penetrated his anger, and the reality of what he'd done started to set in. He'd just ruined whatever slim-to-none chance he'd had of forging some sort of amicable relationship with Gretchen's parents—and with Gretchen herself, for that matter.

Maybe his mother was right. Maybe he was more like Jesse than he wanted to admit. Where else did these outbursts come from? With a sigh of regret, he turned his back on Gretchen's father and faced the women standing near the library door. Mimi West's face might have been carved from alabaster. Gretchen's was streaked with tears.

"I'm sorry," he said, uncertain if the apology was for Gretchen or her mother. Without another word, he strode past them into the spacious foyer, snatched his hat from the antique hall tree and crammed it on his head.

The door swung wide on well-oiled hinges. He was down the portico steps in seconds, wriggling his fingers into the pocket of his snug-fitting jeans, searching for the keys.

*Fool. Fool. Fool.*

The chant pounded through his head with every beat of his heart. He yanked open the truck door and climbed into the cab. Gretchen was a nineties woman, certainly not the kind who wanted other people fighting her battles for her. He'd probably just thrown away the only chance he'd have to marry the woman he loved.

His hand stilled on the keys he'd just thrust into the ignition. *Loved?* The sobering realization that he'd been fooling himself swept over him like a dousing of cold water. He didn't just want Gretchen, and he wasn't just infatuated with her. He didn't want to do the right thing just because of the baby. He loved her.

He loved her, but he knew he wasn't right for her, which would only bring her more unhappiness. God knew she'd had enough of that. "And that's why you've been fighting the idea of marrying her," he said aloud.

His resistance was rooted not only in his insecurity and fear of failure, but in his desire to keep from adding more misery to her life.

Well, he'd just blown that all to heck. He doubted if Gretchen would ever speak to him again, much less marry him. That thought brought a sharp pang of regret to his heart. He turned the key in the ignition, and the truck's engine growled to life. He pushed in the clutch and reached for the stick shift. A movement from the mansion's doorway caught his attention.

Gretchen was running down the steps, waving her arms. He rolled down the window, certain a dressing-down was imminent, but instead of stopping, she ran around the front of the truck. He watched in surprise as she wrenched open the passenger door and climbed in beside him.

"What are you doing?"

Her smile was tremulous; her eyes were swimming with unshed tears. "Going with you."

"But your mother has dinner waiting."

"I never liked veal," she said, reaching for her safety belt. "And I've been craving lasagna."

Gabe just sat there trying to comprehend what it all meant.

"Well, come on, cowboy. Get this buggy in gear. The baby and I are starving."

Obediently he shifted into first. They were at the fancy, wrought-iron gates before either of them spoke again. And then, all Gretchen said was "Thanks."

He turned toward her with a questioning look.

"That should have been said a long time ago," she stated. "I was just too much of a coward to say it."

# CHAPTER NINE

THE DAY OF THE WEDDING dawned clear and cold, something no one could have predicted, since winter in Louisiana is notoriously unpredictable. Eden said she'd seen December and January days when the temperature hovered in the seventies. Gretchen was glad the weather was cooperating, since her winter white gown was made of velvet.

She was a bundle of nerves and, as Gramps would have said, worn to a frazzle. Every spare minute of the past week had been spent rearranging her closets and drawers to make room for Gabe's things, both at the house in Fort Worth and at her small ranch near Frisco.

They weren't having a honeymoon, but she'd done her best to catch up on some things at Westways so they could take a few days to settle into their new roles. With that, and trying to coordinate a hundred minute wedding details with Eden, Gretchen felt as if she was on a merry-go-round stuck on fast. She had a nagging headache, an aching back, and her stomach roiled with nerves.

She was beginning to think her parents weren't coming when Eden ushered Mimi into the bedroom she was using, then vanished with a smile.

"Mother! You came!"

"Of course I came," Mimi said, sweeping her daughter into a Georgio-scented embrace. "Just because that rude man said all those terrible—"

"Not now, Mother, please." Gretchen's voice held a firm note she was unaccustomed to using with her mother. "That rude man is about to become my husband."

Mimi stiffened, then stepped back and scoured her daughter with a critical eye. Gretchen fought the childish impulse to squirm beneath the scrutiny that swept from her stockinged feet to her dark hair, which she'd pulled back into a knot at the nape of her neck. The severe style seemed perfect for the dress and would complement the garland of flowers she would attach momentarily.

"You look lovely, sugar," Mimi said. Was that foreign glitter in her mother's eye a tear? "Did Nicole design your dress?"

"Yes."

"You don't show at all."

Involuntarily Gretchen's hand moved to her abdomen. The dress's dropped-waist design hid the fact that she was starting to grow thicker around the middle. "It's an illusion," she said with a humorless smile. "All done with smoke and mirrors. Did Dad come?"

"Of course he did."

Gretchen gave a small sigh of relief. Tyrell and Mimi might be less than perfect, and their actions might have caused her a lot of pain in the past, but they were still her parents, and she wanted them to share this important day with her. She wanted them to be happy for her, though it seemed that might be too much to hope for. She would have to be satisfied with their coming to her wedding.

There was a rap on the door and Jody stuck her head in. "Ford and Mariah just got here," she announced. Then with a wide smile, she said, "You look gorgeous."

"Thanks." Gretchen motioned for Jody to step inside. "Jody, I'd like for you to meet my mother, Mimi West. Mother, this is Gabe's sister, Jody."

"I'm pleased to meet you Mrs. West," Jody said in her best schoolgirl voice. "We're very proud to have Gretchen become a part of our family."

Mimi blinked. Gretchen knew that her mother had never considered the possibility that her daughter might not be welcome in the Butler family, or that they might harbor the same resentment toward her that the Wests felt for Gabe.

A stiff smile made a cursory appearance on Mimi's burgundy-hued lips. "It's a pleasure meeting you, too," she said with faultless courtesy.

Jody glanced at the bedside clock. "You'd better get the flowers in your hair," she told Gretchen with a grin. "If we don't get this over with, Gabe's gonna have a heart attack."

Gretchen couldn't hide her surprise. He'd been cool and composed when Dirk had flown them to Calloway Corners on Thursday for the bachelor party his brothers had planned, and he'd been fine during the rehearsal the night before. In true wedding tradition, she hadn't seen him all day, but she couldn't imagine him getting rattled over anything. "He's nervous?"

"Nervous?" Jody said with a laugh. "He's as jumpy as a drop of water on a hot griddle."

Gretchen felt the knot of nerves in her stomach ease somewhat. She reached for the garland of white and burgundy roses with a steady hand. There was something comforting in knowing that Gabe was as nervous as she was.

JESSE CALLOWAY sat at the kitchen table, a bottle of Jack Daniel's in one hand, a shot glass in the other. It was the first time he'd touched hard liquor since he'd left the joint, partly because he was trying to do better for Sarah's sake, and partly because he knew it was high time he changed his ways.

The counseling sessions he'd had with Mariah's husband before Christmas had helped ease the pain of his transition back into society and his former life, but he'd stopped going after a few weeks. Ford had made him take a good hard look at himself, and he wasn't sure he liked what he saw. It was clear that his actions had affected his family, but acknowledging the wrongs he'd done meant trying to mend the damage. That meant change, and change was something that made him very uncomfortable. The sameness of his prison days had become a habit.

Everyone kept talking about how hard it must be on Sarah and the boys to have him back, and even though everyone said they knew it must be difficult for him, no one had any idea just how difficult.

Everyone and everything had changed in eighteen years. The boys he'd left behind were grown men who'd made lives for themselves. And from the beginning, they'd made it abundantly clear that they didn't intend to take any guff from him.

And Sarah. He'd left his wife a sweet-tempered, malleable woman and had come home to find her independent, opinionated and, worse, pretty darn vocal about those opinions. He didn't cotton to the idea of women thinking for themselves.

Hannah had done the same thing way back when Gabe was just a little tyke. She'd told him that she'd finally grown up, finally saw him for what he was, and that their relationship was over. She didn't want to be a mistress. She wanted to be a wife and mother. Wanted to be in the PTA and a Cub Scout den mother. She didn't want to slink around to the No Tell Motel for the rest of her life.

She'd told him that he didn't love her, he just wanted her. She'd said he needed to wake up to the fact that he loved Sarah before it was too late. And she'd gone a step further and said that Sarah was too good for him.

That had hurt, but she'd been right. He'd realized that long before he got out of prison. Sarah was a saint, and he *wasn't* good enough for her. Still, the changes in her rankled, even if, truth be told, he found her much more interesting. He raised the bottle to his lips.

*Be honest, Jesse. Face the truth.*

The nagging voice that came from some dark place inside him taunted him with the same refrain he'd heard often since coming home. It was time to face the truth about what he'd done to himself, his family and the community—but facing the truth took more guts than it seemed he had.

The fact was, he was scared. Scared of all the changes that had happened while he was serving time. Scared to face the people in town. Scared he couldn't live up to Sarah's expectations. Scared he'd lose her.

But strangely enough, it was the freedom that he'd craved for eighteen interminable years that scared him the most. There was no one to tell him when to get up, when to go to bed, when to go get some exercise. No cameras to watch his every move. No guards at every corner.

There were no locked doors. The really funny thing was that even though crime was almost nonexistent in the area and few residents locked up their houses during the daytime, it was he who latched the doors when he left, he who made sure they were secured at night. Locked doors made him feel safer somehow. Maybe, as Ford had suggested, the locked doors were symbolic of his reluctance to face the changes he'd found.

Ford Dunning made a lot of sense and, unlike Sarah and the boys, he never condemned. Jesse appreciated that. Ford had also done his best to make him see that his drinking was just a crutch, a way to avoid facing the truth. He knew the preacher was right, and for Sarah's sake, he'd cut back to a few beers a week.

Today was different, though. Today, beer wouldn't do, Jesse thought, drinking straight from the bottle of bourbon. It was a special occasion: Gabe's wedding day. Only whiskey could ease the ache that burned in his chest. Though he'd come to tentative understandings with Jericho and Daniel, he and Gabe were like two strangers who went through the motions of holding a conversation, but said nothing.

Oh, Gabe had told him about the upcoming nuptials and that the woman, Tyrell West's daughter, was pregnant. But he hadn't elaborated on his feelings, hadn't asked for advice or blessing. All he'd said was that he figured Jesse had a right to know.

Jesse glanced at the clock and downed another big swallow of the whiskey. Even now, Gabe and that woman from Texas were tying the knot. Jericho and Daniel were there—at his brother's daughter's home. Hannah was there. And Joel. Susan and Becca. Ben's girls and their husbands. All one big happy family united for the joyous occasion.

He hadn't been invited. Gabe was his son, and he hadn't been invited to the wedding. Jesse knew the reason, but his heart wouldn't accept that reason. Damn it! he thought, slamming the bottle onto the table. It wasn't fair that he'd been excluded. It wasn't fair that he was sitting here alone and everyone else was there. It just wasn't fair.

GABE PACED the bedroom that had been slated as his dressing room. His hands were sweating and his knees felt weak. He was about to do it. About to become a husband and ultimately a father. About to make Gretchen his wife.

Everything had happened so fast he hadn't given much thought to all that would entail. This wasn't just for a few weeks or until the baby came; it was for life. Through the ups and downs. Through good times and bad. Through disappointments and maybe betrayals like those Sarah Calloway and even Joel had suffered. Not that Hannah had ever been anything other than a model wife, but Joel had stayed in his marriage despite his uncertainty about his wife's feelings, jealous of her protectiveness toward her son and unsure how she'd feel about a child they might have together.

Gabe felt he'd come to a crossroads. He was settling down, and that meant, in his mind at least, it was time to mend fences. He had to start somewhere, and Joel was as good a place as any.

He'd given a lot of thought to his stepfather since he and his mother had talked at Christmas. In spite of Joel's animosity toward him and his jealousy of

Jesse—a situation Gabe now understood—he knew his stepfather was a good man. He hadn't been afraid to marry a woman with a past and an illegitimate son. Joel might not love him the way he loved Jody, but at least he hadn't been ashamed to let him carry the Butler name, an unselfish gesture that deserved some sort of thanks.

Ultimately Gabe had asked his stepfather to be his best man. The decision had pleased his mother, and Joel had accepted with a surprised thanks. It was too soon to tell how the gesture might affect their relationship, but at least Joel knew Gabe was willing to try to make things better between them, and Gabe knew Joel was willing to meet him halfway.

THE FAMILIAR STRAINS of the "Wedding March" wafted from the Logan living room down the hallway to the master bedroom. Tess played well, Gretchen noted as she paused in the doorway to take her father's arm. Tyrell was austere and uncommunicative, but at least he was here. In step, they started toward the guests.

As they walked through the double doors into the living room, it seemed as though hundreds of eyes were focused on her. In fact, there weren't that many. Nicole was the only friend she'd invited; none of Westways Productions employees were able to make the wedding. Mimi sat in a place of prominence near the fireplace. Gabe's brothers and Susan and Becca were in attendance, as well as the Calloway sisters and their families. Gabe had invited Lucas Tanner. Gretchen didn't miss the wary, uncomfortable look in Nicole's eyes.

Gabe was heart-stoppingly handsome in new black jeans topped by a tuxedo shirt and black tails. Joel Butler stood next to him. She thought his choice for best man was an excellent one.

Her gaze moved to her groom's freshly shaved face. The ice blue eyes were unreadable as he stared back at her. The mouth that had once driven her to a delicious frenzy was unsmiling beneath his neatly trimmed mustache. He slipped his tongue over his lips in a nervous gesture, and her breath hung in her throat at the memory of her own tongue tracing the full curve of his bottom lip, of her lips nibbling, tasting, exploring.

Tyrell led her to within a foot of Gabe, who took her hand in his. The warm strength of his fingers and the roughness of the calluses were comforting; the whiff of a musky masculine cologne was not. The sensual scent generated a sudden longing to be held close to him, to hear that deep gravelly voice whispering to her about all the things he wanted to do—all the things he'd done.

Her gaze met his. He knew what she was thinking, she realized on a wave of panic. Her tongue made a brief foray of its own, wetting lips that had gone desert dry.

From somewhere far away, she heard Ford ask who gave her in marriage, heard her father's voice reply that he did. A part of her realized that his answer was reluctant, grudging, but it didn't matter. Her heart pounded, and blood rushed through her veins at an alarming rate, making her feel dizzy and light-headed.

Gabe's fingers tightened on hers. She dragged her gaze away from his and answered whatever question Ford had asked. She prayed, in a moment of anxiety, that her answer was the right one. The next few moments were surreal, as if she was standing far away and observing the age-old ceremony, instead of participating in it.

And then, suddenly, she heard the words, "You may kiss your bride."

She felt Gabe's arms slide around her, and the fog surrounding her lifted. The icy feeling holding her rigid at his side melted as he drew her close. His mouth was warm, commanding. This was no brief, chaste kiss, but rather a wordless demand that she give him the sweetness he knew her mouth held—and give it willingly.

Her lips parted beneath his. She was helpless to do otherwise. The touch of his mouth liquefied her bones, dissolving her into a hot puddle of need, a terribly demoralizing reaction for any woman to admit. She felt the fleeting touch of his tongue and then, as quickly, the kiss ended and he pulled away.

She heard Ford introduce them as Mr. and Mrs. Gabe Butler and felt Gabe's arm go around her shoulders as he turned to face the guests. They were smiling, laughing. Almost as one, they surged to their feet, and Gretchen found herself enveloped in a loving cocoon of hugs, kisses and congratulations. It was over. For better or worse, she and Gabriel Butler were husband and wife.

IN PREPARATION for the reception, Eden was filling the silver coffee service, and her sisters were stirring the last ingredients into the punch. Nicole had been given the job of cutting the cake, a task she undertook with a smile—somewhat strained—firmly in place. She prayed that the reception would be short and sweet.

She'd observed the ceremony with a strange combination of joy and jealousy. It had been a touchingly beautiful wedding, although a simple one.

Jericho was the official photographer, snapping dozens of pictures of Gabe and Gretchen while he kept up a stream of silly chatter to coax smiles from the newlyweds.

Tess had played the piano, and E. Z. Ellis, who'd flown in for the afternoon from his latest tour, had joined her in a special rendition of the Carpenters' "White Lace and Promises." Then, with no accompaniment but his guitar, E.Z. had sung Extreme's "More than Words" with a gentle fervor that had brought tears to more than one eye—including Nicole's.

She was thrilled that her best friend had found a husband, and even more thrilled that she was going to have a baby. But those same causes for happiness were also at the root of her envy. It wasn't that she didn't want these things for Gretchen; it was just that she wanted them—desperately wanted them—for herself, too.

Lucas's presence didn't help the feelings churning inside her. At first, she couldn't believe it when he'd strolled through the front door, even though she knew she should have been prepared. After all, he and Gabe had hit it off from the first.

"You look gorgeous in teal."

Nicole looked up with a small gasp. She'd been so busy cutting the cake she hadn't noticed Lucas's approach. In an impeccably cut gray suit, he looked pretty gorgeous himself.

"Thanks," she said, making a concerted effort to gather her composure. "You look pretty spiffy yourself."

"Need any help?"

Like his presence, the offer caught her off guard. She shook her head and resumed her cutting. Around them, she heard the hum of half a dozen conversations. Laughter. Childish voices pleading for cake. Suddenly those noises irritated her, just as his presence irritated her.

"Men don't serve wedding cake."

"Why not?"

Releasing a sigh of exasperation, she brushed back a wayward strand of hair with an impatient hand. "I don't know. Tradition, I suppose." Her tone was unmistakably testy.

"Why are you so cranky?"

"I'm not!"

"Oh, yes, you are." He reached out and swept his index finger along her cheekbone. She flinched at the touch and watched as he put his finger in his mouth.

"Frosting." He smiled. "Good frosting."

"What do you want, Lucas?" she asked in a waspish voice, unable to keep up the idle chitchat any longer.

"I thought we agreed we could be civil. Friends."

He was right. They had agreed to that. But five years ago she hadn't realized that her feelings for him wouldn't go away. She hadn't known how much of a strain just being friends could be. Being with him, loving him and knowing there was no hope of their ever finding happiness together was tantamount to watching someone pull the legs off a harmless insect, a painful and unnecessarily cruel act.

She drew a deep breath and met his questioning gaze with a candid look of her own. "We did, but since I've started running into you every few weeks, I'm finding that's impossible."

"It's hard for me, too."

Her eyes widened at the confession.

"Why is that, do you suppose?" he asked.

She shook her head and looked down at the cake.

"I guess we're ready to start serving," Eden said, her voice brimming with cheer. "I see you're first in line, Lucas."

"It looks delicious," he said. "And the flowers and decorations are first-rate."

"Thanks. I enjoyed helping out."

Nicole listened to the superficial talk, uncertain whether to shake her sister-in-law or embrace her for bringing the conversation with Lucas to an end.

"Okay, gang, we're ready," Eden called.

Mimi West grimaced and cast a long-suffering look at her husband, who gave a negligent shrug.

"Gabe, you and Gretchen come on."

At the moan of disappointment that went up from the kids, Gretchen said, "Why don't we let the kids go first."

"And get them out of the way," fiery-haired Jo added, a mischievous gleam in her green eyes. "Good thinking, Gretchen. I knew I liked you the first time I saw you. Come on, Carmen," she said to her seven-year-old. "You and Jody can help carry the kids' plates into the other room."

The children were served and banished to the netherlands of the kitchen. Afterward the adults were given cake and punch or champagne. As usual, when there was a gathering of people in the Logan home, there was a lot of joking and a lot of laughter. A lot of love. Nicole hoped Gretchen's parents saw that. She hoped they wouldn't make things hard for Gabe, who was looking a little glassy-eyed from too many trips to the punch bowl.

With everyone served at last, Nicole placed cake for her and Jody on delicate china plates while Jody poured them each a cup of punch.

"Thanks," Nicole said, smiling and glancing around for a place to sit. Eden and Jo waved for her to join them, but even as she complied, she was aware of Lucas across the room, deep in discussion with Gabe. To keep from making conversation herself, Nicole concentrated on her food and the other guests.

She saw that Jody and Jason had found a corner and were forehead to forehead, whispering together as young people did, as she and Lucas once had, back when they were innocent and so much in love. She felt the sting of tears beneath her eyelids and blinked them back as she cast a surreptitious glance Lucas's way.

He was looking at her.

She dropped her gaze and took a deep breath. It wasn't like her to be cowardly, not since she'd learned the truth about her past and had put it all behind her. But this was different somehow. Lucas was her past, and facing it—facing him—was terrifying.

"Are you all right?" Jo asked, snapping the thread of pain binding Nicole to the past.

She glanced up. "I'm fine."

"You're awfully quiet," Eden said.

"I'm just tired."

"Aren't we all."

"Can I borrow her for a moment?" The masculine query caused Nicole and the others to look up. Lucas

stood smiling down at them. Eden looked from him to
Nicole as if to ask if the request met with her ap-
proval. "I need a refill on the cake," Lucas explained.

"Surely."

Though her answer was pleasant, Nicole got to her
feet with a definite lack of enthusiasm. Lucas took her
elbow and guided her to the table, where he tugged her
plate from her hands and set it on top of his.

"Let's go outside," he said, angling his head toward the door and taking her arm again. "We need to
talk."

"I thought you wanted more cake."

"I lied."

Something in his eyes made Nicole's heart race.
"Gretchen's about to change into her going-away
outfit," she hedged.

"She'll have plenty of help," Lucas said. "Please."

The simple plea swayed her. Without a word, she
followed him out onto the front porch.

ALL GABE HAD TO DO to get ready to leave was swap
his tails and tuxedo shirt for a chambray shirt and
sport coat. He grabbed his suitcase from the bed and
turned toward the male faces grinning at him. He
didn't see Gretchen's father or Joel. And his brothers
were conspicuously absent. God only knew what they
were doing.

"Thanks, E.Z. The singing was fantastic as usual."

"No problem, man," the famous rock singer said.

Gabe looked at Ford, who'd given him a good
talking-to the day before about patience and pregnant women and marriage in general. "Ford...what
can I say?"

"Thanks is sufficient."

Gabe took the preacher's outstretched hand. "Thanks." He turned to Tess's husband. "Seth..."

Seth Taylor grinned. "Yeah, yeah, I know. Keep an eye on Jody and Jason."

"Right!" Gabe said amid a round of laughter.

"Did I hear my name?" Jason piped up from behind the group.

"Yeah, you did," Gabe said with mock severity. "Keep your darn hands to yourself when you're with my sister."

"You don't have to worry about Jody. She's the original iron maiden."

"Why doesn't that ease my mind?" Gabe asked. He looked for Nick, who was standing just inside the doorway. "Nick, it was great. I appreciate you and Eden taking this on. She's a talented lady, and a fine one."

"That she is," Nick said, shaking Gabe's hand. "And it was our pleasure."

Jericho and Daniel pushed into the room, lazy smiles on their lips, devilry in their eyes. "Congratulations, Gabe," Jericho said, pulling him into a fierce embrace. "You did good."

Gabe felt close to tears. He nodded, pulled free and turned to Daniel, whose face wore a suspiciously sappy look of joy.

"Come here," Daniel said, draping an arm around Gabe's neck and hugging him close. "I just want to tell you one thing."

"What?"

"You're a sucker!" He locked his arm tightly around Gabe's neck and scrubbed his knuckles against the top of Gabe's head.

Another round of hoots bombarded the room as Gabe broke free with a blistering curse. Unable to believe he'd fallen for Daniel's old trick, he ran his fingers through his hair and looked at Jericho. "Is my hair okay?"

Jericho puckered up and made a couple of smacking kissing noises in Gabe's direction. "Simply mahvelous."

With a surly snarl, Gabe told his brother exactly what he could do with his Billy Crystal imitation, then asked, "Where's Lucas?"

"I saw him and Nicole go outside a few minutes ago," Jason said. Eyebrows lifted and a loud chorus of "Ahhs!" followed the announcement.

"You got everything?" Nick asked.

"I think so."

Nick handed him a towel. "You'd better take this."

Gabe felt the color drain from his face. He looked from the towel to the group of men gathered around him. All wore smiles of counterfeit innocence. "You guys didn't mess with my truck, did you?"

Jericho patted him on the shoulder. "Of course we did. It's tradition. We did, however, refrain from putting Limburger cheese on the engine in consideration of your bride's delicate condition."

"We were afraid she'd hurl," Jason said with a wide grin.

"You didn't use shoe polish, did you?" Gabe cast a beseeching look heavenward. "Please, God, don't let them have used shoe polish. It's a new truck."

"Gabe! You'd better come out here."

The tenor of Lucas's voice sliced through the laughter and brought instant silence. Gabe searched for his friend's face among the crowd of well-wishers.

When he found it, the worry in Lucas's eyes sent Gabe's heart plummeting.

"What's wrong? Is something wrong with Gretchen?" He heard the panic in his own voice and struggled to get it under control.

Lucas shook his head. "It's Jesse. He's outside, drunker'n Cooter Brown, trying to pick a fight with your stepdad."

# CHAPTER TEN

GABE STEPPED OUT onto the front porch and took in the situation in one glance, unable to believe what he was seeing. Pain and anger coiled inside him, like a cobra and a rattler trying to mate.

Jesse—obviously, sloppily drunk—had parked at the end of the long line of cars and was standing at the entrance of the white picket fence, a bottle of whiskey in one hand, the other motioning boldly as he said something to Hannah and Joel.

Gretchen's father was standing on the porch, a glass of champagne in his hand, a closed look on his face. Gabe could imagine what was going through his mind.

Gabe cursed beneath his breath. Dear God, hadn't Jesse done enough to him and Hannah without this? Blind panic quickly replaced his anger. Where was Susan? If the sheriff saw Jesse's condition, she'd throw him in jail in a heartbeat, his parole would be revoked, and he'd be Angola-bound before nightfall.

"Please," Gabe said beneath his breath. "Please..." He wasn't even aware that he spoke, and if he had been, he couldn't have said what he was pleading for.

Forcing himself to walk normally, he crossed the porch and went down the steps. Blood pumped through his veins, and he felt a strange sort of queasy exhilaration at the thought of the upcoming confrontation.

Jesse looked up as he approached, a sneer on his face. Joel took the opportunity to pull Hannah back a couple of steps and insinuate himself between her and her former lover.

"Well, well, well. The bridegroom cometh."

"Quoting scripture now, Jesse?" Gabe asked, coming to a stop a couple of yards from his dad.

"Go back inside, son," Hannah said in a quavering voice. "We can handle this. You don't need this sort of problem on your wedding day."

Gabe offered her a crooked smile. "Hell, Mama, none of us needs this any day." Facing Jesse, he asked, "What are you doing here?"

"I got as much right to be here as they do." Jesse waved a hand toward Joel and Hannah.

Gabe felt his blood pressure rise another notch. He knew what Jesse was getting at. If Hannah was allowed to attend her son's wedding, why wasn't he? After all, they were equally at fault. Gabe also knew that if Jesse hadn't consumed the better part of a fifth of Jack Daniel's, he'd be able to grasp the answer to that one.

He hooked his thumbs in the pockets of his new black jeans and fixed Jesse with a challenging look. "How do you figure that?"

The question gave Jesse pause, which awarded Gabe a feeling of perverse delight. He'd put his dad between a rock and a hard place, the same place Jesse Calloway's boys had spent the better part of their lives.

If he planned to press his right to attend the wedding, he'd have to claim Gabe as his son, something

Gabe didn't expect to happen this side of the grave.
Still, there was that nebulous possibility....

"Damn you to an everlasting hell!" Jesse yelled,
fulfilling Gabe's expectations. "I spent time with you
when you were a kid."

Memories of his conversation with Hannah swam
through Gabe's head. Memories of all the tears she'd
cried and all the fights she'd had with Joel. Memories
of the fishing and hunting trips he'd missed out on
with his stepdad because Jesse had lured him away for
reasons only he could fathom.

"Yeah, you spent time with me—for your own
selfish purposes," Gabe shot back, his fury rising
along with his voice. "Because you wanted to get back
at Mama... and even Joel. Not because I meant anything to you."

"That's a damned lie!"

Jesse's shock was clear, but Gabe was too angry to
see—or to care.

"Is it?"

Jesse swore. "I taught you boys everythin' you
know about cattle and horseflesh, and every one of
you acts like the trouble in your lives is all my fault,"
he railed.

"No, Jesse, it isn't all your fault, but a heck of a lot
of it is."

"All right," he said with a nod. "All right. If that's
the way you feel. But damn it—" his voice broke
"—you could've asked me to be your best man!"

"No," Gabe said in an implacable tone, "I
couldn't, because you aren't."

The tortured look in Jesse's eyes faded. His face
turned red, and renewed anger glittered in his eyes. His
hands clenched into white-knuckled fists. Gabe half-

way expected him to attack him with the bottle of whiskey, but all Jesse did was ask, "Why not Jericho or Daniel, then?"

Jesse waved toward the house, where his sons waited. Quite a crowd was gathered on the porch. Nicole, Lucas and all the other men stood watching with wary, ready looks on their faces. But this was Gabe's fight, and they wouldn't intervene unless it was absolutely necessary.

As for Jesse's question, Gabe respected his mother too much to ask Jericho or Daniel to stand up with him. They understood why he'd chosen Joel and were content with that decision.

"Jericho and Daniel are good men, but Joel took me and Mama in when everyone else in town was looking down their noses at us. He gave me his name, Jesse, something a lot of men wouldn't have the guts to do."

The implication was crystal clear: Joel had the guts to do what Jesse hadn't. For a moment, Jesse just stood there, staring at Gabe. Then, with a bellow of rage, he lowered his head and charged. Joel cursed. Hannah screamed his name.

The women inside the house heard the horror in that scream. The Calloway sisters exchanged startled looks. Mimi West was clearly disconcerted. Becca Harris turned pasty white. Susan Calloway, Jody and Gretchen rushed to the window.

"Damn you, Jesse," Susan grated as she turned her back on the scene unfolding outside. "Damn you."

In perfect synchronization, Gretchen and Jody whirled and raced to the bedroom door, heedless of Susan's cry to come back....

GABE STEPPED ASIDE seconds before Jesse's shoulder would have made contact. The older man lost his balance, doing a belly flop in a sea of winter-dead saint augustine grass. The whiskey bottle shattered against a decorative rock Nick had brought Eden from Arkansas.

Hannah began to sob. Joel put his arm around her and drew her close. From the porch, Gretchen called Gabe's name. Gabe didn't even glance her way. Anger was an icy fist knotted in his belly. Pain was a burning fire in his chest. He was beyond hearing, beyond listening to reason.

Cursing Gabe, Jesse pushed himself to his knees.

"Stay there, old man," Gabe warned, taking two steps backward.

Jesse's crude reply sent Hannah's hands over her ears. He got to his feet, swaying to and fro. He raised his fist at Gabe. "You'll respect me, you bastard!"

Gabe flinched but recovered quickly. The flame of agony in his chest increased. His eyes glittered with defiance and a fine sheen of tears he wasn't aware of. "Well, you're partly right, Jesse. I am a bastard. But my respect is earned, not demanded."

Fists raised, Jesse took a step toward him.

"Don't." Gabe choked out the warning and held out a stiff arm to keep his dad at a distance. A single tear trickled from the corner of his eye. "Please don't."

Ignoring the plea, Jesse gave a mighty bellow and came swinging. This time, Gabe did the only thing he could do. The thing he'd dreaded doing but had known he'd have to do one day. The thing he'd dreamed of doing for more years than he could remember.

His fist connected with Jesse's jaw in a solid blow he felt to the center of his soul. Jesse's head snapped back and his eyes grew wide with shock before he fell to the ground and lay there, unmoving.

Gabe's hands shook and his knees felt as if they would give way any second. His stomach churned with delayed reaction. He fought the urge to vomit as he stared down at Jesse's prone form, trying to comprehend the magnitude of what he'd done.

Jesse hadn't shaved that morning, and the salt and pepper of his scruffy beard was pitiful-looking. He had lines Gabe hadn't noticed before, around his mouth and eyes and on his neck. A feeling of remorse swept through him on a wave of knife-sharp sorrow. How could this be his enemy? He was just a self-indulgent, aging man who'd gotten drunk too many times and hurt too many people and now was paying for his sins.

The anger drained from Gabe then, and with it, all the old resentment. It occurred to him with startling clarity that he couldn't change his past, and there was no use letting it eat him up anymore. It just wasn't worth it.

He'd embarked on a new life moments ago. The only thing he could do was try to do better with his family than Jesse had. Try to be the father he'd always dreamed of having to his and Gretchen's child.

He brushed at his eyes with the back of his hand and turned to Hannah. "I'm sorry, Mama," he said, reaching out to touch her cheek with his fingertips.

With her lips pressed tightly together to hold back her sobs, Hannah caught his hand with hers and shook her head. He pressed a kiss to her cheek and turned toward the house.

No one said a word to him as he made the trek back, but Gretchen—wide-eyed and pale—ran down the steps toward him. He wasn't sure what to expect. He never knew what to expect from her. She met him halfway, and he was surprised to see tears swimming in her eyes. Her hands gripped his shirtfront, and she leaned against him, as if her legs were too weak to support her.

"Are you all right?" she asked.

The anxious question surprised him as much as the tears.

"Yeah."

"Thank God," she said with a sob. Then, without another word, all the starch went out of her and she crumpled at his feet.

A gasp went up from the crowd gathered on the porch. Gabe's heart plummeted. Instantly he knelt beside her and laid a hand against her forehead. She felt cool to his touch but, dear God, she was so pale. His heart began to pound with heavy, sickening beats.

"Bring her inside."

The calm reason in Hannah's voice broke the spell of fear. He scooped Gretchen into his arms and carried her inside the house, where he was bombarded with a flurry of concerned questions about what had happened.

"She just fainted," Hannah said. "Too much excitement, I imagine. She'll be all right in a minute. Where do you want Gabe to put her, Eden?"

"The bedroom she was using will be fine," Eden said.

Gabe carried her through the house and laid her on the Battenburg comforter. The instant he put her down, he was shuffled aside while the women clucked and fluttered around her like a flock of anxious hens.

Nicole put her hand on Gretchen's forehead and brushed back her hair. Jo poured a glass of water from a carafe on the bedside table. Eden loosened the waistband of Gretchen's skirt. Tess slipped off her shoes. Mimi West edged Hannah aside, tapping her daughter's cheek with gentle fingers and speaking her name softly.

Susan Calloway took Gabe's arm and drew him to the door. He cast one last look over his shoulder as she guided him toward the living room. "She'll be all right," Susan said.

"Are you sure?"

"She's in good hands." Jericho's wife grinned up at him. "I fainted at the drop of a hat when I was pregnant. Overexertion or a whiff of something that made me sick—lots of stuff."

Gabe blew out a troubled breath and shoved a hand through his tousled hair. "I can't believe this happened. Not today. Her parents already think I'm the scum of the earth."

"Don't worry about them. If they can't see your true colors, they aren't worth worrying about."

"Easy for you to say."

The living room was quiet. Gabe glanced out the window. The front yard was deserted.

"Where is everyone?" he asked with a frown.

Susan's eyes were wide with innocence. She shrugged. "Mr. West went to get some cigarettes. Lucas left. Someone told me that Jericho and Daniel went home."

"Home? Why would they go home?" He looked out the window again. Both his brothers' vehicles were sitting in the circular driveway, but Jesse and his truck were gone. Jericho and Daniel must have taken Jesse home.

Gabe looked askance at Susan. "I guess this little stunt of Jesse's violates his parole," he said.

"What stunt?" Susan asked guilelessly.

Gabe shot her a questioning look.

"Did something happen outside?" she asked. "I didn't see anything."

"Jesse showed up drunk and—"

"Did he?"

"Susan, I decked him."

"You did?"

"Yeah. Everybody saw it."

Susan covered his mouth with her hand. "Son, I just keep throwin' 'em and you keep missin' 'em," she said in a perfect imitation of the blustery cartoon character Foghorn Leghorn. "You must've landed on your head too many times back when you were bull riding."

Suddenly he realized what Susan was doing. She was going to let the incident slide.

"Yeah," he said thoughtfully. "Maybe I did."

Susan shrugged and started to pace the large living room. "They tell me Jesse showed up here drunk and picked a fight with your mom and Joel, and when you went out to intervene he came at you and you decked him." She cast him a stern look. "Now if I'd *seen* that happen and if there were charges pressed, it would definitely be a parole violation. But I didn't see or hear a thing. One of the kids wanted me to explain how the siren on the patrol car works, so I was off in the kitchen playing Officer Friendly."

She spread her hands.

"When I went outside to check it out, there was no body on the ground, no truck. Without proof, it's all just hearsay. Gossip." She shrugged. "For all I know, Jesse drove himself home."

Gabe crossed to her and took her by the shoulders. He pressed a kiss to her forehead. "Thanks."

She raised her eyebrows, but a glint of laughter lurked in her eyes. "For what?"

"Just being you, I guess," he said. "Jericho is a lucky man."

"That's what I keep telling him," Susan said, smiling.

"Gabe!"

The sound of Nicole's voice sent him spinning around. She was standing in the living-room doorway, wringing her hands.

"Gretchen's awake. She wants you."

His heart leapt like a bronc just let out of the chute, and he brushed past them both, his long legs carrying him toward the woman who'd become such a major part of his life without his ever knowing how.

He found her sitting on the edge of the bed, a glass of juice between her palms. She looked up, and the stark paleness of her face struck a chord of panic in his heart. He took a hesitant step toward her. Quietly the women hovering around her slipped from the room.

"I can't believe that happened," she said.

*Here it comes,* Gabe thought. He heaved a lusty sigh. "Neither can I."

"What did happen?"

Embarrassed and strangely afraid, he turned away and went to the window, staring out at the spot the altercation had taken place. The rock that had shattered Jesse's bottle was still wet.

"Jesse was drunk. He'd worked himself into a tizzy because he wasn't invited to the wedding and I'd asked Joel to be my best man."

From behind him, Gretchen's voice came softly. "It seems to me that by not acknowledging you as his son, Jesse Calloway forfeited his right to take part in the important happenings of your life. Asking Joel to stand up with you was an excellent idea—for a lot of reasons."

"That's what I thought. And more or less what I told Jesse. I guess he didn't see it that way." Gabe gave a bitter laugh. "I'll bet your mama and daddy weren't too thrilled."

"The Wests have had their share of public quarrels."

Gabe had the feeling she was just trying to make him feel better. It wasn't working. He didn't want her pity, and he was reasonably sure he'd never feel better again. He drew a heavy breath. "I imagine you're already regretting being tied to the Calloways."

"I'm not tied to the Calloways," she told him, "though, from what I've seen, most of them are pretty decent people. I'm tied to the Butlers, remember?"

"You don't need this. No one needs this. If you want to have the marriage annulled, I'll understand."

The corners of her mouth lifted in a wry smile. "You should know me better than that by now. I don't bail out at the first sign of trouble. You're right, cowboy. With a business to run, my own family problems, a new husband and a baby on the way, I don't need this, but neither do you." She set down the glass of juice and reached for her bouquet. "I'm part of your life now, Gabe, for better or worse, remember? Yin to your yang. Pretzels to your beer..."

Gabe saw her smile and felt a reluctant grin tugging at his own lips. "Pond to my scum?"

"Yeah," she said, humor glinting in her eyes. "Now, can we get out of here?"

"Now?" he asked. "You still look pretty washed out, and you've got these terrible circles under your eyes."

"Flattery will get you nowhere, cowboy," she said with a lift of her eyebrows. "I'm just tired. Tired of all this wedding brouhaha and past ready to get out of here and get on with our lives."

Our lives. Her life linked to his. Forever. A sobering thought.

"Nick took our things out to the chopper, and Dirk's waiting for us." She slid off the side of the high bed, then reached back to steady herself. "Uh-oh! My head's still swimming."

"No problem." At her side in three long strides, Gabe scooped her into his arms. She sucked in a surprised breath and hooked her arms around his neck. Their eyes met, startled blue to blue. Her scent—warm woman and a woodsy perfume he was beginning to associate with her—filled his nostrils and swam through him with drugging intensity. He thought of kissing her but decided it would be foolhardy.

"I guess Dirk's out back," he said inanely.

She nodded. Gabe turned toward the door, calling himself ten kinds of fool, but uncertain whether he was a fool for not kissing her or for marrying her.

He was still wondering minutes later as the chopper rose smoothly from the ground. He watched the smiling, waving people grow smaller and smaller and wondered if, this time, he'd taken a tougher bull by the horns than he could deal with.

With her hands clasped at her breasts, Nicole watched the helicopter's vertical ascent while the rest of the wedding guests started back to the house. She uttered a silent prayer that, in spite of the odds stacked against them, Gretchen would find the happiness she deserved in Gabe Butler's arms.

"They'll be okay."

Nicole turned toward the sound of Lucas's voice. He was standing close to her, so close her heart had begun to thud in a remembered cadence that brought to mind visions best forgotten, feelings best left in the ashes of their burned-out love.

"Is that a promise?"

"Yeah," he said with conviction, "it is. I'm not saying the road won't be rocky, but I've come to know Gabe pretty well since I moved here, and he's an all-right guy. Not only that, but they love each other."

"Gabe loves Gretchen?" Nicole couldn't hide her surprise. "Did he tell you that?"

"He didn't have to. It's written all over him."

Nicole cast one last look at the disappearing helicopter. Was Lucas right? She hoped so.

"How about dinner?"

She glanced at Lucas sharply, the invitation catching her off guard. "You want to have dinner with me?"

Lucas nodded. "We didn't get to finish our conversation, thanks to Jesse."

Nicole felt the blood drain from her face. "Maybe his coming here was for the best, Lucas. All we'll do is stir up old memories and resurrect all the old anger and pain."

"Maybe so," he said, "but we have to deal with it."

"We tried dealing with it five years ago, remember? It didn't work."

"You're wrong, Nicole," he said, reaching out a finger and tracing the curve of her jaw. "We didn't try to deal with it. We tried to pick up where we'd left off before..." His voice trailed off as he sought the right words—words that wouldn't hurt.

"Before Keith caught us together, beat you up and raped me," she interjected with brutal frankness. "Before my mother decided I had to abort your child."

The color leeched from his face, leaving it a sickly gray beneath his tan. "Yeah," he managed to choke out, "before that."

"There's no sense flogging a dead horse," she told him, turning to walk away. She'd gone no more than two steps when she felt his fingers on her upper arm. She stopped and turned to face the anguish in his eyes.

"We didn't deal with it," he said again. "We just tried to act as if it never happened."

Nicole stared into his earnest dark eyes. He was right. They had tried to date, tried to recapture the old feelings. But they'd never talked about how her stepbrother's betrayal and their parents' lies had ruined their lives. They'd tried to act as if none of it had ever happened, which was impossible. All it had done was lie there between them like a festering wound.

"Come to my place," he said. "There are some things I need to say to you. Some things you need to hear."

"Your place?" She heard the panic in her voice. It was one thing to consider going to dinner with Lucas in a public place and quite another to think of being alone with him in his house. The latter implied an intimacy she wasn't sure she could handle.

"I'll fix you one of my omelets."

Nicole saw the glimmer of a smile in his eyes. She was a little surprised he remembered how much she liked the omelets he'd learned to make from his mother.

"You remembered."

His gaze was steady, intense. "I haven't forgotten anything."

There was something about the way he uttered those words, or maybe something she saw in his eyes, that made her think he wasn't talking about all the bad things that had happened to them, but about the good.

Was it a mistake to go with him? Was she up to resurrecting all the old demons it had taken her so long to rid herself of? More importantly, would spending time with Lucas cause the love she still felt for him to deepen to the point that it became unbearable?

She glanced up at him, and the look in his eyes caused the breath to hang in her throat. Caused her pulse and her heart to race. It was a plea, she thought. A plea for her to listen to what he had to say. A plea to let him get it all out, to look at it, take it apart, so that he could be rid of it. As painful as it might be for both of them, she knew that sometimes a scab had to be ripped off so a wound could heal properly.

Healing was something she needed, too. Desperately. And she knew he was right. Neither of them had come to terms with the past, and neither of them could experience that healing until they did.

"All right," she said at last. "Omelets at your place. I'll follow you there."

The relief on Lucas's face was sobering. This meant a lot to him. To her, too, if she was honest.

"You can ride with me."

Nicole shook her head. "No, thanks. I'll take my car."

He gave her a reluctant nod. He knew she needed the security of knowing she could leave if her emotions got out of hand.

"Let me change out of this dress. I won't be but a minute," she said, preceding him onto the back porch.

"I'll be out front. Waiting."

THE PLACE Lucas had rented was in Doyline, a five-minute drive from Calloway Corners. It was a small frame house with a handkerchief-size front yard and lots of flower beds. Nicole imagined it would be a profusion of color and scent come spring. She pulled into the driveway behind his truck and followed him through the front door, her heart pounding heavily with every step.

"Home sweet home," he said with a wide sweep of his hand.

It looked like Lucas, she thought. All traditional styling with subtle hues of browns and greens and whites and an abundance of wood furniture, predominantly oak. A wood to match the man: strong and hard.

There was a small fireplace at the back of the room, and above it hung a landscape she knew he'd painted himself. He'd always been good, she thought, crossing the room to examine the picture of a fawn hiding in a thicket of pine shoots and honeysuckle vines. He'd improved greatly in the years they'd been apart.

"Still painting, I see."

"Dabbling," he said gruffly, as if her comment embarrassed him. "Let me take your coat."

She felt his hands on her shoulders. "Thanks," she said, shrugging out of the three-quarter-length herringbone coat that topped her pearl gray cashmere sweater and black wool slacks.

"You're welcome." The minty scent of his breath wafted over her shoulder. With her heart still beating heavily, she tilted her head back and looked up at him, knowing as she did so that she was playing a dangerous game. Her entire future hung in the balance of what happened between her and Lucas during the next hours, the next moments, the next heartbeat.

He lifted his hand to her throat, circling it with gentle fingers, tipping her head back against his shoulder with the faintest pressure.

*Insanity!* her mind screamed as his fingers moved up to her ear and toyed with the diamond and pearl studs piercing her lobe. Without taking his eyes from hers, his fingers traveled around the shell of her ear and behind, eliciting a delicate shiver of excitement.

*Don't let him do this. Don't let him hurt you again.*

Her mind gave good advice, but her ever-hopeful heart was helpless to make her mouth form the words to stop him. His fingers caressed the curve of her arched neck and the fragile hollow where her collarbones met. His touch kindled little flames that spread through her like wildfire across a parched prairie.

She felt herself go limp against him and hated herself for her lack of backbone. She turned her cheek toward his touch and berated herself for behaving foolishly, yet she didn't stop him as he lowered his head.

The touch of his mouth was as familiar as the reaction that unfurled through her like New Year's Eve streamers. Familiar and bittersweet. More sweet than bitter, she thought as his lips moved over hers, urging hers to part. So sweet . . .

Hardly aware of her actions, she turned in his embrace and let him pull her closer, twining her arms around his neck and arching against him with a craving that was both exhilarating and frightening.

His body felt the way she remembered it. Hard. Strong. As needy as hers. He took her face in his hands and lifted his lips from hers. Feeling strangely adrift in a sea of tumultuous emotions, she forced her eyelids open. There was concern in his eyes. And desire.

"I love you." He sounded as if he hated making the admission. Resented that it was fact.

It was what she wanted to hear, what she'd needed to hear five long years ago. "I love you, too," she said. "I never stopped."

Her confession only deepened the anxiety in his eyes. Strangely she understood his concern. Just because they loved each other didn't mean it would work out—did it?

She thought of what he'd said about Gretchen and Gabe and how their road would be rocky, but it would work out because they loved each other. A fragile hope came stealing into her heart. If it was true for her friend, wouldn't it be true for her, too?

"Make love to me."

Lucas shook his head. "Not yet. We need to talk. When we get it all out, then we'll make love with nothing between us. No bad memories. No resentment. Nothing between us but the love."

## CHAPTER ELEVEN

IT WAS STILL DAYLIGHT when Dirk landed the helicopter in the middle of a hay field on Gabe's place near Aledo. Gretchen had fallen asleep almost as soon as Calloway Corners was out of sight, and she hadn't awakened since.

The original plan was for them to go to her ranch near Frisco, but after his run-in with Jesse, Gabe felt an inexplicable need to be in a familiar setting. Since Gretchen was asleep, he made the decision to change destinations without consulting her.

When Dirk set the chopper down and cut the engine, Gabe tried to shake Gretchen awake without success. She was dead to the world. He felt a powerful tug of sympathy and sorrow. She'd been through a lot the past few months—ever since she'd taken up with him.

Leaving her where she was for the moment, he took the suitcases to the house and unlocked the back door. Evening shadows gathered in the corners of the rooms. He flipped on the lights and was instantly aware of how badly the house needed some paint and repair. The furniture was worn and dated, too. It had been fine for him, but with a woman around, it definitely needed some sprucing up.

Thank goodness he'd had Ramona come in to clean while he was gone. And if his housekeeper was as thoughtful as usual, he knew he'd find plenty to eat in the cupboards and freezer.

Contemplating renovations, he went back for Gretchen, thanked the pilot and told him they'd call when they needed him. Then he carried her into the master bedroom, put her in the middle of the double bed and eased her out of her coat, all without waking her. Unfolding the colorful crocheted afghan that lay at the foot of the bed, he drew it up over her and tiptoed from the room.

She was still sleeping when he finished eating a plateful of bacon and scrambled eggs, and later, when weariness overtook him and he climbed onto the bed beside her at the end of the ten-o'clock news. He lay there wondering if he should try again to rouse her or if he should let her sleep.

She was probably just exhausted. He was pretty bushed, too. He pulled the afghan up over him and closed his eyes with a sigh. As wedding days went, it had been a strange one.

"IT WON'T BE LONG before we have another wedding," Eden said to Nick as they finished washing the last of the crystal punch cups.

It was almost bedtime. She had fed her sisters and their families a simple dinner of vegetable soup and cornbread after all the guests had departed and Nicole had disappeared with Lucas. It was almost time for the ten-o'clock news, and Nick's sister was still nowhere to be seen. Eden took that as a good sign.

"Yeah," Nick said. "Daniel's wedding will be here before we know it."

"I'm not talking about Daniel." Eden pulled the plug on the sink and dried her hands on her apron. "I'm talking about your sister and Lucas Tanner."

Nick paused with a cup in his hand and a thoughtful expression on his face. "Nicole and Lucas? No way."

"They left together more than six hours ago," Eden said.

"Sweetheart, spending a few hours together doesn't mean wedding bells will be ringing."

"It does mean there's a spark still there, though. And for Nicole's sake, I hope she can fan it into a blazing inferno. It's time she found some happiness. God knows she's been through enough pain and loneliness."

"I agree with that," Nick said. "So has Lucas, for that matter. But they couldn't make a go of it five years ago, and nothing's changed since then."

"Of course it has," Eden said with that gently forceful way of hers. "They're both older and both still unattached."

"Lucas may be recently divorced, but he's bound to be carrying around some baggage from that failed relationship. I don't call that unattached. Besides, he just got out of one marriage. I doubt he's anxious to jump out of the frying pan into the fire."

Eden untied her apron. "We'll see."

"I hate it when you say that," Nick said, setting down the last cup and tossing his towel next to her discarded apron.

She put her arms around his waist and wrinkled her nose at him. "Because you know I'm usually right when I say it."

Nick shook his head, a reasonable facsimile of awe in his eyes. "So smart," he murmured. "And humble, too."

"Go ahead. Make fun of me. I'm tough. I can take it."

"Tough!" He laughed. "You're a cream puff."

"A cream puff!"

"Yeah," he said, straight-faced. "A cream puff. Crusty on the outside and full of mush inside."

She narrowed her eyes and gave his arm a punch. "Thanks loads."

Nick laughed and slid his hands down to her bottom. He settled her against him in a way that was both very satisfying and very unsatisfying and lowered his head to nuzzle her neck. "A cream puff," he said again, this time with conviction. "So sweet and soft and delicious that I keep coming back for more."

"You'd better," she said, raising her lips for his kiss. "Always."

NICOLE AWOKE in the garage apartment just before dawn. She'd stayed with Lucas for hours, just talking. About their past and the ways their parents' behavior had affected their lives. About the pain they felt over the loss of the child they'd created together. About their hopes for the future.

Long before his antique mantel clock chimed midnight, any inclination they might have had for spending the remainder of the night making love had faded beneath the onslaught of old memories.

Lucas had been right. There was no way they could hope to have a future together until they buried the past, and there was no way to bury the past until they took a good look at it, saw it for what it was and placed the blame where it rightfully belonged. What they'd done had been agonizing but necessary.

Nicole had learned that, five years earlier, when they'd tried to resurrect their love, Lucas had still blamed her for aborting his baby.

"I loved you, but I was angry about the abortion, even though your mother and the doctors were the ones who insisted upon it. Even finding out that she believed she had a legitimate reason didn't help. I'd blamed you so long I couldn't shift that blame to your mother."

"She thought she was doing the right thing," Nicole reminded him. "She thought we were half brother and sister."

"I know," Lucas said. "I've had plenty of time to think about it from every angle." He swore. "It's hard to believe that people's actions can have such a profound effect on others."

"They do, though. Gabe Butler is another prime example of someone who's suffered for his parents' actions. So are Jericho and Daniel, for that matter."

"The sins of the father, huh?" Lucas asked with a wan smile.

"I don't think it's that we're being punished for their sins. It's just that everything we do or say has a domino effect. The old action/reaction theory at work. Reaping what you sow and all that."

"It makes me want to be very careful with the rest of my life," Lucas told her. "I don't want to make things any harder for the kids I might have by willfully putting obstacles in the way of their happiness."

At the mention of children, Nicole grew still. "Why didn't you and Carol have any children?"

Lucas didn't speak for several seconds. Finally he explained, "I married a woman I didn't love to try and forget you." His eyes met hers. "It didn't work. I made myself believe that just because she was good and sweet and giving, she could become to me what you'd been, take your place in my heart. I was wrong and I was selfish. That one mistake made two people miserable. To have brought children into that marriage would have been even more wrong, especially since it didn't last."

They'd talked about it all: their parents, Keith and the happiness Nick had found with Eden. When they'd finished, Nicole felt better—freer somehow—but strangely awkward, too; baring your soul was as embarrassing as it was liberating. Exhausted, she'd told him that she was going home, that she'd see him the following day.

Technically it was the following day, even though darkness still shrouded the apartment. There would be awkwardness between them now, she thought, getting up and heading for the bathroom. She drew her gown over her head and stared at the reflection of her naked body in the mirror of the medicine chest. They'd stripped themselves of ego and to reveal who they really were and how they really felt. They'd both wonder if they'd said too much—or not enough. They'd be embarrassed because they'd opened their hearts and let all their feelings out, good and bad. Now their concern would be whether or not they could live with what they'd seen—the ugly, still-raw wounds and the jagged scars from the past.

Their first encounter would be the most embarrassing, and the more time that passed, the harder that meeting would be. Someone had to make the first move. Lucas had done it yesterday by forcing her to confront their pain together. Today was her turn.

Out of the shower, she dressed in a baggy sweat suit that had seen better days, got into Nick's station wagon and drove to Lucas's house. As she pulled into the driveway, she noticed a light on in the kitchen. He was awake. Afraid she'd lose her nerve if she thought about the wisdom of her actions for too long, she turned off the engine and got out of the car.

The distance to the front door looked at least the length of a football field, but she finally made it. She pressed the doorbell and heard the melodic chiming from somewhere in the bowels of the house. In a matter of seconds, Lucas was pulling the door open.

His dark hair was mussed, as if he'd run his fingers through it repeatedly. He hadn't shaved. All he had on was a pair of wash-softened jeans. He hadn't bothered to snap them, and they dipped scandalously low over his hard stomach. Without saying anything, he stepped aside to let her in. She closed the door behind her.

Wordlessly she reached for the bottom of the sweatshirt and drew it over her head. Lucas drew in a sharp breath when he saw she was wearing nothing underneath. Ignoring him, she kicked off her shoes and started to shimmy out of the sweatpants.

"Nicole..."

The soft cotton puddled on the floor. "Shh," she said, placing her fingers over his lips and stepping free of the sweats. "Shh."

Lucas seemed to stop breathing. Her hands found the zipper of his jeans and ground it downward slowly. There was no awkwardness as he shed them. Like her, he wore nothing beneath.

Nicole took his hands and carried them to her breasts, then closed her eyes because his touch felt so good. For several seconds neither spoke. Neither could. Then she opened her eyes and looked up at him. Love and hope shimmered in their dark depths.

"Nothing between us, Lucas, remember?" she whispered. "Nothing but the love."

WEAK WINTER SUNLIGHT greeted Gretchen when she opened her eyes and encountered an unfamiliar light fixture attached to the ceiling. Fighting a feeling of disorientation and an overwhelming weariness, she raised herself to her elbows and looked around. Nothing about the Southwestern-style bedroom looked familiar. She had no idea where she was.

She realized she was still wearing the skirt and sweater she'd changed into before leaving Calloway Corners, but someone had loosened the waistband. Gabe. She must be at Gabe's place near Aledo, though she had no recollection of getting there.

She remembered the fight between Gabe and Jesse and recalled coming around in Eden's bedroom after she'd fainted. She also recalled Gabe carrying her to the helicopter and Dirk taking off. Beyond that, her mind was a total blank. Where was he, and what had happened to their plans to go to Frisco? She looked at the clock and gasped. What had happened to her wedding night?

Swinging her feet over the edge of the bed, she stood, only to find that her legs were as shaky as a newborn foal's. The first thing she had to do was find a bathroom and then a toothbrush and then something to eat.

She called out for Gabe, but when he didn't respond, she showered and changed into some slacks with an elasticized waist and another baggy sweater. After adding a touch of eye makeup, she was ready to raid Gabe's refrigerator. She found eggs and bacon and sausage in the fridge, and cereal and pancake mix in the pantry. She didn't think she could handle anything so substantial, so she poured herself a glass of orange juice and popped a couple of slices of bread into the toaster. While the toast browned, she carried her juice to the kitchen window.

Winter sunshine shed its warmth on a brown pasture. A cluster of naked oak trees huddled near one corner of a weathered barn to her left. A couple of corrals held quarter-horse mares who looked ready to foal.

Movement at the barn's door caught Gretchen's attention. Gabe was leading a sorrel mare outside. A huge Airedale terrier followed at his heels. Her new husband—her heart skipped a beat at the thought—wore jeans, boots and a goose-down vest over a burgundy-and-navy plaid flannel shirt. The denim stretched tautly over thighs that had grown hard and muscular from hours in the saddle. They fit the rest of him in a way that sent a wave of pure sexual longing spiraling through her.

She remembered the way it felt being held in his arms, the way it felt when he slid into her so gently, yet so forcefully. A little groan of frustration escaped into the quiet of the room. She wanted her wedding night, darn it! But how was she going to convince Gabe to give it to her? Outright seduction?

As plans went, it had its merits and its drawbacks. Normally she wouldn't doubt her ability to lure him

into her bed, but this wasn't a normal situation, and
she was no longer the slim, trim woman he'd once
made love to. At four and a half months pregnant, she
was beginning to lose her shape.

She watched as Gabe put the mare in the corral and
unsnapped the lead from her halter. Instead of walking away, the mare bumped his chest with her nose.
Gretchen saw Gabe smile. He drew something from
his pocket and offered it to the horse on his outstretched hand. Sugar, no doubt. The mare lipped the
treat from his palm, and he rubbed her between the
ears.

Watching the exchange, the Airedale began to bark,
almost as if he was jealous of the attention his master
was lavishing on the horse. Gabe reached into the
other pocket and drew out a treat for the dog, who
ingested it with one snap of his jaws. As he had with
the mare, Gabe rubbed the dog's head and gave him
several pats on the neck.

He was good with the animals, Gretchen thought.
It was obvious he loved them. A kernel of insight settled into her troubled heart. If he was so patient and
kind to animals and his fans, didn't it follow that he
would be the same with their child—and with her?

The confusion and heaviness that had filled her
heart on awaking vanished like the doggie treat from
Gabe's fingers. Toast forgotten, she set the glass on
the countertop and stepped onto the back porch. Almost as if he sensed her presence, he turned and
looked at her. The smile was gone. His face wore a
wary, waiting expression.

She crossed the wide expanse of lawn and climbed
onto the bottom board of the fence. "Good morning."

"Mornin'."

The Airedale slithered beneath the board and began sniffing her shoes and legs. "Who's your buddy?" she asked, extending her hand for the dog to examine.

"The monster is called Klutz," Gabe informed her with a wry smile.

"Klutz?"

He nodded. "For reasons that will be very obvious if you spend much time with him inside a closed area."

"He's beautiful."

"He's a pretty fine specimen, all right."

"It looks like you have some mares getting ready to foal."

"Seven in all," he told her, pride and pleasure in his voice. "I have some yearlings and a few older horses I'm training."

"I didn't know you raised quarter horses."

The gaze that met hers was filled with a hint of humor and an undeniable awareness. "I guess we never got around to talking about it."

His deep voice held a note of intimacy he made no attempt to hide. He was flirting with her! Heartbreaker that he was, she knew his actions were as natural as drawing his next breath. Wasn't it that gentle teasing that had first caught her attention?

She sighed, uncertain whether she should be flattered or offended by his behavior. On the one hand, he played coy when she told him she expected their marriage to be a real one; on the other, he was behaving as if consummating their vows was definitely in his thoughts.

"I can't rodeo forever," he told her, approaching the fence and resting his forearm on the top rail. "A man has to have something to fall back on. I know stock, but growing up, I got my bellyful of cattle.''

"So you decided to raise horses?''

He nodded. "There's a demand for good horses, whether it's for rodeo or ranch use, and good horses fetch good prices. It's taken me five years to get what I have, but they're quality mares and they were covered by the best stallions I could afford.''

"You've been holding out on me,'' she said with raised eyebrows.

"How's that?'' he asked.

"You're not just a rodeo clown.''

"Most of us are more than we seem on the outside.''

She couldn't argue with that. It was just what she'd been trying to make him see about *her*. But now didn't seem like the time to point that out.

"Show me your horses,'' she begged.

The request seemed to take him by surprise. "Why?''

"Because you're my husband, and everything about you interests me.'' He looked even more surprised. "And like you said earlier, we never got around to getting to know each other—we just jumped right into the heavy stuff. It occurred to me that finding out more about each other might make the next few months easier on us both.''

"You've got a point,'' he said. "Go change your shoes and grab your coat, and I'll give you the grand tour.''

An hour later, Gretchen had been introduced to each horse on the farm. She had also heard that Gabe got his start when someone named Dizzy Crenshaw left this ranch and his horses to Gabe when he was killed at a rodeo five years earlier.

As they headed back to the house, she said, "So besides bullfighting for a living, you're a horse breeder." She lifted her eyebrows and adopted an exaggerated Texas drawl. "Why, Mr. Butler, you're not a cowboy at all. You're a businessman."

Even though she said it teasingly, his face grew red. He was embarrassed that she'd found out about his sideline, but for the life of her, she didn't know why. Could it be that, in his eyes, his small band of horses was nothing compared to the West wealth?

The grin that sent his mustache hiking up at one corner was cocky and mocking. "Hell, darlin'," he shot back. "I'm not just another pretty face."

"You certainly aren't. Though you're that, too," she said, deliberately letting her lashes veil her eyes in a falsely shy fashion.

"Flirtin' with me will get you nowhere, lady," he said. "I'm a married man."

"And don't you forget it."

"I'm not likely to after that little stunt you pulled yesterday." His smile slipped, and he grew suddenly sober. "What was that all about, anyway? You scared me to death."

"I scared you to death? What happened was that *you* scared me to death—duking it out with your dad in the front yard. I was afraid you'd get hurt."

"You were worried about me?" he asked as if the idea of anyone worrying about him was a foreign one.

"Does that surprise you?"

"I guess it does. No one but my mom ever cared a whit about me, except maybe Jericho and Daniel."

Gretchen's heart ached for him, even though she thought he'd been lucky to have three people who cared about him. After her grandfather had died she'd had no one.

The day passed pleasantly, if uneventfully. That afternoon, while Gabe was out repairing one of the stalls, Gretchen decided to watch the movie *8 Seconds* on cable, so that she'd get a better idea of the kind of life he led. The account of Lane Frost's life was bittersweet; she saw several parallels between the likable young bull rider's relationship with his father and Gabe and Jesse's relationship.

She was so engrossed in the tale she didn't hear Gabe come in. But she did hear his sharp intake of breath when the bull hit Lane from behind, killing him almost instantly. The sound drew her attention, but before she could say anything, Gabe was striding toward the kitchen.

The movie forgotten, Gretchen rose to her feet and followed him. She found him on the back porch clinging to one of the upright posts and staring into the horizon. When he heard the back door close, she saw him take a surreptitious swipe at his eyes.

"Are you all right?" she asked, going to him and leaning her hip against the cross rail. His profile looked etched in stone.

"I'm fine," he said tersely. "But I never see that movie that I don't think about Dizzy."

"You mentioned him earlier," Gretchen said. "Who was he?"

"He was a rodeo rider who worked part-time at the sale barn when I was a kid."

"He must have thought a lot of you to leave you the place when he died."

"Yeah, I guess he did."

"Tell me about him."

"So you can find out more about me?" he asked, looking at her with a quizzical lift of his eyebrows.

"Yes."

He must have sensed she wouldn't let up until he told her, so he said, "Dizzy was in his early twenties when I met him. I was eight. He taught me everything I needed to know about bronc and bull riding and more than I should've learned about the wilder side of life."

"He sounds like an interesting character."

Gabe smiled reminiscently. "Now that's what I'd call a real understatement."

"So he's the one who got you interested in rodeo?"

"I was always interested in it. I guess it was born and bred in me. Jesse rode in his younger days." He turned and looked back at the pasture. "My brothers and I wanted to be like him when we were kids, back before we realized he was all shine and no substance."

"All that glitters isn't gold, huh?" she said, turning to put her hands on the rail. They stood side by side, staring out across the rolling pasture.

"You got it. Jericho and Daniel sort of grew away from rodeo after junior high school, but I stuck with it. When Jesse shot Becca's dad, it was all I had to live for. As soon as I graduated, I set out with Dizzy, and for a while, life was nothing but traveling the circuit—wine, women and dance halls. I guess that's when I earned my reputation."

Gretchen's grip on the wooden rail tightened. She couldn't stop or deny the pang of pain and envy at hearing about the other women in his life. "There were a lot of women, I suppose?"

"More than there should've been." He shrugged. "After a while, it all started running together, and I realized none of it meant anything to me but the riding. That's when I got serious about it, and it started paying off.

"Then, about ten years ago, Dizzy fractured his skull. The doctors told him he ought to quit riding. He said there was no way he was giving up rodeo. He was conceived at the rodeo and he'd die at the rodeo. So he became a clown and eventually got his wish."

The statement was spoken so casually that, for a moment, Gretchen thought she'd heard wrong. She turned her head to look up at him. "He was killed bullfighting?"

Gabe nodded and let his gaze meet hers for a moment. "I'd drawn a particularly nasty bull that day, and I'd had too much to drink the night before. If I'd been able to stay on him, Dizzy would still be alive today."

She couldn't stifle her soft gasp. Dizzy had been killed trying to save Gabe. Clearly the guilt still gnawed at him even after five years. "You don't know that," she said. "Anything could have happened to him."

He shook his head. "I know."

"Is that when you quit riding?"

He nodded again. "The very next night, I made up my face the way Dizzy did, put on his clown outfit and took his place. I was only going to do it once, as a sort of tribute to him, but when I got out there and saw the real terror on some of those young cowboy's faces, I knew it wasn't just a silly job or an acting role."

He turned and looked her straight in the eye. "Good clowns make it look easy. But it's not easy and it's not funny." His eyes held an earnest belief. "It's more than being a stand-up comedian. It's a real job with real responsibilities. Besides a repertoire of corny jokes, it takes courage and skill and quick wits to try and figure out the best course of action to take when a two-thousand-pound bull is bearing down on you with blood in his eye and hate in his heart."

Picturing the scene he described, Gretchen felt the bottom drop out of her stomach. "So you're really in a lot of danger when you're out there."

His smile was grim, humorless. "It's no walk in the park." He turned to her and forced a smile to his lips. It didn't quite reach his eyes. "Heard enough?"

"Yes." She didn't want to hear any more about how much danger he was in. She didn't want to think about it.

"Then how about I take you to the Bearcat Café for an Elaine-burger and some carrot cake?"

He'd told her earlier today about the giant burger topped with chili, onions and the other condiments that made it a gastrointestinal delight—or nightmare, if her recurring heartburn kicked in.

"That sounds heavenly." She went to find a more comfortable pair of shoes, her mind filled with the things he'd told her about his work and wishing she hadn't asked.

JESSE LAY ON THE SOFA, an ice bag on his swollen bottom lip, watching a classic Western. He'd just taken two more painkillers, but following his unaccustomed binge the day before, his head not only felt twice its size, but as if a herd of elephants was stomp-

ing around in it. The slightest movement sent fresh
waves of agony and an accompanying nausea eddy-
ing through his aching body.

He had a raw elbow where he'd landed when he
charged Gabe, a knot on the back of his head where
he'd hit the ground when Gabe slugged him, a split lip
and a bruise the size of Gabe's fist on the side of his
chin. To add insult to injury, he had a couple of loose
teeth, which, along with his roiling stomach, had made
eating Sarah's leftover roast-beef lunch hell.

He sighed. Sarah. She was mad at him, no doubt
about that. The last thing he remembered about going to Eden's place was seeing Gabe's fist coming at
him. When he woke up, he was being put to bed by
Jericho and Daniel.

Sarah had stood nearby. Even drunk, he'd recognized the disgust on her face. She hadn't asked what
happened; she'd just told him that if he got sick he
expected him to clean up after himself. Then she'd
turned and left the room.

At the time, he'd been too drunk to care. Today was
a different matter. He expected some commiseration,
but all she'd done was give him the cold shoulder ever
since he crawled out of bed to face the day. When,
showered and shaved—as well as he could with his
shaking hands and mangled face—he'd come out for
breakfast, she told him she was late for Sunday school
and that if he wanted to eat, he could help himself to
a bowl of cereal.

Lunch had been more of the same. As soon as the
dishes were loaded into the dishwasher, she'd come out
of the bedroom with her coat and purse. When he'd
asked where she was going, she'd said simply, "Out."
Seeing the challenge in her eyes, he hadn't pressed for

a more specific answer. Sarah didn't take too well to pressing these days.

She'd gotten home about thirty minutes ago and had gone straight to the bedroom without a word. He supposed she was taking a nap—or still pouting.

As if on cue, he heard the bedroom door open and the click of her shoes on the hardwood flooring of the hallway. He was shocked to see she had a suitcase in each hand. Trepidation pervaded him, chilling him to the bone. The fear fueled an irrational anger. He bolted into a sitting position; the elephants in his head began to stampede.

Grabbing his head, he snarled, "Where the hell do you think you're going?"

Sarah's cheeks flamed with color. "I've told you not to curse in my house. And as for where I'm going, I'm going to the abused women's shelter."

"Abused!" he thundered. "Hell, woman, I've never laid a hand on you, and you're not going anywhere until you tell me what this is all about!"

"For your information, there are different kinds of abuse, Jesse Calloway, and I've suffered most of them at your hands." She turned on her heel and started toward the door. "I'm leaving you."

His blood ran cold. Dear God, she was all he had left in the world. Oh, he'd made his peace with Jericho and Daniel, but too late for it to make a difference. They had their lives, and those lives didn't include him. And his stupidity yesterday had ended whatever shaky relationship he'd had with Gabe. He couldn't lose Sarah.

"Why would you want to do that, sugar?" he asked, changing tactics and using the cajoling voice that had once worked wonders when she was miffed at him.

Sarah was unmoved.

"I know you don't want me drinkin'. I don't know why I did it. It won't happen again, I promise."

"Not till the next time. I've heard your promises before and I'm sick of them."

"Sugar—"

"I'm tired, Jesse," she told him with a heavy voice. "I'm tired of carrying the burden of being Jesse Calloway's wife. I've put up with your shenanigans for more than thirty-five years. I've lived with your drinking, your gambling and your whoring while the people of Webster Parish talked about us behind our backs. I stayed faithful to you while you were in prison for killing a man—"

"It was an accident!"

She might as well not have heard for all the difference it made. Her anger had a full head of steam, and she plowed forward.

"I'd have thought that growing older and spending time in prison would make you stop and think before you went off and did something so stupid."

"Stupid!"

"Stupid!" Sarah set the suitcases down and planted her fists on her hips. "Obviously you don't care what you do or who you hurt as long as Jesse Calloway gets what he wants. From what Jericho told me, your behavior yesterday proves that."

He sighed. He knew that what he'd done had embarrassed not only Gabe and his new wife's family, but the other Calloways, as well—Jericho and Daniel included. But he didn't want to think about that now.

Ignoring her reference to the day before, he said, "I've done my damned—" he caught the curse word before it was fully formed "—darnedest to change my ways since I've been back. I've put up with a lot from you."

"You've put up with a lot from *me?* Like what?"

"You working at the sale barn, for one thing. Acting like you're somebody important to the business. Not staying home and cooking for me the way you used to."

"Are we back to that?" she cried. "I *am* important to the business. I know it backward, forward and sideways. I know every bill that's owed and every penny that goes out or comes in, which, I might point out, is more than you ever did. The business was in better shape when you came home in September than it ever was when you ran things. You were too busy having a good time and messing around with every woman in town to pay proper attention to what was going on!"

The truth pierced Jesse's heart like a needle-sharp arrow, but he'd be darned if he'd let her know. "That's how you see it?" he asked coldly.

"No, Jesse. That's how it is." The anger had drained from her voice. All that was left was weariness. "People change. Life changes us. But you're caught in some sort of time warp. You're not twenty-five anymore, Jesse. It's time you took a good hard look at yourself and your actions, and asked yourself if you want to spend the rest of your life—however long that might be—making the people around you miserable. Making yourself miserable."

With his current aches and pains making him acutely aware of his age and mortality, Jesse couldn't think of a smart comeback. He simply stared at her.

"I've done my best by you all these years," she went on. "I've been ridiculed, talked about and pitied. All I've ever wanted from you was your love. If I couldn't have that, I wanted your respect. Lacking that, a little consideration of my feelings would have gone a long way.

"I've asked very little of you since you came home. But you obviously don't care about my feelings, or you wouldn't have stopped going to counseling. You're selfish, Jesse, not to mention foolish. Now you've gone and made an idiot of yourself by showing up drunk at Gabe's wedding. The whole town's talking about us again."

"People in this town are always talking about something," he grumbled.

"Well, I'm tired of it being about me. I'm finished with it." She picked up the suitcases. "And I'm finished with you."

"What am I going to tell everyone?" Jesse demanded. "What am I going to tell the boys?"

"I'll explain to the boys," Sarah said, going to the door. "But as for everyone else . . ." Her voice trailed away and she shrugged. "I don't know, Jesse. I guess you'll have to do what I've done all these years—just try to ignore the talk and go about your business. Frankly I don't care."

Jesse watched in stunned amazement as the door banged shut behind her. He heard the car door slam, heard the engine start. Surging to his feet and cursing the pain in his head, he rushed to the front door and flung it open, just in time to see the car disappear down the road.

"Damned women's rights," he muttered, slamming the door with such force the noise reverberated through the house and his head. Clutching his throbbing temples, he shuffled back to the sofa and eased himself into a horizontal position, willing the pounding in his brain to cease and asking himself what he was going to do now.

# CHAPTER TWELVE

GABE WAS LYING in a field somewhere, flat on his back in the lush grass, trying to sleep. The scent of wildflowers surrounded him, and butterflies filled the air, wings fluttering, colors flashing in the sunlight. One landed on his forehead, then his nose, his chin. Delicate wings brushed his eyelids, his cheeks and his mouth.

He reached up to brush the pesky insect away, and his hand encountered the unexpected softness of a woman's hair. Like something from a fairy tale, the butterfly had metamorphosed into a beautiful fairy with a diamond crown and gossamer wings. Before he realized there was something familiar about her, she touched her mouth to his.

"Kiss me, Gabe," the fairy begged, her full red lips promising sweet delight. "I want you."

He wanted her, too, more than he'd ever wanted a mortal woman. He slid his arms around her and answered the pressure of her mouth with a passionate willingness, thinking he'd never made love to a fairy before. Fairy princesses were way out of his league.

He rolled over, and when he did, the fairy gave a little groan. His eyes flew open, and he realized he'd been dreaming. He wasn't in a field of flowers, and there was no fairy princess in his arms. He was in his bedroom, in his bed, Gretchen pinned beneath him in a tangle of covers. But one thing was the same—fairy or woman, he still wanted her. Badly.

She wanted him, too. She'd made that clear before the wedding. He'd avoided consummating their marriage the night before by deliberately staying up late to "go over his books" to make sure everything was clear for his accountant's monthly scrutiny. When he'd finally tiptoed into the bedroom, she'd been asleep, and he'd drawn a sigh of relief at being granted the reprieve.

Now, with the dream so fresh in his mind, his silly stance on not making love seemed just that. They were married. Why dwell on how a physical relationship would cloud the issue between them if their marriage fell apart? Pain was pain. Regret was regret. And at that moment his pain was very real. Why cling to his noble gesture of celibacy? Why make a martyr of himself? Why not take what she offered, do what they both wanted?

As he lowered his head to kiss her, she clutched him and gave another groan. He felt her nails gouging the flesh of his shoulders. This time he was awake and there was no mistaking the sound for what it was. It wasn't a groan of pleasure; it was a groan of discomfort. The frown that puckered her forehead confirmed it.

"What's the matter?" he asked, rolling away from her.

"I had a bad pain."

Panic and fear vied for the upper hand. "Where?"

Gretchen's hand moved to her abdomen. "Down low."

He was up in a flash, heading for the closet. "Get dressed. I'm taking you to the doctor."

"I don't need to go to the doctor."

"You fainted the other day, and that was the second pain you've had. You need to see a doctor."

"Aches and pains are part of pregnancy. In case you haven't noticed, my body is changing. Things are moving, stretching . . ."

It made sense, but his still-pounding heart wasn't convinced. "Are you sure?"

"Positive."

He didn't fail to notice that the conviction in her voice didn't reach her eyes. Those blue eyes held more than a hint of anxiety. That, too, made sense. Even though the doctor had cautioned her about what to expect, she was facing uncharted territory. She was bound to have moments of fear and uncertainty. He forced himself to calm down. He had to set the example. He'd play it cool and be on the watch for any sign of excessive pain.

"Okay," he said with a nod. "Go ahead and get dressed. I'll rustle up some breakfast."

The look in her eyes was something between pleading and coyness. "I'd rather have you."

The brazen statement took him aback. He'd never met a woman like Gretchen before. She looked every inch a lady, but there was a bold earthy streak in her that cropped up occasionally, just enough to break the spoiled-rich-woman stereotype, just enough to keep him off balance and his interest level high.

The flirtatiousness that was an ingrained part of him surfaced, along with a sexy grin. "Not on your life, sweetheart," he said, rubbing his palm over his bare chest in a deliberately suggestive gesture. "It's Wheaties for you."

In a typical macho reaction, he was pleased by the way Gretchen's gaze followed the movements of his hand.

"Breakfast of champions, huh?" she asked with a smile. "Just in case the baby is a little bull-riding buckaroo?"

He winked at her. "Or a goat-ropin', barrel-racin' rodeo queen with a rear end just like her mama's," he said, suddenly intrigued by the thought of a little girl who looked like Gretchen.

She sighed. "Bring on the Wheaties."

The phone beside the bed rang and Gretchen reached for it automatically. "Hello. Oh, hi, Jericho. No. He's right here." She handed the receiver to Gabe. "Jericho," she said unnecessarily.

Gabe took the phone, and Gretchen went into the bathroom to give him privacy. "Hey, brother! What's goin' on?"

"I might ask you that," Jericho said. "I never expected to find you in Aledo, but I thought I'd leave a message on your machine in case I couldn't locate you anywhere else."

"What's up?" Gabe asked. If Jericho was trying to track him down, something momentous had happened.

"I thought I'd better call you with the latest news," his brother said, "before you heard it through the grapevine."

Gabe's first thought was that Susan had been forced to report Jesse's actions, after all, and that his parole had been revoked. "You sound pretty down, so it must be something to do with Jesse," Gabe said.

"How'd you know?"

"Intuition. What's he gone and done now?"

"It isn't him this time," Jericho said. "Well, indirectly, it is, I guess. They've split up."

"Split up? Who? Jesse and Sarah? Come on."

"She called me and Daniel and told us she had to talk to us. She said that Pop's barging in drunk on your wedding reception was the last straw. She was tired of his selfishness and tired of being whispered about. She's packed her bags and left him. I don't mind telling you, it knocked me and Daniel for a loop."

"I'll bet," Gabe sympathized, trying to picture his mother leaving Joel, but unable to. "I wouldn't worry too much if I were you. Sarah's a sensible woman. She'll go back to him soon."

"I don't know. Pop seems to think this is it."

"You've talked to him?"

"Daniel and I drove over to the house after we talked to Mama."

Concern roughened Jericho's voice. Gabe's heart ached for his brothers. And for Sarah. God knew she'd been through enough. "Where's she staying?"

"Right now she's at that shelter for abused women Jo and E.Z. helped Ford open in November. Ford has a psychologist who comes in a few hours a week free of charge, and Mama's going to talk to her tomorrow. But Susan was volunteering there today, and Mama told her that Pop's hurt her for the last time."

"And what does Jesse say?"

"You know Pop," Jericho said. "He's being a hard case. He's spouting stuff like if she thinks he's going to sit around and wait for her to come back, she's sadly mistaken. Ditto for begging her to come home. He said she'd gotten too highfalutin, trying to do a man's job. He was complaining because she hadn't stayed home and taken care of him the way she was supposed to since he got out of prison. He's glad she's gone. Et cetera, et cetera, et cetera.''

"Which translates to..."

"He's mad as hell, but even more to the point, he's running scared and damned if he'll show it."

"Well, no offense, but I say bravo for Sarah. She deserves better than Jesse Calloway."

"But who'd have ever thought she'd do the leaving?"

"Stranger things have happened."

"I suppose so," Jericho said morosely. "But this is Mama. I can't believe she'd up and walk out on him. She loves him, Gabe."

"Yeah, well, sometimes that isn't enough. My mom is a testimony to that. What did loving Jesse Calloway ever get her or Sarah except heartache?" Gabe paused. "Who knows? Maybe this will open Jesse's eyes and make him see he can't keep getting away with treating people like dirt."

"That's what Susan said."

"Susan's a smart lady."

"She is that."

"Speaking of Susan, how's married life?"

"Wonderful," Jericho said. "How's Gretchen?"

"Worn-out, I think. Stressed. She's slept the clock around since we got here."

"Slept!" Jericho's taunting laughter grated on Gabe's nerves. "How the mighty have fallen."

Gabe felt the heat rush to his face at his brother's blatant mockery of his sexual prowess. "Yeah, well, things are a little different with us than with you and Susan."

"Not that different," Jericho said. "Let me re mind you of a couple of things you seem to have for gotten. She wanted to marry you, so what are you afraid of?"

"That I'll get in too deep. That she'll change her mind in a few weeks or months or years."

Jericho's voice was suddenly serious. "You're afraid to invest in a real relationship because it'll hurt too much if she leaves you? But that could happen to any of us. Susan could leave me at any moment. Heck, Mama just left Pop."

"Maybe you're right."

"You love her, don't you?"

"Yeah, I guess I do."

"Then tell her," Jericho urged.

"Tell her? I can't do that."

"Why not?" Jericho asked. He sighed. "What you have, brother mine, is a case of Calloway cowardice the basis of which is a general lack of self-esteem. Even though your successful career should prove you're as good as anyone else, the minute you drive over the Webster Parish County line, your lack of self worth emerges and you have the sudden overwhelm ing need to head to the Midnight Hour and bolster your courage."

Gabe was stunned by the depth of Jericho's under standing of both his feelings and his actions. "How do you know?"

"I know, because I suffered from a bad case my self."

"I'm not a Calloway."

"Oh, yes, you are, and Pop has screwed up your life as much, if not more, than he has mine and Daniel's. Don't let him hurt you anymore."

"How can I stop it, Jericho? How did you stop it?"

"Pop and I made a sort of peace. Susan helped. But the best thing you can do is stop letting the fact that he's never claimed you eat away at you. That's his loss, not yours. You're a great guy, and I'm proud to call you my brother."

Gabe felt an unfamiliar thickness in his throat. He struggled to speak without giving away that tears were close at hand. "It sounds good in theory, but how do I break the habits of a lifetime?"

"Take a lesson from my mother and walk away from all the bad stuff that goes with being associated with Jesse Calloway," Jericho said. "Then focus on something positive, like loving Gretchen and your baby."

Jericho's suggestion had merit, but Gabe didn't know if he had what it took to walk away. "I think you missed your calling," he told his brother. "You ought to go over to that shelter and give that psychologist a run for her money."

Jericho laughed. "Armchair psychology, bro. I got my diploma out of a box of Cracker Jacks."

"Works for me."

"I hope it does," Jericho said, his tone solemn again. "I really hope it does. Oops! I gotta go."

"Susan calling?"

"Nope. Bonnie. She needs me to put her hair up in a ponytail."

Gabe smiled as he thought of Susan's six-year-old daughter. "You've taken to that fatherhood stuff like a duck to water, haven't you?"

"I guess I have." Jericho sounded more than a little defensive.

"Chill, big brother. I think it's great you're so happy. I mean that."

"It'll happen for you, too, if you let it."

"We'll see. Tell Daniel and Becca hello, and I'll give you a call when Gretchen and I head that way."

"Will do."

"Thanks for calling. I'll think about what you told me." They said their goodbyes, and Gabe recradled the phone, his mind preoccupied with Jericho's advice. His brother was right. Being Jesse Calloway's son had had an impact on his life, had helped make him the man he was, just as it had Jericho and Daniel, but even though there was some of Jesse in him, there was a lot of Hannah in him, too.

His mom always said that a person chose how they would behave and how they would react to a given situation. And for the most part, he knew he'd chosen to be decent and upright. Honest and straightforward. If he lost his temper occasionally, it was no more than anyone did.

There was nothing written anywhere that said he had to continue paying for being Jesse's blood. Like Sarah, he'd already paid dearly. Jericho was right, it was time to do what Sarah had done: walk off and leave the past. Get on with the future and his new life, which included a wife he'd come to love and an unborn child he was beginning to look forward to.

A smile curved his lips, and the heaviness that had lain on his heart for so long lifted. His greatest fear was that their marriage wouldn't work, but as Jericho had pointed out, that was anyone's fear.

He was thinking about that when Gretchen walked out of the bathroom a few moments later, wearing a burgundy satin sleep shirt. She looked like a fresh-faced teenager with her sleek brown hair drawn back into a ponytail and her flawless complexion free of cosmetics.

His reaction was instant and typically male. He wanted to kiss her pretty lips, wanted to kiss her all over. Without thinking about what he was going to do, he strode across the bedroom and took her by the shoulders.

She looked up at him, obviously surprised by his actions.

"I changed my mind about breakfast," he said, before his mouth swooped and took hers in a hungry kiss.

Her response was gratifying. Her arms circled his middle, and she seemed to melt against him, clinging tightly. A little whimper escaped her. She pulled away and spoke his name, her voice thick with emotion. He raised his head to look at her. Expecting passion, he was surprised at the fear in her eyes. Anxiety ambushed his desire, a swift, painless kill.

"What is it?"

Tears filmed her eyes. Her lips trembled. "I'm spotting."

THE NEXT FEW HOURS at the hospital in Fort Worth were a nightmare of trepidation and self-recriminations. It had all started the day he had the fight with Jesse and she'd fainted. He should have made her go to the doctor this morning when she'd first complained of the pain. He should never have had the argument with her parents. He shouldn't have done anything to cause her to worry or put her under any undue stress.

When he said as much to Gretchen's obstetrician when he came out to report on how she was doing, the doctor only smiled and said, "Ideally, every woman needs an emotionally stress-free pregnancy, but stress isn't necessarily the cause of spontaneous abortions."

"She's going to lose the baby." Gabe made the statement in a cold, emotionless voice. Inside, he was a quivering mass of fear. Inside, he was crying out that it wasn't fair. Inside, he was praying it wouldn't happen.

"That's certainly a possibility, but not if I can help it," Phil Mason told him. "It isn't as if she's hemorrhaging badly. She's just spotting. I want to keep her overnight for observation and run a couple of more tests...see how she reacts to the medication I've given her."

Gabe nodded.

"We did an ultrasound and everything looks good, right on schedule. Size, heartbeat, everything." The doctor shrugged. "She may never have another moment's trouble. If she looks okay tomorrow morning, she'll be out of here by suppertime. When she goes home, I want her to have complete bed rest for a week, and I mean rest. No sex. I'll want to see her again then. And we'll go from there."

Gabe wasn't sure if he felt disappointed or relieved at the doctor's orders.

The doctor must have seen the look in his eyes. "I know it's a heck of a way to spend a honeymoon, but it's necessary."

"No problem."

Dr. Mason smiled wearily and slapped him on the shoulder. "You look like death warmed over. Why don't you go home and get some rest? She'll need you to be at her beck and call when she goes home.''

"I don't want to leave her."

He offered Gabe another droll smile. ''I figured you'd say that. At least go buy yourself a good magazine or paperback. Everything in the waiting room is months old.''

"Thanks, Doctor," Gabe said with a final, parting smile. "I will."

THREE EVENINGS LATER, Gretchen lay on the sofa—none too happy about her imposed inactivity—while Gabe fixed grilled cheese sandwiches and tomato soup for their dinner. When she'd suggested that she could do it, he'd looked at her with an expression akin to outright horror. The only thing he'd let her get up for was to go to the bathroom and a shower.

Winter weather permitting, he also allowed her to go outside and lie on the chaise in the sunshine, but insisted on carrying her back and forth. He was taking such good care of her he was about to drive her insane. She knew he was concerned about her and the baby, and she was worried, too, but that concern didn't make it any easier for a person who was used to filling every moment to the brim to be reduced to invalid status.

Actually it wasn't Gabe's concern that was getting on her nerves—that was touching, even if he did tend to go overboard with it. What was making her crazy was that she couldn't do anything but read and watch television. Hoping to bone up on the competition's techniques, she'd watched all the music-video channels until every video was ingrained in her mind and she'd come to despise all the songs—rock, alternative or country.

But if she was honest, she'd admit that the thing that had her the most upset was that this medical crisis had interrupted the consummation of her marriage. She knew that initially Gabe was worried about too much physical intimacy making things worse if the marriage didn't work out, but something must have been said during his telephone conversation with Jericho to render a change of heart, or he wouldn't have kissed her the way he had.

She reached out and turned on the brass lamp to dispel the gloom settling into the room. She wanted him. She hurt with wanting him, but he seemed strangely relieved to have the situation taken out of his hands, even temporarily. When this crisis was over, she supposed she'd have to take the bull by the horns the way she had throughout their strange relationship, and seduce him.

She was thinking about that strategy when she heard a knock on the door. "I'll get it!"

"You stay put!" Gabe bellowed from the kitchen.

He strode into the room, a dish towel tied around his narrow hips, an egg turner in his hand and a look of irritation on his rugged face.

Unlocking the front door, he flung it open. Nicole burst into the dusk-shrouded room like a ray of summer sunshine, flinging her arms around Gabe's neck and pressing a kiss to his whisker-rough cheek. He returned the hug with a little more enthusiasm than Gretchen thought necessary.

Wishing she'd taken time to put on makeup, Gretchen pushed a hand through hair she hadn't washed that day and drew the afghan higher. Nicole glowed with health and happiness. Feeling ugly and useless, Gretchen couldn't help a sudden stab of jealousy.

"Gosh, you smell good, Gabe," Nicole said with an almost giddy laugh. "Like cold outdoors and pheromones."

"That's horse manure and sweat, sweetheart," Gabe said with a wicked grin.

Gretchen pressed her lips together. Funny. Until now, she'd forgotten what a flirt her husband was. Until now, she'd never realized that Nicole was a flirt, too.

"What the heck happened to you?" Gabe asked Nicole, finally putting some distance between them. "You win the lottery or something?"

"Yeah," Gretchen said from her place of exile. "What are you so disgustingly cheerful about, and what are you doing busting in on my honeymoon, anyway?"

If Nicole noticed Gretchen's sarcasm, she chose to ignore it, along with the question about her cheerfulness. "Gretchen! Hi!" she said brightly as she crossed to the sofa. "Gabe called and told me you were under the weather. I was worried about you." She thrust a box at her. "Here. I brought you a box of Godiva chocolates."

*Great. Just what every pregnant woman who's losing her figure needs.* "Gee, thanks," Gretchen said, forcing a smile. "You're a real friend." This round of sarcasm bypassed Nicole, too.

"I know how much you like them," she said, her face aglow. She sniffed and turned to Gabe. "Is something burning?"

"Damn! The grilled cheese." Without another word, he spun on his heel and stalked back to the kitchen.

Nicole raised her eyebrows. "What's the matter with him?"

"He has a lot to do around here and can't get it done for playing nursemaid."

"Ah," Nicole replied.

"I finally insisted he go outside this afternoon," Gretchen said. "He spent a couple hours cleaning stalls and seemed to be in a little better mood when he came in. That was before he burned the grilled cheese."

"Do you think he'd be offended if I offered to finish dinner?"

Gretchen's smile was so thin it was almost nonexistent. She struggled to reply civilly. "Highly."

"Yeah. You're right. So," Nicole went on, "how are you feeling?"

"Much better, thank you. The spotting has stopped, and I'm pretty much just lying around like a lazy slug when I have a mountain of work back in Fort Worth."

"I thought this was your honeymoon."

"So did I," Gretchen said as cheerfully as she could manage with Nicole and Gabe's flirting and her own frumpishness uppermost in her mind. "So what brings you out this way?"

"When Gabe called and told me you were stuck in bed, I thought I'd come and stay and give him a break. If that's okay," she tacked on.

"Why wouldn't it be okay?" Gretchen asked as sweetly as possible.

"Because you're ticked off at me for some reason," Nicole said bluntly.

"I'm surprised you managed to notice since you were so busy coming on to my husband."

The comment struck Nicole dumb for a few seconds. Then she burst out laughing. "That's priceless," she said between giggles.

"I'm glad you find it amusing."

Nicole struggled to compose her features and subdue her laughter. "Gretchen, you're married to a hunk, no doubt about that, but you must be having a major attack of low self-esteem if you thought you saw any serious flirting going on between me and Gabe."

"It looked like flirting to me." Adopting her best Nicole voice, Gretchen trilled, "'Gosh, you smell good. Like cold outdoors and pheromones.'"

"Hey, I'm not dead yet. I can still appreciate the finer things in life," Nicole said. "Actually I'm happier than I've been in years, and I guess it's spilling over into everything I do."

Gretchen clutched a throw pillow to her breasts and said, "You do have an obnoxiously cheerful glow about you."

"I'm glad to see you aren't too green with envy to notice."

Gretchen had the grace to blush. "I'm sorry, but you'd be feeling a little put out with the world if your honeymoon was canceled, too."

"I'm sure I would."

"So, what's made you so high on life?"

A serene smile curved Nicole's lips. "Lucas."

"Lucas?"

Nicole nodded. "He cornered me at the reception and said we needed to talk, that there were things we never settled five years ago. After you and Gabe flew off, I went to his place and we talked until almost midnight."

"Talked?" Gretchen asked with a lift of her eyebrows.

"Talked. The good stuff didn't happen until the next morning when I went back and seduced him."

"You seduced Lucas?"

"Yeah," Nicole said with a nod. Her eyes shimmered with a brightness that matched her smile. "He says he loves me, and I know I still love him, and I think it's going to be okay this time, Gretchen. I really do. There may even be wedding bells in our future."

WIDE AWAKE, Gretchen lay next to a softly snoring Gabe. He was lying on his side with his back toward her. There was something comforting about the sound of his breathing. Not as comforting as being in his arms, but reassuring nonetheless. She inched closer and slid her arm around his waist, placing her cheek against his wide back and inhaling the clean scent of soap and deodorant.

He stirred, and she lay very still, hardly daring to breathe. If he woke up, she would pretend she was asleep. She couldn't be blamed for seeking his warmth in sleep, could she? He quieted, and she pressed closer, thinking about her talk with Nicole.

As soon as she'd heard about Nicole and Lucas, her jealousy vanished like a wisp of smoke and she'd apologized for her behavior. Nicole had just laughed and told her to chalk up her moodiness to hormone changes, which Gretchen was glad to do; it was as good an excuse as any.

She thought about Nicole's confession of seducing Lucas and smiled into the darkness when she remembered that just before her friend's arrival, she'd been thinking about doing the same thing herself.

"You're playing with fire."

At the sound of Gabe's voice, Gretchen gasped and raised herself to one elbow. Only when his fingers circled her wrist did she realize that her hand had drifted dangerously low on his stomach. Still holding on to her, he shifted to his back and looked at her in the moonlit room.

"The doctor said bed rest." The deep rumble of his voice was sleepy and sexy.

"I've rested so much I can't even sleep," she whispered, lowering her head and letting her lips graze his in a light kiss.

"He said no sex." The reminder was given as she trailed hot, openmouthed kisses across his chest.

Her lips hovered over his navel. "There are all kinds of sex, cowboy," she taunted softly.

His breath left him in a soft hiss of desire.

"Hell, woman, I'm tired of fighting you," he said, his voice a thread of sound. "Go ahead. Have your way with me."

Gretchen's mouth curved into a smile of satisfaction. That was exactly what she had in mind.

## CHAPTER THIRTEEN

THE FIRST DAY of spring came with its promise of better things to come. Gretchen's pregnancy had progressed without further problems. She did her best to obey the doctor's orders within the confines of a stressful job, and as a result experienced only occasional backaches and bouts of cramping.

The baby—she wouldn't let Phil Mason tell her what he thought it was—seemed to be thriving. In her seventh month and feeling awkward and clumsy, she longed for the day she and Gabe would bring their son or daughter home from the hospital.

She was never sure if The Seduction, as she thought of that night in January, had worked any wonders with her marriage or not. All she knew was that when she was able to return to "regular sexual activities," she sometimes thought she might die from pleasure.

She was frightened occasionally, after they'd spent a particularly satisfying night together, fearing that what she and Gabe shared was too perfect, too good to last. She understood now why he'd been afraid to get too close to her.

Her husband was a hard man to gauge. He seemed satisfied with their love life and could play the role of gentle or demanding lover with equal skill. He was helpful and did his share of the household chores without complaint. In true macho fashion, he insisted on paying half of the monthly bills at the farm in Frisco and would have demanded to do the same with the house on Elizabeth Avenue if she hadn't convinced him that certain monies in her trust had been designated for that purpose.

After the doctor allowed her to go back to work—telling her to delegate, put in shorter hours and avoid as much stress as possible—she opted to spend the workdays in town. Gabe tried city living, but after a week in Fort Worth, with nothing to do but watch Gretchen work, he'd had enough. He decided to spend the weekdays in Aledo, waiting for the spring rodeo season to start and making sure he was there if his mares needed help foaling.

He made it a point to spend Wednesdays with Gretchen so he could check up on her and take her to lunch. On Friday evenings, he went to Frisco, or she joined him at the old Crenshaw place until late Sunday night when Dirk flew her back to Fort Worth.

But even though the helicopter made their nomadic marriage work with extraordinary ease, neither was crazy about the arrangement. Because of her work, Gabe saw the necessity of keeping the house in town, but he thought that alternating weekend homes was ridiculous. No one needed two ranches.

Gretchen wanted him with her in bed every night and spent a lot of time thinking about ways to change things. So far, neither of them had come up with a workable solution, so they kept on with the arrangement. Neither was willing to upset their truce by challenging the status quo.

For the most part, Gabe seemed content, but there were times he withdrew from her, and no amount of cajoling could bring him out. Sometimes she caught him staring at her with a look in his pale blue eyes she could only describe as lost.

The look frightened her. It made her worry that her advancing pregnancy was a turnoff to him. It made her fear that he regretted ever meeting her and being forced to give up his bachelor life-style. It made her feel lost herself.

Used to facing problems head-on, she longed to go to him and demand to know what was wrong, or press his head to her breasts and assure him that whatever was bothering him would be all right.

Knowing he would reject either of those overtures, she usually took him into the bedroom and made love to him with every ounce of skill and love she possessed. If he still feared losing her or their marriage ending, making love was the only way she could assure him that was the farthest thing from her mind.

Whenever he smiled at her with that lazy, mocking smile and said, "Damn, woman, you're going to kill me yet," Gretchen knew she'd done what she'd set out to do. She'd tamed his wild heart for the moment, and if it was something she had to do daily, then that's what she'd do. She'd never turned down a challenge and never would.

Gabe knew his moods fluctuated between bliss, boredom and belligerent determination to make his marriage work. Gretchen seemed happy, and the sex was great, but there were times when thoughts of the future scared him to death.

He knew he couldn't rodeo forever, and even though he'd told Gretchen he wasn't quitting until he was ready, he'd been giving it a lot of consideration lately. Watching *8 Seconds* in January had brought back all the horror of Dizzy's death. That, combined with Gretchen's bout of spotting, had made him very aware of how quickly life could be snatched away. He'd started thinking of his own mortality, something that had seldom crossed his mind in the past.

He realized he didn't want to be an absentee father, traveling the circuit while his child grew up. Unlike some wives, Gretchen's work prohibited her traveling with him, and even if it didn't, a life on the road wasn't something he'd wish on anyone.

The hard fact was that if he wanted to be there to watch his son or daughter grow up, there would have to be some radical changes made in his life. He was willing to make changes, but he just wasn't certain what they might be or how to go about setting them in place. He couldn't retire from rodeo without having some way to make a living, and he couldn't get enough money to build his string of mares without bullfighting. It was the old catch-22 situation.

He'd been able to save most of the money he'd made the previous season, earmarking it to buy more good mares, but with Gretchen spending time at the ranch, he'd begun to think about how run-down the place was and how badly it needed renovations. It had been fine for him and Dizzy, but a woman like Gretchen needed a finer setting. He was torn between using the money to fix up the place for her or following his initial plan to buy more horses to secure their future.

Another alternative was to sell his ranch and move his stock to her place near Frisco, but he wasn't crazy about the location, and he hated getting rid of his last tie to Dizzy. Would Gretchen consider selling out and using his place as their country home?

Sometimes, without realizing he was doing so, he found himself staring at her with a fearful intensity, almost as if he could look inside her pretty head and see what she wanted. Invariably she caught him. He wondered what she saw in his eyes, because without exception, she maneuvered him to bed and loved him until the doubts and fears were swept away by the turbulence of their lovemaking.

He was no fool, though. He knew that the lovemaking was just a stopgap measure. There would be no real stability in their relationship until they came to some agreement on some very basic problems.

Lacking the initiative to address those problems, he felt in limbo, as if he was waiting for something momentous to happen—a sign of sorts that would make his path clear. He had a vague notion that the "something" was the birth of their baby, but he wasn't sure; he'd know it when it happened, though. Until then, he contented himself with taking each day as it came and seeing what happened.

ON THE LAST WEDNESDAY in March, three things happened. His best mare died trying to deliver a stillborn foal. Gretchen called the ranch to see if he was coming to take her to lunch and heard a strange woman answer the phone. And Tyrell West paid Gabe an impromptu visit and found him in the arms of a voluptuous Hispanic woman with a cloud of raven hair. As "somethings" went, the day was memorable.

After losing the mare, Gabe was prowling around outside, alternately cursing and fighting the unmanly urge to cry. Dolores Juanita Cartright, the vet who'd taken care of the stock way back when it was Dizzy's and she was straight out of vet school, had gone into the house to make some coffee while Gabe tried to get a grip on his seesawing emotions. D.J.'s teenage sons cared for the horses when Gabe was out of town, and of all people, she knew how devastating his loss was. As a longtime friend, as well as his veterinarian, she was willing to shuffle her appointments back an hour or so to help get him through the initial feelings of loss and grief.

The mare, a former cutting horse, was as good as money could buy, both in temperament and ability. Replacing her was vital; Gabe needed to keep building his brood-mare base, but finding the financing to do so was a problem, especially since he was still debating whether to renovate the house.

When D.J. came outside, she was carrying two mugs of coffee and had a couple of packaged sweet rolls clutched in her teeth. As she handed Gabe his comfort food, she said, "Somebody called while I was inside."

"Who was it?" he asked, ripping open the roll.

She shook her head, the cloud of curly dark hair flying. "I don't know. They hung up before I could ask."

He shrugged. "Probably a wrong number."

GRETCHEN STARED at the telephone in her office with all the abhorrence of someone looking at a three-headed creature. Some woman was with Gabe at the house in Aledo. Hearing the distinctly Hispanic, distinctly feminine voice on the other end of the line had come as such a shock she hadn't known what to say, so she'd hung up.

Tears sprang to her eyes, and her trembling hands crept up to cover her quivering lips. Of all the things she'd thought might happen between her and Gabe, this hadn't been on the list.

Maybe it was just a neighbor. Maybe. But who? And why? A better question might be how she was going to handle the situation. Should she confront Gabe or pretend innocence and see if he offered an explanation?

D.J. AND GABE DRANK their coffee and ate their rolls in a companionable silence. D.J.'s veering-toward-plump body slouched against the corral fence; Gabe rested one foot on the bottom rail and set his coffee mug on a post.

"I know losing Bandita is a major obstacle, but you'll overcome it," the veterinarian said, licking the powdered-sugar icing from her fingers.

"I suppose."

"I'll be on the lookout for a replacement mare."

"Finding a good mare isn't the problem, Dee," he told her. "Finding the money is. It isn't just me anymore. I have a wife and baby to think about now."

He didn't say he had a *rich* wife to think about. He didn't have to. D. J. Cartright was well aware of the West family's money and power.

"Won't Gretchen help you?"

Gabe shot her an angry glance. "I can't ask her to do that."

"Can't or won't?"

"It's the same thing."

"A typical male response," D.J. said, rolling her eyes. "Look, Gabriel, you're married to this woman.

Legally, what's yours is hers and what's hers is yours—unless you signed a prenuptial agreement.''

''I didn't, but that's not the way I see it.''

''Of course it isn't. You're a man, and you seem to be under the assumption that you have something to prove to her, or maybe not to her, but to her family.'' D.J. narrowed her eyes and regarded him with sudden comprehension. ''Or maybe you're trying to prove something to yourself, eh, hombre?''

''Back off, Dee,'' Gabe said.

With a cheerful smile, D.J. told him exactly what he could do with that remark. Then she put her hand on his arm and looked up at him with complete empathy. ''As a Mexican married to a white man, I understand your feelings, my friend, but you don't have to prove anything to anyone. Marriage is a partnership. It's being there for the other person. It's sharing the good and the bad. It's trying to figure out what to do next, together.'' She shook his arm, as if that would make him see the importance of what she was saying. ''Together,'' she said again.

It made a lot of sense, and something told him she was right. While it was true that he wanted to impress the Wests with his ability to provide for their daughter, D.J. had hit the nail on the head when she said that what he was really trying to do was prove his worth to himself.

''You're a wise woman, Doc,'' he said, smiling down at her.

''And gorgeous, too,'' she quipped, batting her eyelids, tossing her midnight hair and laughing up at him.

He laughed, too, and put his arms around her. ''Thanks,'' he said, giving her a friendly hug.

"What are friends for?" she said. She put her arms around his neck, returned the hug and then leaned back in his arms.

Neither of them had any idea that Tyrell West was anywhere in the county until he cleared his throat and asked, "Am I interrupting something?"

One look at his father-in-law's cold eyes and Gabe knew he was in for an uncomfortable visit. He wasn't looking forward to the inquisition that was bound to take place, but there was no chance of getting out of it, so he did the only thing a well-mannered country boy could do. He introduced D.J. to Gretchen's father, thanked her, deliberately gave her another hug, then sent her on her way. Finally he invited his father-in-law inside.

Tyrell looked around the clean but shabby surroundings with a definite air of superiority.

"Would you like some coffee?" Gabe asked, determined to observe all the neighborly amenities. "D.J. just made a fresh pot."

"No, thank you. This isn't a social call."

"What kind of call is it then?" Gabe asked, pouring the steaming liquid into his cup.

"I wanted to talk to you about your future. Yours and Gretchen's."

"It's nice of you to be concerned," Gabe responded with barely veiled sarcasm.

"In spite of what she's told you, I'm very concerned about Gretchen's welfare, and that of her baby. She is my daughter."

Gabe couldn't argue with that.

"I've done a little checking into your background, and it seems you have a way with the ladies," Tyrell said. "The little scene I interrupted a few moments ago only lends credence to your reputation."

"Reputations have a way of getting blown out of proportion, Mr. West," Gabe said, trying to hold on to his temper. "I don't deny having sown my share of wild oats—as I imagine you have—but that was when I was much younger and before I married Gretchen." He took a deep breath. "As for the little scene you interrupted, it wasn't what it appeared to be."

Tyrell's cold smile seemed to say he'd heard that excuse before. "You don't owe me any explanations."

"On the contrary," Gabe said, "I believe I do. D.J. is the local veterinarian. Not only that, she and her family are close friends of mine. I lost a prize mare and foal this morning. I was upset, and she was trying to cheer me up. For what it's worth, I hug her in front of her husband, too."

"Do you think Gretchen would believe that story if she'd seen what I did—or if she knew about it?" West asked the question with a lift of his heavy eyebrows.

"Gretchen has no reason to doubt me. And she has no way of knowing about this, anyway... unless someone tells her."

Tyrell only smiled that frosty smile. Gabe had little doubt that as soon as his esteemed father-in-law left, the first thing he'd do was call Gretchen from his cell phone and tell her what he'd interrupted.

"That doesn't have to happen," Tyrell said.

"Not if you love Gretchen, it doesn't," Gabe agreed.

"Oh, I love her, all right. So much that I'd do anything to make her happy. Right now she thinks that's you. But I know my daughter. She's like a will-o'-the-wisp. The only thing constant in her life is change."

"She has many and varied interests," Gabe conceded. "That's why she's so fascinating."

"She's always liked thwarting me," West said with a thoughtful expression. "That hasn't changed just because she's gotten older."

"On the contrary," Gabe said. "She's a woman, not a kid who goes against Daddy's wishes just for spite."

"You don't know her as well as you think you do, Mr. Butler, so you'd better listen up. Gretchen is willful, and she likes shocking her mother and me. When she finds something she knows we don't approve of, she goes after it with single-minded determination."

For the first time since Tyrell West had arrived, Gabe's confidence faltered. He thought about Nicole's telling him how Gretchen had set up her company without any help from her parents, and how she'd badgered, cajoled and otherwise browbeat the crew working on the video until it was as near perfection as it could possibly be. And he thought about her relentless pursuit of him.

Like the shrewd businessman he was, West noted the chink in Gabe's armor and pushed in the tip of the knife. "Right now, that shocking something is you. For obvious reasons, her mother and I don't approve of you—your background and all," he said with a vague wave of his hand. "So that makes you eminently desirable to her. Next year it will be something or someone else."

Gabe felt his confidence ebb back. If there was one thing Gretchen had convinced him of, it was that his background had no bearing on how she felt about being married to him. In fact, she'd made a big deal of wanting a real marriage, a lasting relationship, a traditional, happy family—with him. The picture her father painted of her was not only incorrect, it was insulting. He had a sudden suspicion about where the conversation was headed.

"What are you getting at?"

"A simple solution."

Before he spoke, Gabe took a sip of his coffee and let his gaze meet Tyrell's over the rim of the cup. "What kind of solution?"

"I give you a large sum of money. In return, I don't say anything to Gretchen about what I saw today, and you come up with some excuse to end the marriage."

Gabe couldn't believe the audacity of the man. No wonder Gretchen had grown up thinking she wasn't loved. No doubt her life had been a series of manipulations and "solutions."

"What about the baby?" Gabe asked.

"I'm talking about a great deal of money," West said. "Did I mention that?" His mouth curved in another of those chilly smiles. "I've always believed a clean cut is best," he continued in a smooth, soothing tone. "It's less painful in the long run."

Gabe longed to smash his fist into West's gloating, handsome face, but refused to give the older man the satisfaction.

Gretchen's dad must have taken Gabe's silence for consideration. "It would mean the difference between struggling to put together a nice band of brood mares and breeding to the best studs money can buy. Money spent in the right place can mean instant success."

The muscle in Gabe's jaw knotted. "That's true."

"It's a big decision," Tyrell said. "I don't expect your answer right now. Think about it a few days—say, a week. That should give you plenty of time to weigh your options and think up a good excuse for Gretchen."

"That sounds like a good idea."

"I'll give you a call next week, then." Without bothering to say goodbye, Gretchen's dad headed for the door. Gabe watched him go, clutching the mug of coffee in a white-knuckled grip. When he heard the Lincoln start up, he hurled the mug at the kitchen door. It shattered on impact, splattering brown liquid over walls, cabinets and tile. Even knowing he'd have to clean it up, Gabe felt immensely better.

GRETCHEN'S DAY had gone downhill fast after she'd called the ranch. She was nervous and irritable, and the sharpness of her tongue had her crew walking on eggshells until quitting time. She had a headache, a backache, her feet were swollen and her stomach felt queasy. To make matters worse, she'd been rear-ended at a red light, and by the time the police were finished with their reports, she was almost in tears.

Seeing she was pregnant, they'd wanted to call the paramedics and have her checked over at the hospital, but she insisted that both she and the baby were fine; it was a minor accident and her bumper was hardly dented. All she wanted to do was go home and have a hot shower, a quart of butter pecan ice cream and a good cry—not necessarily in that order.

She was walking into the kitchen of her house on Elizabeth Avenue when the phone began to ring. Closing the door with her foot, she hurried to the cordless wall phone and plucked the receiver from the base.

"Hello."

"Hey," Gabe said. "It's me. Where've you been? I've been trying to call."

Her first impulse was to tell him about the accident and elicit the sympathy she knew would follow, but her stubborn pride kicked in. "The traffic was pretty bad."

"I should have known," he said. "I was getting worried."

"Really?" she asked in an accommodating tone. "That's sweet." She stepped out of her shoes and made a face at the receiver. Her voice was all honeyed innocence as she asked, "What's happening out there? I expected to see you for lunch."

"I know, but I lost a mare and foal this morning."

Although he made the statement without any discernible emotion, Gretchen felt a stab of pain. "Which one?"

"Bandita. My vet, D.J., came out, but it was too late."

This time she heard a definite thickness in Gabe's voice and felt the prickle of tears in her own eyes. She knew how much he loved all his horses, and she knew how little he could afford the loss of his best mare. "I'm sorry."

"Yeah, me, too."

"Would you like to talk about it?"

"Thanks, but not right now."

Gretchen couldn't deny the hurt his answer brought. She was trying to think of some way to respond when he said, "I called to tell you I'm going out of town for a few days. I've got a lot on my mind right now, and this has thrown me for a loop. I was counting on that foal. I need to step back and regroup. If it won't throw a kink in any of your plans, I'd like to take a few days to get away from here and think things through, just be by myself awhile.''

Gretchen felt that painful constriction of her heart again. He didn't feel as if he could talk to her. She wondered if he ever would.

*''Don't worry if Gabe feels the need to go off by himself sometimes. Separating themselves from the world so they can get a better perspective on how they fit in is a habit all Jesse Calloway's boys have.''*

The words of wisdom, spoken by Susan Quinlin Calloway on Gretchen's wedding day, slipped into her mind. It had been just before the fracas between Gabe and Jesse, and every woman in the room was tossing out advice on how to make a success of her marriage. When Susan had made the statement, she'd put her hand on Gretchen's shoulder and looked her in the eye. Gretchen had known then that Jericho's wife had had to come to terms with this problem herself. And she knew it was a need of her own husband's she would have to learn to deal with.

It might be easier if the memory of a cheerful feminine voice answering his phone wasn't so fresh in her mind, or if she could rid herself of the nagging fear that when he left for wherever he was going, he would take that woman with him.

''You do whatever you have to do,'' she said, unable to mask the dejection in her voice.

''Look,'' he said, picking up on it in a heartbeat, ''I don't have to go. If you need me—''

The sound of her thoughts almost drowned out the rest of his sentence. *Of course I need you. I need you*

*to hold me close and tell me you love me and that*
*whoever that woman was, she means nothing to you.*

"—I can always go another time."

She rubbed at her throbbing temple, where a sudden headache pounded out a labored rhythm. "No. Go ahead. I'm just tired. I had a rough day, too. We shot some footage for the new Harlan Dugan video, and I had to start editing the Mary Chapin Carpenter."

"You need to delegate more," he told her. "Is there anything I can do to help?"

*Come home and rub my back and massage my feet and hold me.*

"Nothing," she said. "Maybe tomorrow will be easier. Where are you going?"

"I'm not sure. I heard about a good mare for sale down near San Antonio, and Joel told me about one he'd heard about up in Arkansas. If I go up there, I'll probably stop by Calloway Corners to see Jericho and Daniel. Little Bit isn't far off from foaling, so I'll be back Sunday evening. It's her first foal and I want to be here."

"Who's going to take care of the horses?"

"D.J.'s boys."

"Do you need to...stop by here for anything?" *Like to tell me goodbye and that you'll miss me?*

"I don't think so." A note of amusement crept into his voice. "Ramona came today, so I have plenty of clean underwear."

Ramona!

A sweet, cleansing relief swept through Gretchen. A foolish smile curved her lips. Why hadn't she thought about the housekeeper before? It was Ramona who'd answered the telephone!

"Then I guess you're all set." The assuaging of her fear made her charitable. "Do you want to take the chopper?"

"No, thanks. I do my best thinking while I'm driving."

With a sigh, she realized she'd run out of ploys to get him to stop by and see her, as well as excuses to keep him on the phone. "I'll see you Sunday, then."

"Yeah. I'll stop by before I come back out here."

"Great!" she said, forcing some enthusiasm into her voice. "I'll miss you," she added, unable to stop the words.

"I'll miss you, too."

The confession, unexpected and rumbled softly into the telephone, almost convinced her that he would. "Well, then—"

"Gretchen."

"Yes?" she asked eagerly, thankful that he'd interrupted her goodbye.

"Promise me you'll take care of yourself."

The tentative happiness she'd felt a moment before vanished, and a chill tripped down her spine. Something about the words sounded like goodbye. She buried her teeth in her bottom lip to control its sudden trembling and blinked back a startling rush of tears.

"Gretchen?"

"Yeah. I'm here and I will. You be careful, too," she managed to choke out. "Goodbye."

She managed to push the off button before the tears overcame her. It was a long time before she got them under control.

# CHAPTER FOURTEEN

GABE LEFT that evening for San Antonio to look at the mare, which he did, telling the man he'd get back to him. He was halfway to Louisiana the next morning when he realized he should have gone ahead and written the man a check. He'd be hard-pressed to find another mare as good, but his heart wasn't in purchasing a new horse. It was back in Fort Worth with Gretchen. She'd sounded really tired. Depressed, even. He wondered if her dad had said something to her about D.J. But if he had, wouldn't she have confronted him? Gabe couldn't shake the feeling that something was wrong, that he shouldn't have left, even though, with his next breath, he chided himself for making something out of nothing. He and D.J. were just old friends. It was Gretchen he loved.

That was the real kicker. He loved her, and the things Tyrell had told him had triggered the old Calloway curse of insecurity and quickened his fear of losing her. Would she get tired of him when the newness wore off their relationship, as her father predicted?

He divided his attention between that problem and how to handle Tyrell West's proposition. Of course he'd refuse the insulting offer. West's trying to pay him off was one thing; trying to coerce him into giving up all his paternal rights was something else—as if he'd

evér consider either option after all he'd been through
with Jesse.

Though it was a thorn in his side, his father-in-law's
visit had helped bring definition to Gabe's most
pressing problem: how to provide for his wife and a
child when his rodeo days were over.

Gretchen had made a big deal about not caring
about the money, but he didn't want her thinking he
was less of a man because he couldn't provide for her.

He fought the urge to stop at a gas station and call
Gretchen just to hear her voice, because he knew that
wouldn't really help. He was doing the right thing by
giving himself a few days. He'd go to Calloway Corners, talk to his brothers and give Gretchen a call over
the weekend. Hopefully, by the time he got back to
Fort Worth on Sunday night, his future would look a
little brighter.

FOR A FRIDAY EVENING, the occupancy of the Midnight Hour was amazingly sparse, which made it an
ideal place for Gabe to tell Jericho, over a couple of
greasy cheeseburgers and a beer or two, about his
conversation with Gretchen's father.

"The sorry sun of a gun," Jericho said when Gabe
finished his tale. "You aren't going to take him up on
it, are you." It was a statement, not a question.

"Of course not. I called him early this afternoon
and told him exactly what he could do with his big
check. He wasn't too happy, but I figure having
someone turn him down will be a character-building
experience." Gabe released a big breath. "I hope he
doesn't blow the whistle about D.J."

Jericho tipped his beer bottle to his lips. "It isn't as if you did anything wrong. Just tell Gretchen the truth."

Gabe grinned. "Oh, yeah. The truth. Why didn't I think of that? I don't know if I should tell Gretchen about her dad's little offer or not. I don't want to help widen the rift between them. He's a sorry sun of a buck, but he is her father."

"See how it goes," Jericho suggested.

"Yeah. At least this has made me think long and hard about the future, and I believe I've come up with something."

"Which is?"

"Sell both farms. I know I can get top dollar for my place. Aledo is a hot little bedroom community right now. Things are moving north of Dallas, too, and I'm sure Gretchen could sell for a tidy profit."

"I can't see you living in town, Bubba."

"We wouldn't. We could use the money from her place to buy another and use what I get from mine to buy breeding stock. Or vice versa."

"Not bad," Jericho said with a contemplative nod. "It ought to fly."

"I hope Gretchen thinks so."

"You won't know if you don't ask."

Gabe lifted his beer and regarded the brown bottle thoughtfully for a moment. "I'll talk to her when I go back Sunday evening."

"Good."

"How're things going with your mom and Jesse?"

"Still separated. Mama's rented herself a little two-bedroom house and bought a bunch of new furniture. Got a new hairdo and went to Dallas and bought a whole new wardrobe. Pop's furious. He thinks she's seeing someone else.''

"Is she?''

Jericho cocked an eyebrow. "Mama?''

Gabe grinned back. "Stupid question, huh? Is Jesse still drinking?''

"Not to my knowledge. He's talked to Ford a couple of times—in an unofficial capacity. Ford says he's lonely, that he misses Mama, but he's in denial. He still wants to place the fault for everything that happened to him on someone else, instead of taking his share of the blame.''

"I could've told him that, and I'm no shrink.''

Jericho laughed wryly. "Ford also says that while Pop was in Angola, the world changed and he didn't, and it's going to take him a while to come to terms with those changes. I'm trying my best to be more understanding.'' He glanced at his watch. "Speaking of understanding, Susan is—usually. But if I come home late with Miller breath, she'll have my hide.''

Gabe's chuckle was warm but taunting. "Henpecked already?''

"Yeah, I guess I am,'' Jericho said. The twinkle in his eyes didn't quite mask the look of seriousness Gabe saw there. "Want to make something of it?''

Gabe held up both hands. "Not me. Actually,'' he said, tongue-in-cheek, "it looks damn good on you.''

Jericho grinned. "It feels damned good.''

GRETCHEN WAS in the editing room late Friday afternoon when her assistant announced that her father was there to see her. With a weary hand, she pushed a swath of hair from her face and arched her back against a nagging ache. "Tell him I'll see him in my office."

Tyrell, looking handsome but irritated, was waiting for her when she walked in a few minutes later. "Hi, Dad," she said with a cheerfulness she was far from feeling. "What's up?"

"I came to talk to you about your husband."

Gretchen's heart sank like a dinghy that had been hit by a shotgun blast. "What about Gabe?"

"Did you know he was seeing another woman?"

Gretchen felt as if he'd punched her in the stomach. A deep pain exploded inside her, followed by shock waves of misery. She crossed her arms over her stomach, swollen with Gabe's baby, and felt it constrict into a tight, hard knot.

Swallowing back a sudden nausea, she managed to say, "I don't believe you."

"I saw them myself."

Though Tyrell wasn't above telling a lie to suit his purposes, the look in his eyes told her that this wasn't one of them. She couldn't breathe, couldn't think. Crossing the room on shaking legs, she sank into the leather chair behind her desk. She closed her eyes and leaned back, drawing in great gulping breaths and doing her best not to go to pieces at the image that surfaced in her mind.

"Are you all right?" Anxiety laced her father's voice.

Gretchen opened her misery-filled eyes. "What do you care?"

"I care, or I wouldn't have told you. He's no good for you, Gretchen. Your mother and I have known it from the first time we saw him. You should be glad I

found out what he was before he took you for everything you have.''

She saw the satisfaction in her father's eyes and
wondered why it pleased him so much to tell her
something he knew would hurt her. That was almost
as devastating as hearing about Gabe's betrayal.

''How could you possibly know what's good for
me, Dad?'' she cried. Leaning forward, she placed her
palms on the desktop and pushed herself to her feet.
''You don't know anything about me. If you did,
you'd know that Gabriel Butler is the best thing that's
ever happened to me. If you'd stop looking down your
nose, you'd see that he's a good, decent man who's
managed to make something of himself despite the
things he's had to overcome.''

''Damn it, Gretchen, he's a clown!''

''Yes, he is. And do you know what he does besides tell corny jokes? He saves lives, Daddy. Just like
fire fighters and policemen. He may have saved my
life. At the very least, he's given me the life of a baby
I might never have had without him.''

''I understand about the baby,'' her father said. ''I
know you've always wanted one, but did you have to
marry him?''

''Yes, I did. I love him, Daddy. But love is a concept you don't know much about, just like you don't
know much about saving lives. All you know how to
do is destroy them.''

Suddenly drained of energy and acutely aware of her
aching back, she sank down in the chair. ''On that
note, I think you'd better leave.''

''I told you for your own good,'' he said.

''No, you didn't. You told me because you want
your way—as usual—and you'll do anything to get it.''

"I saw what I saw, and I saw him with a pretty, young Hispanic woman in his arms, laughing and teasing."

Gretchen's heart was breaking, but she'd never let her father know. "Maybe there's a logical explanation."

Tyrell's face flamed with color. "And maybe you're a fool." Turning on his heel, he yanked open the door and stormed out, slamming it behind him. The sound reverberated through the room and the hollow chambers of Gretchen's numbed mind.

"Undoubtedly," she whispered into the silence of the room. Laying her head on the desk, she let the bitter tears flow.

She had no idea how long she sat there crying, but eventually the tears stopped and she realized two things. One, it was almost time to leave for the day, and two, she had to go to the bathroom.

Rising wearily, heavily, she went into the small cubicle attached to her office. She wished she hadn't. Dear God, she was spotting again!

GRETCHEN AWOKE feeling groggy and strangely out of sorts. The gray light in the hospital room told her that the night had finally passed. The roundness of her tummy told her that everything was all right with Gabe's baby.

Her fingers clutched the sheets in a white-knuckled grip. Though she knew the fault couldn't be laid solely at her father's feet, his satisfied announcement that he'd seen Gabe in another woman's arms had likely triggered last night's trauma.

When she'd seen the blood on her panties, she'd panicked. She had no idea where Gabe was, so she called 911 and Nicole, who'd arrived at the studio immediately after the ambulance. A short while later, Dr. Mason had worked his particular magic, and though he was concerned that she'd spotted twice, he seemed fairly confident that the incident would pass.

Again he maintained that everything seemed perfectly fine with the baby, though it was beginning to look as if Gretchen might have a premature delivery. The longer she could hold on, the better for all concerned. Then, telling her he hated to do it, he confined her to bed for the rest of her pregnancy.

But she'd been halfway expecting the ultimatum, and as much as it galled her to have to delegate her responsibilities at the studio for the next couple of months, she was willing to do whatever it took to see that this baby arrived in the world safe and sound.

She had talked to her mother first thing this morning, and Mimi had already taken it upon herself to arrange full-time live-in help. If all went well, Gretchen would be going home after lunch.

She was just finishing a breakfast she didn't want but knew she should eat when the door to her room cracked open and Nicole poked her head inside. "Hi," she said with a bright smile. "How're you feeling?"

"Better," Gretchen said with a sigh. "More in control. The spotting has stopped."

Clearly relieved, Nicole crossed the room to the bed. "Thank God!" She squeezed Gretchen's hand. "Do you feel like telling me what happened? You were so hysterical when I got to the studio yesterday evening that I just got bits and pieces, the main one being that your dad said he saw Gabe with another woman."

"That's what he said."

"Do you want to talk about it, or will it upset you?"

"I don't mind." Gretchen told Nicole about her call to the ranch and the woman answering. "When Gabe told me later that Ramona had come in, I figured that my hormones were playing havoc with my judgment and I'd been a fool. I told myself it must have been her."

"What makes you think it wasn't?"

"My dad said that the woman he saw in Gabe's arms was young and pretty. Ramona's sixty if she's a day." Gretchen's eyes brimmed with tears. "Daddy said they were laughing and teasing."

Nicole held up a hand and smiled. "Hold the tears. I think I can solve this mystery."

"What are you talking about?"

"Didn't you say that Gabe lost a mare?"

"A mare and foal. So?"

"You said the vet came. Did Gabe by any chance call the vet by name?"

Gretchen nodded. "He said D.J. had come, but it was too late."

Nicole began to laugh. "Gretchen, honey, D.J. is Dolores Juanita Cartright. She's everything your daddy described, but he didn't know a couple of very important things. D.J. is very happily married and has six kids, and Gabe has been a friend of the family for years."

A tentative hope began to take hold of Gretchen's heart. "How do you know all that?"

"Gabe sent pictures of her with foals she helped deliver to Eden and Nick. I've seen them. I guess they teased him like crazy the first time they saw photos of her. Eden met her a year or so ago and says she's a wonderful person."

"Do you really think that's who he was with?"

"I'd bet my life on it," Nicole said. "So you just put that little worry right out of your mind and concentrate on getting strong. By the way," she added, "where is Gabe?"

"I don't know. He said something about going to San Antonio and maybe on to Calloway Corners and up to Arkansas."

"Do you mean he doesn't know you're in the hospital?"

Gretchen shook her head.

Nicole patted her hand. "You just lie back and let me handle things. I'm going to find that husband of yours and get him back here pronto."

WHEN GABE AWOKE at nine o'clock on Saturday, it was to a perfect spring day. The air was crystal clear, sunshine shimmered on the surface of the pond, and bird song melded with the sounds of lowing cattle. Even Joel's rogue bull was grazing peacefully. It was the kind of morning that lent credence to the saying, "God's in his heaven; all's right with the world."

After his meeting with Jericho at the Midnight Hour the evening before, Gabe had driven to his mother's place and been welcomed with open arms. There were concerned questions about Gretchen's whereabouts and her health. His mother was sympathetic with the loss of his mare and foal; even Joel added his commiserations.

Gabe had noticed a little softening in his stepfather's attitude toward him since he'd been his best man. It was as if each of them had made a silent agreement to let bygones be bygones and make a tentative start on a new relationship.

After eating one of his mother's wonderful desserts, he'd gone to the old house and fallen into an exhausted sleep well before ten o'clock. The rest had done him good—or maybe it was the decision he'd reached. He felt better than he had in weeks.

Now, he showered and dressed and walked the short distance to his mother's, drinking in the scents of spring, absorbing the warmth of the sunshine, wishing Gretchen was there with him. He missed her. Now that he'd made some decisions about their future, he was anxious to share them with her, to get her input.

"What were you trying to do? Sleep your life away?" Hannah asked as he stepped onto the back deck, where pots of purple and yellow pansies danced prettily in the morning breeze.

He grinned as she poured him a mug of coffee from the insulated pot. "Looks that way, doesn't it?" He kissed his mother's cheek and pulled out a chair. "Actually I've been missing a lot of sleep, getting up every couple of hours to check the mares—for all the good it did me," he added.

"Don't dwell on it, son," Hannah said. "You have a lot to be thankful for."

"I know."

"I'm taking a vote. What do you want for breakfast? Jody and Jason haven't eaten yet."

"They're getting pretty thick, aren't they?" Gabe asked with typical big-brother concern.

Hannah gave a noncommittal shrug. "You can never tell with Jody. They've been on again, off again ever since Christmas."

A child's giggle wafted through the screened double doors out onto the deck. "Who's that?" Gabe asked.

"Jason's little brother," Hannah explained. "Tess and Seth went to Alexandria for a funeral, so Jason's baby-sitting this morning. He and Jody are taking Richie fishing."

"And isn't it nice of us," Jody said, pushing through the screen door, followed by Jason and the four-year-old boy, who had inherited his mother's green eyes and light brown hair.

"Richie, this is my big brother, Gabe," Jody said, picking up the child and plopping him into the chair next to Gabe's.

"Hi," Richie said, all twinkling eyes and dimples.

"Hi. I hear you're going fishing," Gabe said.

Richie's smile grew wider. "Yeah, and I'm gonna put fishin' worms in Jody's blouse."

Hannah, Gabe and Jason burst into laughter. "Little pervert," Jody muttered. She pinned Jason with an accusing look. "I suppose you put him up to that?"

"Me?" Jason asked innocently.

"Okay, you two. Stop the arguing," Hannah commanded, "and tell me what you want to eat. This isn't the Holiday Inn, you know. I have things to do."

They decided on sausages and waffles—for Richie's sake—and while Jody helped her mother fix the breakfast, Richie kept Gabe and Jason entertained. Gabe was fascinated by the child's bright inquisitiveness and his disarming smile. For the first time, he seriously thought about having a son and found himself hoping he would.

After demolishing most of his waffle, Richie went in search of butterflies and left the older people lingering over coffee. At Hannah's insistence, Jody started to clear the table. Jason volunteered to help so they could get on with their fishing trip. Gabe was left alone, entranced by the little boy who flitted around the yard like the butterflies he chased, running from flower to flower, stopping to examine leaves and rocks and bugs.

He was watching Richie stick his hand through the barbed-wire fence to try to lure a newborn calf close enough to touch, when he heard a car pull into the lane and recognized it as Lucas Tanner's. Gabe scraped his chair back and went to see what his friend was doing in this part of town.

The first thing he noticed was that Lucas's face was drawn with worry. Probably a fight with Nicole, Gabe thought, which was too bad, since their wedding was scheduled for mid-June.

"Hey," he said, taking the hand Lucas proffered, "how's it going?"

"So-so," Lucas said, releasing Gabe's hand and shoving his own hands into his pockets.

"Okay." Gabe grinned. "I know something's wrong with you and Nicole, so you might as well tell me and get it off your mind."

"It isn't me and Nicole," Lucas said. "Damn, I hate being the one to tell you..."

Gabe's blood ran cold. "Tell me what?"

Lucas's eyes were bleak with despair. "Gretchen was admitted to the hospital last night. She started spotting again."

Gabe felt the color drain from his face, felt a peculiar numbness settle in his hands and feet.

"Nicole called me a little while ago, looking for you..."

Lucas's voice droned on, over the noise of Gabe's thoughts.

"I phoned Jericho right away, and he told me you were here."

Gretchen was spotting again. She—

"Oh, God, no!"

The sentiment was his; the voice was Jody's. The terror in her voice sent him whirling around, Gretchen forgotten. The scene he beheld was a parent's nightmare. Richie had slipped beneath the barbed wire, probably in pursuit of the calf. Joel's bull, in a far corner of the pasture, must have spotted the intruder about the same time Jody saw what was happening.

Lucas cursed. Simultaneously, Gabe and Jody started toward the fence that separated them from Richie. Jody had the advantage of being closer. She had the advantage of tennis shoes and shorts—and youth.

Gabe's legs were longer, his stride stronger, but his jeans and boots were a hindrance he could ill afford. He saw the distance between the bull and Richie close and longed for the sneakers and the baggy pants he wore in the arena. As he ran, his mind was already putting his experience into play, offering and discarding half a dozen possible scenarios.

He saw Jody slip between the strands of wicked wire. Her shirt caught on a barb and she jerked free, uncaring that the shirt was ruined or that the sharp spike left a bloody streak. She called Richie's name. Grinning, he turned and looked at her questioningly.

"Watch out for the bull!" Jody screamed, pointing. "Run!"

Richie turned and saw the bull. Jody called his name again. Gabe added his own hoarse plea. Wide-eyed, Richie turned to look at them. Gabe wasn't sure he'd ever seen such fear on a child's face. He called him again, but, instead of turning and running, Richie froze.

Gabe cursed and ran faster. From the corner of his eye, he saw Hannah and Jason come onto the porch, heard their anguished cries. He spared them a quick glance as Joel stepped through the door. Disbelief added ten years to his stepfather's face. A panicked Jason started across the deck; Gabe yelled for him to stay put. Joel turned and rushed back into the house.

The fence was coming up fast. Gabe would waste precious time if he stopped to crawl between the strands. Making a split-second decision, he put on an extra burst of speed and vaulted over the fence as if he was high-jumping. The boots and tight denim worked against him again. The fabric caught, and he went sprawling onto the ground, shoulder first.

Scrambling to his feet, he saw Jody swing Richie into her arms. Thank God! When Jody turned and saw Gabe, the horror on her face receded a little. She started running toward him and the safety of the yard beyond the fence, but Richie's weight slowed her considerably.

The bull was getting closer with every second. Gabe was closing in on them from the other side. *God, please!*

When Jody reached Gabe, she slowed down, but he yelled for her to keep going and bolted past her, putting himself between her and the bull. Yelling like a banshee, he threw up his arms, waving them wildly, praying the ploy would work and buy Jody and Richie a few precious seconds.

The bull came to a stop a few yards away, snorting and pawing huge clods of dirt from the covering of lush green Bermuda grass. Breathing heavily, Gabe looked into the mean, beady eyes and knew he had his work cut out for him. He cast a quick glance over his shoulder and saw Jody hand Richie to Jason on the other side of the fence.

The bull snorted, garnering Gabe's undivided attention once again. He was on his own. There were no other bullfighters to divert Toro's attention. No pickup men. He had no knowledge of this bull's habits, except that he was one ornery son of a gun. Uncertain how to proceed, Gabe began to back up. The bull gouged up more sod, but he didn't advance.

Encouraged, Gabe tried the gimmick again, moving a little faster. The closer he could get to the fence before he made an all-out run for it, the better chance he'd have. Still the bull didn't advance. Never taking his eyes off the beast, Gabe eased around half a turn and started a sideways retreat.

The bull snorted and took two trotting steps forward. From the yard, Hannah called Gabe's name. The torment he heard in that anguished wail breached his concentration for a fraction of a second, long enough for him to look her way, long enough for the bull to break into a determined lope.

When Gabe realized that the bull was on the move again, he broke into a run himself, using a zigzag pattern he hoped would break the bull's stride and buy him a few feet. He looked toward the terror-stricken group on the other side of the fence. Security was closer, but still so far away.

From behind him, the bull's dissonant, ragged breathing sounded closer than ever. Casting a glance over his shoulder, Gabe saw that the distance between them had dwindled from yards to feet. There was blood in the animal's eye and slimy saliva dripping from his fleshy mouth.

Terror took Gabe in a powerful grip.

He wondered suddenly if Dizzy had felt this same brand of fear as the bull had borne down on him that day five years before. Probably. But Dizzy hadn't had the incentives Gabe did. He'd had no wife, no child on the way. From somewhere deep inside him, Gabe found another burst of speed. He tried not to think about the bull and concentrated on putting one foot in front of the other as fast as he could.

The bull thundered behind him; Gabe felt the hot breath of Satan on his neck. He was less than ten yards from the fence and safety, when his boot slipped in a fresh cow patty and he fell to one knee.

He pushed to his feet.

Tasted the bitterness of fear.

Heard a sharp cracking sound.

Felt something red hot and painful in his side.

He closed his eyes and felt himself go sailing through the air. Behind his closed eyes, he pictured Dizzy's agonized face as the bull tossed him into the air...or was it Lane Frost's face? He thought he called out a name, but he wasn't sure. There was another sharp, cracking sound, and a lot of yelling from somewhere far away.

He hit something hard. Something hard hit him. The musty scent of the bull was all around him, all over him.

His last coherent thought before the darkness overtook him was of Gretchen.

## CHAPTER FIFTEEN

NICOLE WAS GETTING READY to leave the hospital when Lucas tracked her down. A nurse stuck her head in Gretchen's door, told Nicole she had an emergency phone call and handed her a slip of paper with a phone number on it. She recognized the area code as north Louisiana, but the number was unfamiliar. After exchanging a questioning look with Gretchen, Nicole excused herself to make the call.

Lucas answered on the first ring.

"Lucas?" she asked. "Where are you? What's wrong?"

"I'm at Gabe's mother's place. He's been hurt," Lucas told her with brutal bluntness.

"Hurt? How?"

In great detail, Lucas recounted how Gabe had saved both Richie and Jody by putting himself between them and the raging bull. "Gabe slipped, and the bull gored him in the kidney. I didn't know until Joel told me, but Gabe only has one."

A cold fear raised goose bumps on Nicole's chilled flesh. "What are you trying to say?"

There was a lengthy pause before Lucas blew out a harsh breath. His voice shook. "It doesn't look good, Nicole. He's in surgery now. Depending on how things go, they're talking about a possible transplant."

"Dear God!" Nicole breathed. "Do they have anyone in mind?"

"They're doing all that blood-work stuff. The good news is that Joel killed the damned bull. If he'd hit him with the first shot, Gabe wouldn't have been gored. As it was, he was just a couple of seconds too late. Joel is blaming himself."

"Oh, God," Nicole said again as a new thought entered her mind. "Gretchen..."

"That's why I called. I hate to put it all on you, and I know she isn't in the best condition herself, but he's her husband, and she has a right to know what's happened—just in case."

Nicole didn't want to think about what "just in case" meant. Her heart told her he was right about her telling Gretchen, but she worried that the news might worsen Gretchen's condition. Nicole had to keep reminding herself that if *she* was in the hospital and something happened to the man she loved, she'd be furious if the news was kept from her. Unfortunately that didn't make the execution of her task any easier.

Gretchen was propped up in bed when Nicole got back to the room. She took one look at Nicole's face and knew something terrible had happened.

"What's wrong?" she asked.

Nicole heard the note of controlled panic in her voice. She crossed the room and took Gretchen's hand in hers. "Gabe's been hurt."

The last bit of color drained from Gretchen's already pale face. "Hurt? Where? How?"

Nicole strove to tell the tale as calmly as possible. When she was done, Gretchen's eyes flooded with tears. "How badly is he hurt?"

Nicole's gaze shifted from her friend's.

"Nicole!"

Gretchen's anguished cry drew Nicole's gaze back. "The bull gored him. Lucas said it damaged his kidney. He may need a transplant."

Nicole was prepared for sobbing and buckets of tears. Instead, Gretchen fainted. Panicked and guilt-stricken, Nicole rang for the nurse and explained what had happened. The nurse promptly called for help and alerted the doctor, while a bevy of other nurses worked at reviving Gretchen.

At last Gretchen came to. "Let me up," she cried, pushing away the hands that tried to hold her. "My husband is hurt. I've got to go to him."

"You aren't in any condition to go running off," the nurse said. "Now lie back and take a deep breath."

"I can't! Don't you understand? He might be dying."

"Gretchen, Gretchen, settle down now."

The soothing masculine voice came from the doorway, which framed Gretchen's obstetrician.

"Gabe's been hurt, Dr. Mason," she said, tears trickling down her cheeks. "I have to go to Louisiana. I have to see him."

The doctor moved to the side of the bed and took her hand in his. "Take it easy." His familiar voice and touch did what the nurses hadn't been able to do; Gretchen stopped struggling and looked up at him with despair-filled eyes.

"I know you want to be there, but you have to understand that even though your cramping and bleeding have stopped, a trip to Louisiana might very well send you into premature labor."

She gripped his hand and swallowed hard. "He's my husband, Dr. Mason. I love him, and he—" she sniffed "—he might die. I have to go to him."

"Even if it means risking the baby?"

A harsh sob racked Gretchen's body. "You have no idea how much I want this baby," she said, "but I waited a long time to find Gabe. I have to go."

Phil Mason sighed, and she took it as a sign that he was weakening. "I have a helicopter," she told him. "The trip won't be that long. I'll lie down. I won't move, I promise. I'll take my medicine, and I'll put myself in the hospital when I get there."

He shook his head. "Even so, it isn't a good idea. I'm very much against it."

"If you don't release me, I'll just walk out," Gretchen warned.

"There's nothing I can say that will make you change your mind?"

"Nothing," she said with a shake of her head.

"I can't release you. If I do and you lose the baby, I'll be leaving myself wide open for a lawsuit. But if you choose to go, there's nothing I can do to stop you." He patted her hand and stood. "See to it that you take care of yourself."

Gretchen gave him a shaky smile. "I'll do my best."

Forty minutes later, Dirk was flying Gretchen and Nicole east, toward Louisiana. Gretchen prayed for her baby and she prayed for her husband. The possibility of losing either was unthinkable. The possibility of losing both was more than she could bear.

JERICHO BROKE the news to Jesse, telling him the story as Lucas had told it to him and finishing with the news that Gabe was in surgery.

"If they can't patch up the kidney, he'll need a transplant. Finding a compatible donor on short notice might be hard. Daniel and I are the wrong blood type. So are Hannah and Jody."

The implication was clear. If they couldn't find a donor, Gabe would die. Jesse felt his throat tighten and a heaviness fill his chest. "Keep me posted, will you?" he asked gruffly.

"I will," Jericho said, and hung up.

Jesse cradled the receiver, wishing with all his heart that Sarah was here. She'd always been his rock, his stability, the one who made him believe that everything would be okay. But Sarah had been gone for more than two months, and it was beginning to look as if she wasn't coming back.

He rested his elbows on his thighs and clasped his hands between his knees. Maybe he should call Hannah, just to tell her that he was sorry, that he was thinking about her—and Gabe. No. She was probably at the hospital, and on second thought, calling wasn't such a good idea, anyway. All it would do was cause trouble between her and Joel. He didn't relish the thought of that.

He scraped a hand down his whiskery cheek and wished he had a beer—or something stronger. But there was nothing in the house. He hadn't had a drop to drink since Sarah walked out. He'd sworn off the stuff, as much to prove to himself that he could do without it, as to prove it to her. As Reverend Dunning said, life was all about making choices.

He'd learned a lot since he'd started making the occasional call to Mariah's husband. For example, he'd made a number of bad choices in his life, and he'd made them for two reasons, the first being that he'd sought instant gratification and hadn't considered the repercussions.

The second reason was pure selfishness and immaturity. Such as seeing Hannah and making up his mind to have her no matter what the consequences to her or

Sarah or his boys. Such as insinuating himself into Gabe's life just to show Hannah and Joel that he could. Such as a hundred other bad decisions he'd made.

His mouth quirked in a droll smile. Damn if he wasn't developing a conscience in his old age. Or was it character? Maybe he was just finally growing up. Whatever it was, it was a painful process. It meant he'd had to stop placing the blame for the mess he'd made of his life on everyone else and take a good look at what he'd contributed to his condition. It meant being big enough to recognize he'd done wrong and big enough to admit it, no matter how awkward or painful it might be.

He'd admitted a lot of wrongs to Ford Dunning, who said that the next step was to admit them to Sarah, but Jesse knew he wasn't up to that any more than he'd been up to apologizing to Gabe for crashing his wedding reception.

Jesse cleared a sudden obstruction from his throat. Now it might be too late to apologize to Gabe.

He remembered the night his and Hannah's son was born, just a month after Daniel. He remembered how he'd insisted on giving him a biblical name, like his other boys. It was a family tradition, he'd said. But Gabe wasn't really a part of his family and never had been, because claiming him would have hurt Sarah too much—or so Jesse told himself. So Gabe had remained the outcast. Jesse Calloway's bastard.

Jesse knew he'd made Gabe as much a part of his life as he could, and he'd done his best to bring up the three boys together like the brothers they were.

He remembered how Gabe had started riding calves as soon as he was big enough to corner one in a pen. He recalled how tough he'd been, never crying when he got hurt, taking the punishment doled out to him with a stoicism most grown men lacked. He thought about the way Gabe used to follow him around, eager to learn whatever he could about horses and cattle and rodeo. Of all his boys, Gabe was the most like him. Maybe that was why he'd never been able to make a clean break, even though that would have been the best thing for them all.

Jesse thought of all the gossip when Gabe was growing up. Tears pricked behind his eyelids. He'd done what he could to protect Gabe from the rumor-mongers, but it had never been enough.

He knew, too, that Hannah had taken the brunt of the blame for their affair. It was she who'd been branded a home wrecker and a floozy. It was she who struggled to hold her head high in the community while the boys down at the Midnight Hour slapped him on the back and took bets on how long Jesse Calloway could keep two women satisfied.

Putting his marriage in jeopardy had been a foolhardy thing to do. But then, he'd done a lot of foolhardy things in his life. In retrospect, it was amazing that Sarah had stayed as long as she had. And it was no wonder she hadn't come back.

It was time to make some changes, that was for sure. Time to set things right before it was too late. *Please, God, don't let it be too late to make things right with Gabe.*

With a great gulping sob, Jesse lost the battle with his tears. He cried for all the people he'd hurt and for all the wrongs in his life. He cried for what he'd done to Hannah and for causing Sarah so much heartache. He cried for all the hurt he'd caused his boys. And he cried for the son he'd never acknowledged.

LUCAS AND AN AMBULANCE were waiting when Dirk landed the chopper at Shreveport Downtown Airport. With a minimum of effort, Gretchen was loaded into the vehicle and it sped off toward the hospital where Gabe was still undergoing surgery. According to Lucas, Gabe was holding his own.

Telling her friend that she and Lucas would follow in his car, Nicole watched the ambulance disappear down the street and then headed straight for Lucas's arms. He held her so tightly it hurt, but she didn't care.

"Don't let me go," she whispered.

"Never."

She looked up at him through a veil of tears. "Tell me he's going to be all right and that Gretchen won't lose this baby."

"I can't tell you that," Lucas said. "But I can tell you that from what I've seen of him, he's a fighter, and from what you've told me, Gretchen is, too."

She nodded; then, drawing a breath in an attempt to gather her composure, she stepped out of his embrace. "We'd better go. Gretchen will wonder what happened to us."

"Just a minute," he said, catching her hand.

"What?"

"I want you to marry me."

A tremulous half smile curved Nicole's lips. "Of course I'll marry you."

"Now," Lucas said. "Marry me now."

"Now?"

"As soon as possible. I don't want to wait. We've already spent too many years apart. Something might happen."

"Like what?"

"Anything. What happened today made me realize just how uncertain life is, and I don't want to spend another hour without you in mine."

JESSE PAUSED in the doorway of the hospital waiting room. Hannah and Joel were there, as well as their daughter, Jericho, Susan, Daniel and Becca. Ben's four girls and their husbands were there, too, along with the new Calloway mill manager and a dark-haired woman Jesse didn't recognize.

As he stood there, trying to figure out what to say, Eden looked up and saw him.

"Uncle Jesse!" she cried, surging to her feet and casting a worried glance toward Hannah and her husband, who also started to rise.

Hannah reached out and put a hand on Joel's arm. His gaze shifted from Jesse to her troubled blue eyes. Jesse saw Hannah's fingers tighten in warning.

When no one said anything, Jesse realized they were all waiting for him to make the first move. With a dozen pairs of eyes on him, he felt as uncomfortable as a whore in church. His courage faltered, but then he thought of Gabe and knew that he had to go through with it. He also knew that even though what he had to say was meant for everyone, he had to say it to Hannah.

"Jericho said Gabe might need a kidney." He looked directly into the eyes of the woman who'd once shared a great part of his life. The woman who'd given him her love and a son. The woman who was far too good for the likes of him and who deserved whatever happiness she'd found with Joel Butler. The woman who deserved to have her son well and whole.

Hannah nodded.

"I wanted to let you know that I'm willing to give him one of mine," Jesse said in a nervous, quavering voice. He shrugged. "It seems only right, since he's my flesh and blood."

JESSE WAS SITTING in the living room watching the ten-o'clock news and eating a TV dinner when the door-bell rang. Wondering who had come to visit at such a late hour, he shoved aside the TV tray and went to answer it. When he saw who was standing there, his heart skipped a beat.

"Sarah?"

Her smile was tentative, fleeting. "Hello, Jesse. May I come in?"

"Sure," he said, stepping aside. She brushed past him, leaving a cloud of sweet-smelling perfume to tickle his senses. He followed her into the living room and gestured toward his dinner. "I was just having a bite. Can I get you something?"

"No thank you. I ate earlier." She took a look at his meal and shook her head. "No wonder you've lost weight."

He tried to smile. Failed. "I'm not the cook you are. These are easy."

They stood awkwardly. Finally Jesse spoke. "Have a seat."

"I can't stay but a minute," she said, taking him up on the offer as he sat, too. Then, as if she finally realized he must be wondering why she'd come, she said, "I heard about Gabe. I stopped by to see how he's doing."

The gesture surprised and pleased him. "Better than they expected. He was in surgery four hours to repair his kidney. He's in critical condition, but he's stable, and the doctors are hopeful that they won't need to do a transplant."

"Thank God!" Sarah said, and he knew she meant it.

Another silence descended. He poked at his enchilada with his fork and tried to think of something to say. Shooting her a quick glance, he asked, "Would you like a glass of tea?"

She smiled, another swift curving of her lips. "No thank you."

"Jesse—"

"Sarah—"

They spoke simultaneously. "Ladies first," he said, making a sweeping gesture with his arm.

Sarah nodded and forced her gaze to his. "I have a confession to make."

"Oh?"

"I didn't come here just to ask about Gabe." She twisted her hands together in her lap.

"Why did you come, Sarah?" he asked in a gentle, hopeful voice.

She raised her chin and blurted, "Jericho told me what you did this afternoon—owning up to fathering Gabe and offering to give him one of your kidneys."

The comment surprised him even more than her visit. Even though he figured she'd heard, he hadn't expected her to say anything about it—especially not to him. Well, he'd done it, and he wasn't sorry, even if it meant losing Sarah forever. It had been the right decision. He was sure of that.

"It was about time, don't you think?" he said, his unfaltering blue gaze holding hers.

Her eyes glittered with unshed tears. "Yes, it was. Everyone in town's known the truth for years. And I have, too."

"I know."

Sarah's eyes drifted shut at his acknowledgment of her pain. She stood and smoothed her skirt. "I should be going."

"I'll see you out," he told her, rising and following her to the door. He opened it. Immediately the sounds of chirping crickets and singing bullfrogs bombarded them.

"I'm sorry, Sarah," he told her, meaning every word. He was sorry for all the pain he'd caused everyone through the years. Sorry for hurting her and the boys. Sorry for not being the kind of husband she wanted and deserved.

"So am I," she told him. She started across the porch and turned at the steps. "I want you to know that I'm proud of what you did today. It takes a big man to own up to his mistakes."

Without waiting for his reply, she started down the steps.

"Sarah!" His voice halted her at the bottom. She looked back at him questioningly.

"Can I call you sometime?" he asked. "Maybe take you to Minden for some of Cotton's fried chicken? If you have the time," he added hastily.

A soft smile bloomed on her lips. For the space of a heartbeat, she looked eighteen again. She nodded. "Call me," she said. "I'll think about it."

GABE AWOKE the next morning, groggy, but aware of an incredible pain. He struggled to remember why he was hurting so badly, and then the whole thing came rushing back with the force of a freight train.

Richie. Jody. Racing Joel's bull. Losing his footing. He remembered a sharp sound—a rifle shot, he realized now—so one of two things had happened: ei-

ther the bull had got him or Joel had shot him. At the
moment, he didn't care which; he just knew that
whatever had happened, he hurt like a son of a gun
and it had landed him in the hospital.

A sudden thought hit him. Who was taking care of
the horses? That thought led to another: the memory
of Tyrell West coming to the ranch and his threaten-
ing to tell Gretchen he'd seen him in the arms of another woman.

"Gretchen!" His voice was thin and weak.

"Gabe! You're awake!"

He eased his head to the side and saw Gretchen lying in the bed next to his. She looked so beautiful he
felt like crying.

"What are you doing here?" he managed to ask.

"Standing by my man," she quipped. Her light tone
belied the tears trickling down her cheeks. "Maybe I
should say lying by my man. Lucas called Nicole at the
hospital in Fort Worth and told her about the accident. The doctor didn't want me to come, but nothing this side of hell could have stopped me."

Hospital? Doctor? He struggled to make sense of
everything she was saying, but it was hard because his
mind kept floating off somewhere. Then another
memory, this one very important, drifted into his
medicated mind. Just before the fiasco with the bull,
Lucas had come to tell him that Gretchen was in the
hospital in Fort Worth. His heart gave a sickening
lurch. "The baby!"

"The baby is fine," she told him, pushing back the
sheet and sitting on the edge of the bed. "We're both
fine. How about you?"

He managed to lift one corner of his mouth in a
smile. "I feel like I've been ... rode hard and put up
wet."

She slipped off the edge of the bed and crossed the few feet that separated them. "That good, huh?" she asked, laying her hand against his cheek and smiling down at him.

Her face wavered, and he knew he was about to lose consciousness again. But before he did, there were a lot of things he needed to tell her.

"Your dad offered me money to... leave you."

"I hope you told him no," she said.

"Damn straight," he murmured thickly. "An' I figured out how I can provide for you and the baby."

"How?" she asked, smoothing his hair away from his forehead.

Darkness swooped over him and he forced it back. "I can't remember," he confessed before his eyes drifted shut.

He heard her laugh and forced his eyes open again. "...love to hear you laugh," he told her, trying to lift one hand to touch her and finding that it weighed at least a thousand pounds. She carried his hand to her lips. The tears were back in her eyes.

"I love you," she murmured.

He wanted to tell her he loved her, too, but the darkness began to descend again. Oh, well, he thought before the lights went completely out, he'd tell her tomorrow. They would have a lot of tomorrows together.

# EPILOGUE

GABE PASSED the crisis point that night, and by the time his daughter, Whitney, was born five weeks later, he was well on his way to a full recovery. Gretchen took to motherhood like a duck to water, and Gabe found being a father pretty okay, too. Tyrell West hadn't come around yet, but when Mimi had seen how terrified her daughter was at the thought of losing Gabe, she decided to at least give her son-in-law the benefit of the doubt.

When Hannah told Gabe about Jesse's offer, they both wept. Later, when Gabe was able, he and Jesse had a long talk. As Lucas had said, there was no putting the past to rest until it was faced. Gabe and Jesse faced it and laid it to rest. The first time Jesse held Whitney, he cried tears of happiness that he was being allowed a second chance.

He was getting a second chance with Sarah, too. They were dating and seeing Ford Dunning together on a regular basis. Ford held out a lot of hope for their being able to work things out.

Lucas and Nicole eloped as soon as Gabe was out of danger. Nicole moved to Louisiana to be with her husband after leasing her boutique to her manager and opening another shop in Shreveport. Laughing, she said she'd always wanted a chain of boutiques, and she was close enough to Dallas that she could still market her line of clothing there.

When Gabe got home from the hospital, Joel, with tears in his eyes, thanked Gabe for saving Jody's life and apologized to him for the past. Gabe did the same, and asked his stepdad if he'd take him fishing on Lake Bistineau.

Daniel and Becca were married in April, and Susan announced that she was pregnant in May.

The Calloway clan was definitely growing.

Gretchen and Gabe sold both farms, and, at her insistence, they bought a huge parcel of land just a twenty-minute drive from Calloway Corners. Gabe moved the horses, and she planned to move Westways Productions to Shreveport, former home of the Louisiana Hayride. With the riverboat gambling and the resurgence of interest in the downtown area, she felt that, with the right push, the city could be tops in the country-music business again.

Besides, she said, it was important that they be close to Gabe's family. She wanted Whitney to have the luxury of her grandparents' love, just as she had the luxury of Gabe's love.

And so, strangely, the Calloway boys—Jericho, Daniel and Gabe—all wound up in Calloway Corners. They still meet at the Midnight Hour on occasion, not to bolster their courage, but to talk to Duke and have cheeseburgers.

Whoever it was who said you can never go home again was wrong.

# RETURN TO
# CALLOWAY CORNERS

Don't miss these fabulous stories
from the original Calloway Corners series!

# Take 4 bestselling love stories FREE

## Plus get a FREE surprise gift!

## Special Limited-time Offer

**Mail to Harlequin Reader Service®**

3010 Walden Avenue
P.O. Box 1867
Buffalo, N.Y. 14240-1867

**YES!** Please send me 4 free Harlequin Superromance® novels and my free surprise gift. Then send me 4 brand-new novels every month, which I will receive before they appear in bookstores. Bill me at the low price of $3.34 each plus 25¢ delivery and applicable sales tax, if any.* That's the complete price and a savings of over 10% off the cover prices—quite a bargain! I understand that accepting the books and gift places me under no obligation ever to buy any books. I can always return a shipment and cancel at any time. Even if I never buy another book from Harlequin, the 4 free books and the surprise gift are mine to keep forever.

134 BPA A3UN

| | | |
|---|---|---|
| Name | (PLEASE PRINT) | |
| Address | Apt. No. | |
| City | State | Zip |

This offer is limited to one order per household and not valid to present Harlequin Superromance® subscribers. *Terms and prices are subject to change without notice. Sales tax applicable in N.Y.

**As Seen on TV!**

# Free Gift Offer

With a Free Gift proof-of-purchase
from any Harlequin® book, you can receive
a beautiful cubic zirconia pendant.

This stunning marquise-shaped stone is a genuine cubic
zirconia—accented by an 18" gold tone necklace.
(Approximate retail value $19.95)

## Send for yours today...
## compliments of ⬦HARLEQUIN®

To receive your free gift, a cubic zirconia pendant, send us one original proof-of-purchase, photocopies not accepted, from the back of any Harlequin Romance®, Harlequin Presents®, Harlequin Temptation®, Harlequin Superromance®, Harlequin Intrigue®, Harlequin American Romance®, or Harlequin Historicals® title available in August, September or October at your favorite retail outlet, together with the Free Gift Certificate, plus a check or money order for $1.65 U.S./$2.15 CAN. (do not send cash) to cover postage and handling, payable to Harlequin Free Gift Offer. We will send you the specified gift. Allow 6 to 8 weeks for delivery. Offer good until October 31, 1996 or while quantities last. Offer valid in the U.S. and Canada only.

# Free Gift Certificate

Name: _____

Address: _____

City: _____ State/Province: _____ Zip/Postal Code: _____

Mail this certificate, one proof-of-purchase and a check or money order for postage and handling to: HARLEQUIN FREE GIFT OFFER 1996. In the U.S.: 3010 Walden Avenue, P.O. Box 9071, Buffalo NY 14269-9057. In Canada: P.O. Box 604, Fort Erie, Ontario L2Z 5X3.

---

## FREE GIFT OFFER
084-KMF

ONE PROOF-OF-PURCHASE

To collect your fabulous FREE GIFT, a cubic zirconia pendant, you must include this original proof-of-purchase for each gift with the properly completed Free Gift Certificate.

---

084-KMF

# REBECCA

## 43 LIGHT STREET

# YORK

# FACE TO FACE

*Bestselling author Rebecca York returns to "43 Light Street"
for an original story of past secrets, deadly deceptions—and
the most intimate betrayal.*

She woke in a hospital—with amnesia…and with child.
According to her rescuer, whose striking face is the last
image she remembers, she's Justine Hollingsworth. But
nothing about her life seems to fit, except for the baby
inside her and Mike Lancer's arms around her. Consumed
by forbidden passion and racked by nameless fear, she
must discover if she is Justine…or the victim of some mind
game. Her life—and her unborn child's—depends on it….

Don't miss *Face To Face*—Available in October, wherever
Harlequin books are sold.

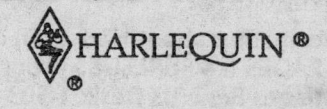 HARLEQUIN ®

43FTF

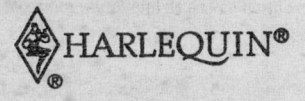